PARALLEL

AUSTIN LAUTERWASSER

To my younger self, because, Austin, you finally did it.

Chapter 1

June 4th,

    I have recently discovered something that can change the world forever. It's something that has been hidden for all these years. I almost missed it, but after analyzing all of the voices and things I've been seeing, I'm about to make the conclusion. I'm the only one who has discovered this. But here I sit, pondering, *what if I'm not the only one?* I can't afford to let this secret escape, at least not yet. It only took me a couple of weeks to finally put all these pieces together, and now that I have, there's so much more to discover. This truly is life changing.

    Following up on my research I came across this old saying, "According to Greek mythology, when humans were made we had four arms and four legs, but the gods split everyone to rid us of our sins and demons, forcing us to find our other halves." It sounds so farfetched that I can't entirely believe it, but under these circumstances I'm afraid I have to.

I wasn't searching for what I found. It found me. I can't quite put my finger on it, but it's so intriguing. I write my thoughts down because I feel I would have a mental overload if I didn't. This still makes me feel sane. But something about this, something about what I found . . . there's a reason it was hidden. I am almost certain that it has wanted to be found for some time now. Everyone has been looking for it, but it's when you don't look for something that you find it.

June 6th,

I can't seem to stay away. Everything about what I found has been so addicting, so captivating, so . . . mysterious. But I don't like what I see; something isn't right. This isn't a happy place, but I need answers. So I go back and I go back and I go back but it isn't by choice . . .

June 9th,

Sometimes it feels like I don't have a mind of my own. It's as if I can't comprehend what is going on, so my mind makes up the rest. Deep down, a part of me knows this is not the case. I used to think this was the best discovery of my life, that nothing could top this. That's the thing, nothing ever could. What I have seen is what no human ever wants to. I can't unsee something; I can't hide what has been discovered. Only *it* has the capability of doing that.

Some nights I wake up to a humming noise and I can't tell if I'm in their world or mine. The hum is an eerie sound with an old tune that shakes me down to my core. I haven't figured out why they do that, and especially why *I* do that. I can't stop humming.

June 13th,

Now that I can't stay away and now that it knows that, there's no going back. I feel something getting closer to me. What I knew is no longer what I know. Everything has shifted, and everything is not what it seems. My worst nightmares have come to life, and what seems to have been imaginary has been nothing less than a reality. It's like I discovered a whole other world. My heart is crippled by my past, and they have the upper hand.

Their appearance is not like ours. I used to think that

these things were human, that they lived and breathed like us, and I've been telling myself that this isn't real. They lack humanity, they're different . . . their motives aren't ones that are—

June 17th,

There's something following me, every room I'm in. Every breath I take, there's something always following behind it. I start to hear voices; I start to hear things other than my thoughts. I don't even recognize myself in the mirror. My reflection is off.

I can't sleep. It's in the room with me now; I can feel its presence. I can feel it get closer to me. Those eyes, oh my God, those eyes.

Those eyes, the color of the moon, so bright and white and mysterious, with a simple but sinister glow to them. One day I woke up and found it sitting next to me, staring at me blankly, and as it sensed my fear a grimace slowly appeared. The eyes were devoid of color as they pierced into me, and took things from my soul that I can never get back.

June 19th,

I can no longer sleep. All I do is sit in my chair in

my dark room. My fingers are in pain. I bit off my fingernails, which helps me refrain from clawing at my walls. Whenever I think I'm alone I hear heavy breathing and a low, dry, sinister cackle. I turn on my lamp and look at my mirror and realize it's me. My reflection wears a smirk, and then it fades.

I play music at all hours of the night to try to drown out the voices and screams. I'm losing myself; I don't know what they want from me. I needed answers and I found a lot more than what I wanted. I've gone there three times now and I have three long cuts on my wrist. I must never forget who I am—I *will* never forget. It's literally hell on earth. They're not like us, they want something they—

June 21st,

I now do not know what I thought I had known. I feel burned where they touch me, hear the screams and cackles, like they're trying to claw their way inside of me. I'm not going to say I'm becoming crazy, because I know I'm already there. The only thing I know is that I can't fight this anymore, whatever *this* is, whatever they are. I stopped feeling my dry blood from clawing and punching myself, from cuts from the broken mirror and broken windows. I can't stop shaking. I'm just a shell of a person. It's dark, it's so dark. What they say to me, what I feel, what I hear, the smell of rotting, burning flesh. I don't like what they show me. I'm just their toy. I didn't mean for any of this to happen. I look down at a shattered piece of a mirror and I keep shaking my head, I keep twitching. I put my hands over my ears and I scream so loud, but no sound comes out. I look at the broken mirror and I find myself smiling, with eyes that are no longer mine, and I realize that I am home . . .

***

The whispers of his words left me feeling even more hollow and broken. I traced the scrawled outlines of where his pen met the paper, as if touching them allowed me to feel him one last time. His overwrought entries were unnerving. I looked at his penciled chicken-scratch drawings. One looked like a young male with a resemblance to Alex, but his eyes had no pupils. Other drawings ranged from an old church, to a younger-looking man with the same pupil-less eyes, to another male with normal eyes. Some of the words etched on the pages were legible, and others weren't words at all.

I put down my older brother's dark gray leather journal and stared off into my room. I found his journal tied to the bottom of his mattress about a week after he died. I read the whole thing over and over again, and this journal still chilled me to the bone. Not even my friends knew about it, just like no one else knew what my brother found. Everyone thought Alex went crazy and killed himself, but even with an autopsy, his cause of death was unknown. It had been about a month, and it was still hard to believe he was gone. Especially with this journal, my memories, and what I thought I knew. I wasn't left with much that proved Alex wasn't crazy. I knew he wasn't. There were so many unanswered questions.

I wanted solace. My life had been nothing but grim for the past few years. Some days I wondered what would happen to me if I didn't find answers to the questions asked in this journal. What would I end up like? Could I live with no closure? Would whatever my brother "found" take me, too? I didn't know what I was going to do and if I should even figure any of this out, but I felt there was a reason he left a journal. But then again, maybe there was no point to it at all.

I grabbed my car keys, stood up and went to my car. It was half past midnight as I made my way to my brother's old place. It had been up for rent but no one wanted it because Alex supposedly killed himself in it.

Driving these familiar streets brought back memories of when I would bring my brother fast food after I got done with my night classes. We would chow down while we played video games. He had all the latest zombie survival games and even our childhood favorites. When I was still in high school he moved fifteen minutes away from the college town we grew up in. I couldn't wait to graduate and follow him. Every now and again when my parents and I fought, I would grab my things and stay at his place for the weekend. Our fights were always over something stupid; disobeying them for instance or not updating them soon enough on my whereabouts. Alex always knew how to make me feel better. We bonded over everything: venting about Mom and Dad, talking about girls and life, and even playing our video games.

He had plans to go to the university, but kept deferring his admission. He took online classes in the meantime, but never completed his gen eds. Alex was always ridiculously smart at math, and toward the end of my junior year I would drive to his place just so he could help me with it. I always thought, with his skills, he would be a marine biologist. Alex loved animals, and if he could have, he

8

would have spent every night at the zoo. Even so, he never had the desire to follow through with his degree. But I could understand where Alex was coming from; If someone had the life he and I did, they wouldn't have desire to go to school either. Losing our parents at a young age really made our lives a darker place.

The memories floated away as I parked my car right in front of his apartment. I got out and started climbing the fire escape; he had lived on the sixth and final floor. This wasn't my first time doing this. As I climbed the familiar ladder I looked through the windows of the fifth floor. It was an entire floor dedicated to storage units. It made the residents of the sixth floor have more storage space beneath their units. Alex loved that, especially when he threw parties, because the people below wouldn't hear the crowd in his apartment. I climbed the rest of the fire escape to his window. I slid it open and a wave of musty air hit me.

I crawled through the window and hopped down onto the creaky wooden floor. The window led straight into the living room. I used my phone's flashlight to make my way to a lamp and turned it on. I looked around and noticed, underneath the crummy paint job, the landlord tried to cover up the words written on the walls. "It's under my skin," one message read. "They watch us all," said another, followed by "Why is it always dark there?" and "Home again." They were all written in Alex's blood. There was still blood by the doorframes, too, but I could only see it if I looked closely. This place made me uneasy, but I was trying to find answers.

My nose wrinkled as I caught the repugnant odor of rotten flesh, a somewhat-permanent smell of the place now. It could have come from an animal that snuck in long ago, but I knew it wasn't. The nauseating stench could be smelled from the bottom of the fire escape and somehow it was a smell I have never recognized. I made a face and walked deeper into the apartment.

The landlord had placed a few chairs, a couch, and other furniture in the apartment to make it look presentable whenever he gave a tour. Nothing of Alex's was left. I made my way to the bathroom and looked in the mirror there, which they had replaced since the last time I had been there. I looked at my reflection and just stared. Part of me felt empty now that Alex was gone, and that this was a dream and he'd come back and tell me he was here to stay. That we could have another drink together and share stories and go to football games. I lowered my head and turned the other way, accepting that would never happen again.

He never said anything about how something was after

him or how he felt like he was going crazy. One of the things that hurt the most was that he never reached out. Not one phone call, not one text, not even a visit in his final week. I could have been there for him. He knew I would have dropped everything for him, so why didn't he reach out to me?

I shook off my thoughts and I walked out of the bathroom and into his bedroom, nothing but a square room with white walls. All the furniture was gone, and the only noise that of the squeaky floorboards. An uneven floorboard caught my eye a few feet away. Why had I never noticed that before? I walked over to it and crouched down so I could pry it up. When I finally got it loose, I shined the light from my phone into the hole and saw a piece of paper. My heart jumped. I picked it up and saw it was a photo of my brother and I, taken the night of my freshman finals. I had been worried about my math test, and Alex told me whether I failed or passed, we were going to drink. This was taken here, in this apartment.

I flipped it over and saw he had written on the back, "Keep the ones you love hidden." Why would he put a picture of us in the floor? And hidden from what?

The sound of creaking floorboards stopped my thoughts and sent chills down my spine, for the sound came from the living room. A soft, cool breeze brushed against my face as I slowly stood up. The creaking continued as I started making my way into the other room. I thought it was the landlord and that he caught me sneaking up here. The rest of the apartment was dark; somehow the lights had turned off. I used my phone's flashlight once more, shining it around the room. I noticed one of the chairs rocking. My heart began to race and my breathing grew quick.

"Who's there?" I heard myself say.

The chair stopped rocking and turned to face me. I saw the silhouette of a human sitting in it. I heard a deep, dry cackle escape its mouth. It slowly reached for the lamp on the end table and turned it on. I found myself asking, "Who are you?"

The lamp came on and flickered like a candle as I made out the silhouette to be my brother. Those eyes, they weren't his. They were the color of the moon. His flesh was all torn up, like he'd been clawing at it.

"Alex?"

The light continued to flicker rapidly and the silhouette's smile grew bigger. He stood up and the sounds of bones cracking pierced the quiet apartment. He took a few steps toward me and spoke in a deep, dark voice.

"I'm home."

With another flicker of the light, he was gone. The light went out and all that was left was the breeze through the open window and goosebumps on my skin. I tried turning on the light, but it wouldn't come back on. I didn't know if what I saw was really there, or if I only imagined it. It felt and looked real. . . but Alex was dead and that was not possible. Alex was dead and he was never coming back. I was simply overwhelmed with the journal and being in his apartment wishing he was back. *He's not back and he's not here and the chair never moved and the lamp never worked,* I thought. I needed to go home and go to bed.

I held on to the picture as I crawled back out of the window and into the night. When I got home, I set the picture down and lay in my bed, taking everything in. *What did I just see? What is going on in my head?*

Each time I closed my eyes, all I pictured were the white holes where Alex's eyes should have been. My anxious heart was still racing and paranoia seeped in. I didn't feel safe anymore in my house. I was scared, thinking about what would happen if Alex followed me home.

I needed to let things be and quit chasing shadows. Maybe Alex *was* crazy. If that was the case, I couldn't let that happen to me, too.

Chapter 2

Day after day, I think it gets easier. That time can heal all wounds and that every smile ever faded will appear again. No matter how many blows I take, I tell myself one more won't hurt. I feel tired and empty, time never slows down to help myself recover, and I feel as if I can't catch a break. Everything I do only reminds myself of where I am in this world and what I lost. All the hope I had went away.

Even before Alex died, I felt lost with no direction, cold and abandoned. Before I graduated high school, things got hard. Our parents passed away during the winter of my senior year. They were driving home from a dinner date for their anniversary when a drunk driver slid through a stop sign, going too fast, and ran right into them, killing them instantly.

I had never experienced loneliness to that extent before. Thank God I had my brother; he was there for me through it all. When I had difficulties picking what school to go to or even with my homework, Alex was always there. When I had nightmares in the middle of the night, I would call Alex and we'd talk it out. When we both struggled with our fears and our losses we'd take each other out fishing, or to the movies.

Alex was always the strong one. He knew what to say and when to say it. He and I rarely fought and when we did, it was over something miniscule. He showed his pain in a different way than I did; he would become a little distant and he'd distract himself with his job, and eventually his girlfriend, Emily. When she came into the picture, not much changed with Alex and me. He still came to me when he wanted to talk and he still chose me to take fishing. I looked up to him. He made me who I am today.

I decided to go to the university that was in the town we grew up in. It was a decision I made before my parents passed away. At that age I didn't want to venture far and it allowed me to still be close to Alex.

The days and nights were still hard, and the memories burned like embers of a slowly dying fire.

The hardest thing in this world was living in it. Losing my parents and now my brother had taken everything out of me. I had never imagined losing all my family at a young age.

Coming back to the present, I placed the white roses on top of the soft soil, took a step back, and looked at the gravestone. I had visited my brother's grave to take everything in and to get the previous night's thoughts out of my head.

I felt the early fall breeze brush up against me and let my thoughts take their course. Something happened to my brother. There had to be more than just him mysteriously dying. I didn't think he was crazy, despite what anyone else thought. But I didn't get what he was trying to do, what he discovered. Nothing made any sense. I told myself I had to be strong and keep moving, but there was only so much I could do alone. At times, I felt like I was going through the motions, that I had no real purpose.

I felt a tear slide down my cheek and was thankful, because that was the only thing I could feel. I guess today was one of those days. I told myself it was going to get better—it had to get better.

My thoughts were soon interrupted by a familiar voice. "Carter, you okay?"

It was my best friend, Jackson King, standing a few feet behind me. His light blond hair was styled up and jelled toward the left side of his head, taking the shape of a wave. He was wearing his favorite slim jeans with tattered holes ripped through them and his favorite black leather jacket with a sky-blue shirt underneath it. Wearing jeans made him appear taller, when in reality he's about six foot one. He's only an inch taller than me, if that, but in football that one inch helped him become a quarterback.

Jackson and I have been friends ever since we were in diapers. Well, I guess we were introduced to each other as babies, but we didn't meet again until kindergarten. Jackson has always been a self-righteous prick, even at that age. We didn't see eye to eye in elementary school, and he was always involved with turning girls who I liked against me.

One particular incident actually sent Jackson and me on the path to becoming friends. One day at the start of first grade, Jackson passed around a note that said I was a bed wetter, which led kids to make fun of me. Eventually they forgot about the rumor and moved on to bigger things, but my overly paranoid mind still thought about that embarrassing day for weeks. His bullying didn't stop there. He eventually started taking the lunches my mom would pack for me, and he would eat all of what he grabbed or just take a few bites then hand it back to me. One day I had enough. I took some of my dad's Gorilla Glue to school and right before lunch, I squeezed some of the tube into the sack lunch. Seconds after I sat down at the lunch table, Jackson made his way over. He dove his grubby little hands into the sack lunch and pulled them out in disgust, freaked out about what was all over his hands. I smiled as I sipped my juice box and told him it was a special type of glue.

He frantically flailed his hands around, which only made the glue dry faster, and before he knew it a couple of his fingers were glued together. That was the first and last time I saw Jackson run off crying. That day was also the first and last time I went to principal's office. After that, he and I started getting along. It was almost like a mutual-respect type of thing. We had to sit in the principal's office together and explain why we did what we did. I think that it's quite hilarious that we became friends after that, because if someone put super glue in my sack lunch today I wouldn't care to get to know them at all.

Our parents were best friends growing up and we were both born around the same time, which kept them close. Growing older, Jackson and I came to a better understanding of each other. From first grade on, we'd always seen each other like brothers. He'd been there for me like one, and that was all I could ask for. We always had each other's backs.

He asked me if I was okay, wearing the cocky grin that he always used. He had always been the "macho man" and all-star jock at our school. Even if he gave off a cocky presence, he was the most modest and yet still self-righteous person I know.

I responded, "Yeah, I'm okay, just been thinking."

"My parents have been asking about ya. I tell them the same things you tell me. They want you to come over sometime soon for supper. I told them you would." He smiled.

"You shouldn't speak for people, Jackson." My tone sounded harsher than I intended.

"You know everything is going to be okay."

"I would like to know when . . ." I mumbled. I turned and faced him. "How long have you been standing there?"

"Long enough to know that you've been here for too long." He gave me his stupid grin once more and took a step forward. "Let's go get a cheeseburger or something. Talk to me—about anything. I feel like I haven't talked to you in forever!"

Even though I wasn't really hungry, I agreed to go with him. I hopped in his car and we drove off to Jersey's Diner and started catching up, getting my mind on other things.

The smell of grease and fast food soon filled my nostrils and the sound of sizzling burgers and fries reminded me that I was hungrier than I thought. We sat ourselves in a spacious booth with hot-pink seats and black-marbled table. The theme captured the cliché 1950s diner look: shiny chrome stools with hot-pink cushions surrounding the bar, black and white tiles on the floor, and low-hanging lamps above the booths. Vibrant neon radiated through the diner and vintage pictures covered the walls. Not only did the theme and food make the place famous, but the bar's black marble counter was specked with colorful mini LED lights. A few moments later, a spunky young brunette came to greet us, wearing a big, friendly smile to match her short, colorful skirt.

"Hello, my name is Jade, and I'll be taking care of you guys this evening," she started. "Can I get you guys anything to drink?" Her smile never left her face and her voice was soft and genuine. It had a husky, raspy tone to it, like she was out at a concert the night before. It was the kind of voice that you didn't hear on every girl.

We both wanted a Coke; she smiled, wrote it down and walked away. Jackson and I exchanged looks and then began laughing.

"You want her and she wants you, man," Jackson eagerly said to me. "We've been here how many times and you still haven't given her your number?"

"Jackson, it's not like that. A girl like her probably already has a boyfriend, and she doesn't want a guy like me," I told him.

"Carter, I'm going to give her your number."

"The hell you are! You want to take a fieldtrip back to elementary school? More specifically to all the times you sabotaged girls liking me?"

"What's your point? Let this be my peace offering. Everyone knew that I had the better jaw line anyway, and frankly, I still do."

"I don't know, Jackson."

"If I wasn't with Brooke, Jade would be my next choice." Jackson gave me his stupid grin and before we knew it, Jade was back with our drinks.

I shook my head and smiled as Jade set our drinks down. She grinned and then asked us, "Are you two ready to order?"

Jade Hamilton was the girl-next-door type, with dark brown hair that fell down to her stomach normally, but when she worked it was put into a high ponytail. When she walked, the air caught her natural curls ever so carefully, giving them a slight bounce. Her ice-blue eyes sparkled and held a fragile innocence. She had an inner radiance, and the way she moved lit up a room. She went to the same university I did, on the opposite side of town. I always thought she was beautiful.

No one knew much about her, but everyone knew how

gorgeous she was. Despite what I told Jackson about her probably having a boyfriend, word on the street was she was always single, mostly because she didn't let just anyone get too close. She was heavily independent and self-sufficient, which made me even more intimidated to talk to her.

She looked at me and smiled confidently, waiting for me to tell her what I wanted.

"I'll take a bacon cheeseburger with no cheese and a side of fries and two milkshakes, one mint chocolate and the other chocolate," I finally said.

She continued to smile as she wrote my order down, and I realized so was Jackson. He gave me subtle hand gestures, insinuating I was missing something.

Rolling my eyes, I added, "Make sure on the chocolate one there's a cherry."

"Aw, thanks, babe, for getting me my shake." Jackson winked and then turned and faced Jade. "I'll have the steakhouse burger cooked medium, with extra ranch and a side of fries."

"All righty," Jade said as she finished writing our orders down. "Anything else I can get you guys?"

Jackson looked at me and smiled. I kicked him underneath the table and responded, "No, thanks, that'll be all."

"All right, I'll get that in for you guys." She closed her notepad and smiled as she turned to another table.

Jackson turned back to look at me and began talking again after he took a sip of his drink. "But really, dude, talk to me, how have you been?" He studied me to see if there was the slightest bit of grief or anxiety over my face.

"To be honest, every day gets better. Or, well, at least I think it does. I mean, I don't really know how I've been if everything feels like it's been the same. At times I get angry and swear at the world and fail to understand why my whole family is dead. Why me? You know? What did I do to deserve this?"

"You're one of the strongest people I know, Carter. I know I could never go through what you have, and I respect you a lot as a person. Everyone looks at you as a strong man, not as a boy who lost his family."

I gazed down and stirred my straw, circling the ice cubes, listening to them clank against the glass. My ears picked up classic rock music from a nearby jukebox. I wanted to tell him what was really on my mind, what I found, and how deep down inside I felt like I was in a mad house. But instead I sat there and felt like a little scared boy. I looked back up at him and gave him my best fake smile. "Thank you. To be honest, I still sometimes have dreams that what happened in the past few years has all been a dream, but I wake up and my life starts the same and the dream is shattered. I wish . . . a part of me still wishes that what happened never happened, and that I didn't have to be the strong guy at the end of the day. If I didn't have my friends around, I don't know where I'd be. These past two months after Alex's funeral have been the most challenging. I understand I can't change the past and I get death is a part of life, but no one teaches you how to deal with it."

Jackson was about to say something when Jade came over, bringing us our milkshakes.

"One for you," she said as she placed the chocolate one in front of Jackson, "and one for you." She set the other one down and looked me straight in the eye and smiled before walking away.

"Look, dude, I didn't mean to bring anything up or make you think about anything that you didn't want to. I just miss you and want to make sure you're all right. What can I say? I'm selfish."

I nodded. "I know, Jackson."

"So, how's college going?" Jackson asked, changing the subject. "I know it's sucking for me, what with seeing

Brooke only a few times a week. She's preparing for med school."

"It's not going too bad," I said. "I'm passing all of my classes. I question if choosing a psychology major was the right one but I can't complain."

"That's awesome, dude! Going the physical training route makes me hopeful in a job I'll be happy with. But it's so fucking hard, at least for me. I mean, this Asian in my health class gets like everything and tutors at least three-fourths of the Caucasians."

I chuckled. "You are so racist."

"The point is, college sucks."

"I agree, a lot of things suck."

"Hey what are you doing tomorrow night? Dallas is having a party and I was thinking you should go. Ya know, maybe invite Jade. Oh, wait, that's right, she doesn't have your number 'cause you're a pussy . . ."

"You are such an ass!" I said. Jackson grinned. "It amazes me how Brooke is still with you."

"Haha, ouch, but what can I say? I'm good in the sheets." He gave me his cocky grin and finished slurping the last of his shake.

"I do have this test to study for, but I haven't seen Dallas since the funeral."

"You haven't seen Dallas since the beginning of July?"

I shrugged. "It's not easy getting out of the house."

"This is the perfect time! Soooo?"

"So, I'll go."

"That's what I like to hear!" I shook my head and saw Jade make her way over to our table with our food.

"Can I get anything else for you guys?"

Jackson kicked me underneath the table again. I smiled and responded, "I think we're good, thank you." Jade smiled and walked away.

"You blew your chance and I am disgusted at you. That's all I have to say." Jackson and I stuffed our faces with our burgers as we continued to make small talk and enjoy the food. Laughing and making jokes let me escape my thoughts for awhile; it felt good to be free. I felt somewhat guilty for shutting my friends out after the funeral. I couldn't help it, though. Everything hurt too much.

We finished our meals and were handed the check. On the back of a napkin was a number written in pen with a smiley face by it.

"I told you she was into you!" Jackson kicked me underneath the table and smiled. "You better put that in your phone and invite her tomorrow night."

"I will, I will!

We walked out to his car. The night was brisk and cloudy, though the crescent moon peeked through. My breath trailed off into mist when I exhaled. The fall days stayed hot as the nights grew cold.

Jackson dropped me off at the graveyard. "Here ya go, babe, home at last." He winked at me while I smiled and shook my head.

I played along. "I had the best time tonight." I blew a kiss and we both started laughing.

"Anyway, dude, I better see you tomorrow at the party with Jade by your side."

"If she says yes, you will."

"Even if she says no, pick her up at that damn diner and take her there."

"You are a sick man!" We laughed and said goodbye as we both drove off to our homes. It was about half past nine when I walked through the door. For being guys, Jackson and I sure could talk.

As I got settled down and changed into something more comfortable, I realized how tired I was. I walked past the living room and into the kitchen to grab a glass of water. I went to take it back to my room but as I walked down the hallway, something stopped me. A dark silhouette of a man caught my eye at the end of the hall. My heart began to race as the figure just stood there. Light crept down the hall, and I looked back to realize I didn't shut the refrigerator all the way. I turned back around and the figure was gone.

A cold rush of air grazed my bare chest as I stood there in my underwear. Before going back to the kitchen I did a double take, but the figure never reappeared. I closed the fridge and started to walk back, but as I walked past my window, I felt another presence. I no longer felt alone, and for some reason, I felt I'd never been alone. I inched my way closer to the window and peered out of it and looked into the night. I gave it a good half minute before realizing nothing was by the glass. But the more time I spent around my window, the more it felt like something never left.

I lay down in my bed and grabbed my brother's journal to re-read a few entries. I stared at the picture of us and looked at the message on the back. It didn't make any sense, and his journal entries made him seem like he was crying out for help.

He said *something* was following him and talked about hearing voices. He also noted *something* found him. I didn't know what he found, but if what I saw at his place and what I saw a few minutes earlier in my own home were

28

related to that *something*, then there was a connection here and my brother wasn't crazy. There was always a thought, though, that maybe what he experienced was just the beginning.

Chapter 3

At quarter past three in the morning, the howling wind roused me from my rest. The more closely I listened, the more I realized it was not just the wind that woke me. I got out of bed and made my way to the bedroom window. Something about the window . . . droplets ran down and made a trail but stopped about halfway down, like something was blocking them. I slowly brought my hand up and touched the window where the droplets should have gone and realized that spot was warm. Everywhere else was ice cold. I only saw my reflection, but the feeling of something there made me wonder.

I pulled my hand away and started to think that I was literally going crazy. I took a few steps back and watched the window. The condensation ran down the middle, where it wouldn't before, and disappeared past the window pane. I didn't know why I got up and I didn't know what was wrong with my window, but I shook the restless thoughts from my mind and headed back to bed.

I woke up late morning to a text from Jackson saying, "Ask Jade to the party. Don't be a pussy."

I chuckled, grabbed the napkin her number was on and

typed up a short message asking her—hopefully un-awkwardly—to Dallas's party. What felt like an eternity, a few moments later she responded, "Good morning, Carter. I'm off tonight so you're in luck! That sounds like a fun time!" I got her address and told her I'd pick her up at seven. That really wasn't so bad, but Jackson could still piss off.

With the fear of rejection out of the way my stomach began doing flips of excitement. I gave myself a pep talk in the mirror, and turned on some music. I took a shower and got ready for the day. As I began doing laundry, I heard a knock on my door. Jackson rarely knocked so I threw that possibility out.

"Coming!"

Expecting to see a neighbor with baked goods of some sort, I opened it up to see my brother's latest ex, Emily. She was holding a banker box. I was confused, yet relieved to see her.

Emily gave me a sincere, sympathetic smile. "Hi, how have you been?" She asked. She and Alex had dated for almost two years and broke up when things started getting a little weird with my brother. She was always nice and super friendly toward me. My parents would have loved her. We hadn't talked much since Alex's funeral, so I was sure she felt a little awkward. Her eyes looked at my floor more than at me, and her feet shifted from time to time.

"I've been staying busy with college and work, but other than that, not too bad!" I played it cool and smiled back.

"That's great! Still majoring in psychology?"

I nodded. "Yeah, for right now, anyway." The wind whipped Emily's hair around her head. She tried holding the box with one hand as she moved her blonde hair away from her face.

"This darn wind!" She gave a small laugh and looked at the box, then to me.

Emily's freckles were always more prominent by the end of summer and into the fall. They sprinkled her rosy cheeks and brought out her iridescent, light blue eyes. Alex loved her freckles. He always called them angel kisses.

"That's great, Carter. I bet you're doing well with that." She changed the subject. "So, I bet you're wondering why I'm here and what this box is for. And I know I should have called first, but it's been in my car and I was in the area so I thought I'd come by."

"Well, I mean, you're always welcome," I told her. "Come on in."

She smiled as she walked through the doorway. "These

are some things of Alex's that I forgot I had. He kept them at my place for some reason and they aren't meant for me, which is why I brought them to you."

"What does he have in there?" She followed me into the living room.

"A lot of notes and papers and scribbles of things with some photos. He told me not to go through them because I wouldn't understand what they are, and he's right. I don't."

She handed the box to me, and I set it down on the coffee table. "Well, thank you for bringing it over."

She smiled. "Yeah, of course!"

"How have you been?"

"Every day gets easier," Emily said. "It's still hard to believe that he's gone, and to be honest . . . he took a little of me with him. I didn't mean for that to sound more dramatic than what it is!"

"No, you're fine! I agree, he took a lot of me with him, too," I reassured her. "Out of curiosity, did he act differently or was he really distant with you before he passed away?"

"In a way, yes, as if he wasn't around. If I texted or called him it would be hours or sometimes days before he would respond, and I just didn't get it. I wasn't happy, and I would worry. I didn't even know if he was happy anymore. He also came off as scared and paranoid and I could never find out why. This led to our breakup around the first week of June. He wasn't the same man I fell in love with anymore."

"I know," I said, "he would be weird with me, too, and he would never talk to me about it. In the end, I wasn't even allowed over at his apartment anymore. He would tell me he was busy with other things. I wish he would have reached out to one of us."

"I don't know what changed him, but whatever it was, I'm sorry to say, it destroyed him."

"Can I ask you something?"

"Of course, Carter."

"Do you think my brother was crazy?"

Emily paused before she answered. I saw sympathy and sorrow in her eyes. She looked away for a little bit and then back at me.

"I loved your brother. He was such a great guy. I know he would have done anything for you and me. I knew him so well and I miss him more than anything, but—" she lost her voice and started to tear up. She took a few small breaths and continued. "But he was different. I'm not going to say crazy, but he was lost in his own world, or at least *some* world. He found something that was on his mind more than you or I were. I don't know what happened and we never will, but no, I don't think he was crazy. He just had his own way of expressing his sanity."

I nodded and we both stood there in silence. I moved closer and gave her a big hug. She hugged me tightly for a few more moments and eventually let go.

"I'm always here for you," she said. "If there's anything I can do or anything you need, please give me a call."

"I will, Emily, thank you, and same to you." We exchanged soft smiles and as she walked away, I closed the door. I walked over to the coffee table and opened the box. I saw Alex's papers, notebooks, and pictures. Some of it took me into the past and some of it took me to a world of Alex's I never knew.

I took some of the frames out and looked at the pictures. A lot were family photos through the years, and some were of only me. One picture wasn't in a frame, but by itself. It appeared to be taken on a tripod while Alex was sitting on the edge of his bed. His bedroom was completely dark and the flash illuminated the area around him. He wasn't staring at the camera, but at what was next to it. He looked tired and scared, but I'll never know why. Dumbfounded by the photo I moved onto the next items.

Many of the notebooks weren't full or only had a few notes written in them. The notes were almost as dark as his journal was. I couldn't make any sense of them.

Why would he keep pictures of us at Emily's place and papers that had nothing on them? I continued to read through some of his notes, and things started to get weird.

"No matter where I go, *they* always seem to follow me. To keep the loved ones safe is only half the battle, for no matter where you go, once they see you, they'll always see you."

I grabbed one of the pictures he'd stashed away in the box and noticed our eyes were all cut out. On the back of the photo he wrote in blue pen, "Our eyes aren't what make us blind."

I traced the outlines of his words in hopes it would give me comfort. He had even hidden things from Emily. My frustration came and went, but reading his words, I only felt sadness. My heart hurt for him. I wish I had been there for him, wish I could have taken all his pain away. I would have helped solve what he couldn't.

My brother couldn't be crazy. There was always logic in a crazy mind—you just had to find it. I pulled another note out of the pile.

"They'll come for her. Emily, my love, don't let them

see you. You're all I've ever wanted, but I feel as if they want you more."

My phone interrupted my thoughts, and I saw Jackson had sent me a text. "So if u want 2 get hammered tonight which I strongly suggest, I have a DD so we're good, dude! C u at Dallas's!"

***

I spent the rest of day catching up on homework and cleaned most of my house. Quarter after six came and I headed out the door. I picked up Jade at her apartment. With butterflies in my stomach and a lump in my throat, I got out and opened the passenger-side door as she walked up to it. She had straightened her hair and wore jean shorts with white Sperry's and a light blue sports jersey.

When she hopped in my car, the smell of her sweet, tasteful perfume engulfed my nose and instantly filled my car. She smiled the same way she always did at the diner."Thanks for picking me up!"

"Well, as much I wanted to let you walk the mile and a half, a part of me told myself to pick you up." I winked at her as she gasped and then laughed. I pulled out of the parking lot and headed towards Dallas's.

"So, I'm really glad you gave me your number—oh, wait, I only have it because I gave you mine first . . ."

I tried my best not to smile as I spoke. "So what if I was playing hard to get?"

She gave me a crooked smile. "I don't really think that's your style."

"And I'm sure you leave your number on half-used napkins and give them to guys all the time."

"Usually only the ones who ask for it."

We both smiled and laughed. The butterflies were still flying all around in my stomach and my cheeks were starting to hurt from smiling so much. I forgot what it was like to have these type of feelings for a girl. I forgot what it was like to really feel happy, even for just a second, and to forget about the world.

"So, you like working at the diner?" I asked.

"It definitely has its moments, but the tips can sometimes make up for the shitty people. Plus, with college and everything I don't really work much, just on the weekends. I mean, I guess I could call you lucky since I don't work tonight." My eyes kept darting from the road to her eyes to her perfect crooked smile and back again.

"Yeah, I could call you lucky, too, since I could have wiped my mouth with that napkin and thrown it away."

She raised her eyebrows as her jaw dropped. She laughed and relaxed her body in my car, growing more comfortable. "Give me your phone."

"Yeah, why's that?" I asked.

"So I can delete my number from it."

She grinned mischievously and I was hooked. I mentally shook my head because if it weren't for Jackson, she wouldn't be in my car right now. *I should really thank him,* I thought, but I wasn't going to tell him that.

"Sorry, Jade," I said. "It looks like we're here, and I think it's best we get inside and not spend our evening on our phones." I gave her a playful grin and she shook her head and smiled. We both got out of the car and made our way to the front door of the house. As we came up to the front porch I could hear music booming out of the walls and closed windows, and noticed cars were parked up and down the street. Dallas's house was just half a mile out of town but didn't tend to get busted, so his place was usually the party house.

Dallas still lived at his parents' house and practically always stayed there while they were away on business trips. They both were CEO's at this large corporation which required them to travel all over. They don't always travel at the same time, but whenever they do, Dallas throws his parties. Dallas was in college full time and had swim practice most nights. He went to high school with Jackson and I, and we've all stayed pretty close.

Jade and I opened the front door and walked into the raging party. The smell of sweat and vodka filled my nose while the loud music filled my ears. Jackson came into the main room with his arm over Brooke's shoulder, both of them smiling and having a good time. They saw us and made their way across the room and through the crowd of people. We met them in the middle, kicking around empty red Solo cups and every now and again sticking to the sticky hardwood floor.

"You guys made it!" Jackson yelled over the music. "Dude, there's like fifty people here right now, but I guess triple that will be here later." His eyes were wide and glossy, and his expression reminded me of a five-year-old who just found out Santa was coming.

"I thought you said the party *started* at seven?"

"I thought it did, too, but then I found out that's when they planned to order pizza . . ."

The girls laughed and I shook my head. I looked around and saw everyone was loosening up and getting lost in the music, something I would love to do.

"Jade, right?" Brooke asked as she reached out her hand.

"Yeah!"

"I'm Brooke, Jackson's girlfriend. You must be Carter's date?"

Jade looked at me and smiled. "Yeah, but just this once."

"That's what I said to this guy too." Brooke playfully shoved Jackson's shoulder. "You wanna go get something to drink?"

"Sure!" Brooke and Jade disappeared into the crowd and left Jackson and I by ourselves.

"I'm glad you came, dude, and I'm glad you finally grew the pair to ask Jade out." Jackson handed me his half-drank beer as he grabbed a random open one.

"Me, too. I needed a night out. Where's Dallas?"

"He's in the other living room playing beer pong, I believe."

"Oh, God, is he drunk yet?"

Jackson took a sip and responded. "Hard saying, but he's winning, last time I checked!"

I looked around the room and took the whole party in. I tuned out the music for a few moments as I just tried to breathe, until something caught my eye. A figure walked down a dark hallway. I barely caught a glimpse of who it was, but it seemed to maybe be a man. It was too dark to tell. I turned my attention back to Jackson and asked, "It's been awhile since I've been here. Where's the bathroom again?"

He pointed to the hallway. "Down there and second door on the right."

I began walking when Jackson spoke again. "Wait, I meant left. No, I was right the first time, definitely on the right." He smiled proudly.

"Thank you." I made my way to the hall, where no one seemed to be, just in time to see the figure turn left down another hallway. Before it disappeared behind the wall, it turned to look at me and gave me a smirk. The moonlight from a nearby window lit up the guy's face, but I didn't have enough time or light to make out who it was. A little spooked, yet curious, I continued to follow the stranger. I turned down the next hallway, which led to a dead end. A few rooms stood to either side of the hall, but I hadn't heard any doors close or open. I crept further down the hall, making my way to the end of it, and felt a soft breeze. I noticed a slightly opened window. And then, ever so faintly, I heard something that wasn't just a whisper in the wind, but a soft and careful voice that sent chills down my spine.

"And now I'm home."

At first I thought it was just in my head, but then I

remembered that quote had been in my brother's journal. I looked out the window and saw no one. I slowly backed up and felt goosebumps crawl up my skin, then felt the wind brush the hairs that stood tall on my arms.

What did I keep seeing and hearing? Were these just figments of my imagination? Maybe I really was reading too much into my brother's journal. But this all just seemed too real.

"Dude, did you miss the bathroom?" Jackson asked from down the hall.

"Uhh, yeah, must have, sorry," I said, turning around. "I thought you said down this hall."

"Well, I didn't. You should go and then come back and join us!"

"Yeah, says the guy who second-guessed where it was at in the first place," I argued. I smiled to reassure him I was kidding, because I didn't really want to deal with a sassy drunk Jackson. I met him in the middle and we walked back down the other hallway.

***

The night went on and people have come and gone, and we all were been having a good time drinking and socializing. Dallas made some food and we passed it around with just a handful of us in his living room. It was sometime past eleven when the party seemed to slow down a little bit, but only because the guests had started drinking so early.

"Did you guys see how drunk Sarah Windsfield got?" Brooke asked.

"Which one was that?" Jade asked.

"She was the redhead who threw up by the pool out back."

Jackson drunkenly chimed in, "Dallas, I'm sorry. I forgot you had a pool." He mumbled to himself as he drank from his cup. We all ignored his comment.

"She was your RA freshman year, correct?" Dallas asked.

Brooke nodded. "Yeah, she always was super quiet and kept to herself."

"I don't think she drank tonight." I said. "In fact, I don't think I ever saw a drink in her hand."

Dallas narrowed his eyes in judgment. "Then why was she here?"

"I think you're right. I don't know who she came with but I always found her by herself." Brooke added.

"Are you sure it was her then?" Jade asked.

"I knew it was. I recognized her freckles and I mean she's not that tall. She had dark patches covering her skin.

They didn't look like a hikey, but they also didn't look like bruises. I don't know it was just weird."

I wanted to explore more with Brooke about that situation. Something didn't seem right but now wasn't the time. Changing the topic, Jackson sat up straight and said, "I want to say congratulations to Dallas. You kicked ass in beer pong even though you broke the table tonight." Jackson and Dallas raised a toast and took a sip.

"How'd you break it?" Brooke asked.

"After my victory, I belly flopped onto the table and it collapsed."

"Why did you feel that was necessary?"

Dallas shrugged, "You watched a girl puke."

Before Brooke could defend herself, I asked Dallas, "So, when will your parents be home?"

"Not until Tuesday night, I believe, so I hope these people's cars will be out of here by then." He laughed, but he was completely serious.

"Do you like it here?" Jade asked.

"What much is there to say? I live with my parents still. Mooching off them helps me save up but they're gone so much that this place is too big for one person. It's time for me to move out but I think I'll wait until I graduate."

"God, all my classes suck this year. They're

challenging and boring," Brooke confessed. We all agreed.

"Yeah, but Brooke, I'm pretty sure you're on your way to be named valedictorian," Dallas argued.

"So that means I can't find classes challenging?" Brooke asked.

"It just means you shouldn't." Dallas took a sip of his drink and we all took his drunk comments as a joke.

"This was a great night to cut back and relax." Jackson stated, moving on from talking about college. We all raised a toast and clanked our bottles and cups together.

"Yeah. Thanks, guys, for coming." Dallas said.

"Yeah, it was great meeting you guys officially," Jade added. She looked at me and we smiled at each other as I wrapped my arm around her on the couch. I watched Jackson lean in and kiss Brooke on the cheek; she smiled at his touch and he moved her blonde locks out of his way. We'd all had a few drinks, but Jade and I didn't want to get too carried away since I did have to take her home.

"You guys can totally crash upstairs or down the hall, wherever you want!" Dallas offered us. "We have tons of bedrooms for tons of activities." He winked at Jade and I.

"Why would you say it like that?" I asked.

He shrugged and took another sip. Dallas shook his head and his brown bangs fell right above his eyes. His hair was short on the sides but longer on top. Dark, earthy colors brought out his soft brown eyes. Dallas was a very down-to-earth guy. He and I weren't really close until about eighth grade, when we both went out for soccer. Believe it or not, Dallas was quieter and more reserved before high school. His parents moved around a lot, so he was the new kid in school up until the fifth grade. He used to swim at his old schools, but when he came to our school district only the high school had the pool. So soccer it was.

"High school was so easy and now life just sucks," Dallas said with a laugh. "We're all in so much debt and everyone is going down different paths. It's just hard to think about."

"Maybe I'm a little drunk, but sometimes I tell myself when my college bills come, I'll say it's not for me and send it back and tell them they have the wrong address," Jackson admitted.

We all stared at him and Brooke spoke for all of us. "Sometimes you're an idiot and it's really not the alcohol's fault."

"I will say that when I get all of my student loans paid off, I'm going to go the liquor store to buy at least fifteen kegs and bottles and bottles of booze and I'll throw the biggest party ever," Dallas said.

"Are those your only plans after college?" I asked.

"I would love to move to Florida and study marine life there," Dallas replied. "Potentially become a certified scuba diver and practically live in the ocean. I've been to Orlando multiple times and ever since the first time I've gone there, I've loved it. Plus, it would be such a great state for you guys to come visit me in. I don't need to list the reasons."

A few drunk strangers came into the living room only to change the music before heading back to their group. The sound of heavy feet treaded across the upstairs floor. It made me remember we weren't the only group left.

Jackson flaunted his cocky smile but it was a little bit bigger and goofier since he was drunk, and we all couldn't help but laugh. "I love you guys."

"I've never been to Florida before." I stated.

"Really?" Brooke asked.

"My parents took me to Disneyland practically every year," Dallas added.

"Did your parents do anything fun for vacation, Jade?" Jackson asked from the other couch.

Jade seemed to hesitate before answering. She sat up straighter causing my arm to fall off her shoulders. "No, we never really have done anything."

"Is there any jungle juice left?" Brooke asked.

"You know, that is a question I can't answer," Dallas replied.

"Here, babe, I'll go find you some! Jackson got up, and before he walked away, he gave Brooke a sloppy, drunk kiss on the cheek. It made all of us uncomfortable. "Hey, by the way, did you guys hear that Victor Kaestner died a few days ago?

"The Victor Kaestner who used to work for the school before he was caught raping children and having kiddie porn?" I asked. "The creepy one?"

"Yeah, the dude was forty-five and he slit his wrists in prison. They said he found a shard of glass hidden in the grass when he went outside one day. He picked it up and took it back with him, and away he went. They even said his cellmates were afraid of him during his last days alive. He was acting strange and unresponsive when the guards shined their flashlights in his eyes. And apparently he was saying some pretty dark things to himself. But of course, that's just what they say. Either way, the dude was fucked up and deserved it." Jackson then turned around to get more jungle juice.

We were all feeling the alcohol, but I was thinking about Jackson's story. The guy had to have been feeling guilty and in a lot of pain for what he did. I couldn't imagine. His last days sounded tragic.

I stood up. "I need to use the restroom. Keep your eyes on drunkie." I said, referring to Jackson. I made my way to the hallway, but not before one girl did. She covered her mouth and ran into the bathroom and slammed the door. I started walking away before I heard what was behind her hand.

"Dallas, do you have any more bathrooms?" I asked.

"Yeah, there are two more upstairs."

"Thanks!" I made my way toward the stairs; cutting through the crowd that remained, and started walking up. A few people were up there, but they didn't stay for long. I made my way down the hall and tried finding a bathroom. One of them was occupied, but I believed Dallas had another one in a bedroom. I opened one of the doors and turned on the light. It appeared I was in Dallas's parents' room, a master bedroom with an attached bathroom and two walk-in closets.

"Hey, dude, you coming into the pool?" a guy asked me from out in the hall.

"No, I'm good."

"Suit yourself." He stumbled down the hall and made a loud noise as if he fell down the steps. I turned my attention back to the bathroom and realized that it was occupied as well. I leaned on the wall and waited for the person to come out. A few moments later, I heard a woman softly humming "You Are My Sunshine." The noise of a drawer closing caught my attention and I turned and saw an older man who looked exactly like Dallas's dad putting something away. My mouth dropped open slightly as he turned and looked at me. The bathroom door opened and the light turned off, but no one came out.

I turned my head back around and his father was gone. I stepped inside the bathroom, turned on the light, and closed the door. I took a deep breath and started peeing. When I finished, I walked out of the bathroom to see both Dallas's mom and dad sitting on their bed staring at me, but nothing came out of their mouths.

"Oh, I'm sorry, I didn't think you guys were home."

They still didn't say anything, and they started smirking as I began to walk out of the room. They turned their heads and their eyes followed me like a creepy old portrait as I continued to make my way out of their room. I quickly went down the steps and made my way back to the group.

"Dallas, I thought you said your parents aren't home."

"They're not. Their flight doesn't come in until Tuesday after their meeting. Why? Are you on LSD?"

I tried my best to calm my racing heart and not let my voice give me away. I needed to brush it off and not make a scene. Assuming they were pretty drunk or at least fairly tipsy, I decided it was best not to worry them.

"Never mind, I don't know what I was getting at."

Jade looked at me and smiled. "Are you sure you're okay to drive?"

"Yeah, I promise." I shook it off. No more than a half hour later, were we all ready to go. I pulled up to Jade's apartment and parked on the side of the road.

"So about deleting my number," she began. I pulled out my phone and handed it to her.

"You still want it deleted?"

She smiled at me. "Thank you for showing me a good time tonight," she said. "Your friends are pretty great."

"So that means . . . ?"

"It means don't get your hopes up, and we'll see how the second one goes."

"Oh, so you think I want a second one?" I said with a smile.

Jade's mouth dropped open in shock and she giggled a little. Even when she stopped, my gaze doesn't leave her eyes and hers didn't leave mine. We both slowly leaned in and before I realized it, our lips were touching and the whole world, at least for a little while, went away. Her lips were soft and fruity. I didn't want to take mine off of hers. I kissed with purpose but was also cautious; I feared if I had kissed too hard I would ruin her delicate lips.

She pulled away and stared at me, biting her lip. Her eyes said it all. "Keep my number."

"I'll think about it." She softly kissed my cheek, opened the door, and hopped out. I waited until she was inside to drive away. Those last few minutes made me feel like I wasn't so crazy after all. I felt that the world was on my side and that what I'd been seeing and hearing lately was nothing but my imagination. Or was that just what a person who has already lost their mind tells themselves?

Chapter 4

I stepped out of the shower and let the steam envelop me as I stared into the mirror, using my towel to wipe it off so I could see my stomach on up. I didn't like what I saw. A few months ago I would have recognized who I was staring at, but now I just saw the mold losing its shape, morphing into something else. As I thought about how my brother felt and what he had gone through in his final days, I was sure he didn't recognize himself all too well either. I'm not saying I was going down the same path, but I could relate to how he must have felt.

My reflection wasn't who I ever thought I would become. I felt like a shell of a person and didn't know how to make it better. I wanted to drown in a storm of emotions and let lightning go through my veins to make me feel anything. I was so hollow, empty.

I wiped more condensation off to get a better look at my face, and noticed something on the mirror. As the steam started to go away, I noticed the remaining condensation formed into what appeared to be a partially formed handprint. I tried to wipe it away, but it remained. I hadn't remembered placing my hand there, but it felt warm. That was weird. The rest of the mirror felt cold to the touch. It reminded me of what happened with the window the other night, when the rain would not rundown a certain spot. I stepped back and the shape slowly evaporated. All that remained was my reflection, staring in despair. Something wasn't right.

I opened up my medicine cabinet and grabbed two orange medication bottles. One was for my insomnia, and the other was for my anxiety. Dust covered the lids. It had been awhile since I took either one of them.

My anxious mind had been up and down throughout the past few years. Sometimes I didn't know what spiked it up or that I even felt anxious until my body gave it away. The anxiety and insomnia went hand in hand; I just thought and thought and worried and thought. My mind would feel suffocated, almost as if it were placed in a plastic bag with the air slowly getting pushed out of it. The sad thing was, I usually didn't know how to talk myself down. My fears and thoughts collided and peaked until I felt like I was left with no stability.

Next to the medications were my therapist's number and a reminder to pick up an anti-depressant if I ever needed it. Ever since my parents passed away I had horrible nightmares of their accident. I wasn't there to witness it, but my mind made up its own story. In my dream I would scream and scream until my mind said *WAKE UP*. When I woke up, I'd be lying in a puddle of sweat, my throat strained and my body trembling in fear and panic.

I saw a therapist for a couple of months after my parents' deaths, and the medication helped severely. The nightmares went away for the most part, but once my brother passed away, everything came rushing back. My therapist thought I suffered from mild depression, so I had a prescription ready for me. I never got it. I only went to therapy two times after my brother died. I didn't want to hear the bullshit anymore about suicide and the steps to recovery. I knew my brother didn't kill himself, and the best way to cope was to move on and heal.

Some days I didn't even notice feeling depressed. I just felt like I wasn't home, that my soul had left for the time being. Some days I just didn't care what my friends said and what they did. I felt unmotivated and unresponsive to my own problems.

What's even worse is that at least once a week, I wake up and I hate that. I hate waking up because I'm a lot happier asleep. My reality is the nightmare. Jade made me happy, but in the back of my head I knew that happiness wouldn't last forever. I knew the scale had to tip one way or the other. Life can't be all good, but it can't be all bad either. With Jade being something good, I was afraid sadness would soon follow.

Call me weak, hopeless, or pathetic, but some days I didn't have it in me to deal with the world. And I was okay with that.

Right then and there a part of me was tempted to take a handful of each just so my mind would calm down. I couldn't do this alone. Jackson knew that I'd suffered from anxiety and depression, but he didn't know the extent of it.

The day my brother died was the last time I took both of my medications. The next day I swore to myself I would get better without the help of drugs. I'd been doing just fine up until this point. A lump in my throat began to form as I started to feel like I was thrown overboard from a boat. I was lost in the rippling waves, swallowing gallons of water. I didn't feel like waving my hands in the air for someone to try to save me. I wanted to be left behind. I wanted it all to stop.

I took a few deep breaths and closed my eyes. I told myself I was going to get out of the water. Today wasn't going to be the day I drowned. I eventually shook the negative thoughts out of my mind and started to come back to reality.

I quickly changed into some clothes and made my way towards the kitchen. I opened up a drawer that was home to many miscellaneous objects, and found a pencil. My mind calmed down even more by just holding it. I dug around and found the perfect journal to doodle in, and sat down at the kitchen table. The autumn air blew through the window and the sound of dead leaves rustled on the sidewalk outside.

I picked up a pencil and started to draw. It was one of my go-to pastimes whenever I felt anxious and my mind seemed too full. I drew whatever was on my mind, and it felt as if the weight of my anxieties would go away. I started drawing when I was in kindergarten. The older I got the less I drew, until my teenage years began and I had trouble sleeping. Whether my sketches were good or not, I didn't care. For me, drawing was the equivalent for jumping into your warm, comfy bed at night.

My mind calmed down the longer I drew, but that didn't keep my thoughts at bay. My brother said he thought he found something, but then he said it found *him*. What did Alex find? What made him go back and back to it? All of this seemed to be happening to me now. If I talked to my friends about it, they were going to think I was crazy. I saw parents that weren't even home, I saw my dead brother and he talked to me, and now I got the sense that something was trying to get my attention.

I didn't know what to do; I didn't know where to go. None of this made any sense, and I had no idea if this was my own imagination or if this was a severe case of schizophrenia. My anxious thoughts led me to put down the pencil and leave my work.

I picked up my laptop on the way as I headed into one of my spare bedrooms I keep important files in. I searched for my family's medical records out of old documents and prescriptions, and scrolled through pages and pages of articles about mental disorders and genetics, and even some paranormal websites on my laptop. But so far as I searched, all roads led in a circle and I was left with nothing. This would be much easier if my parents were still around, but I was done feeling sorry for myself. As I read one more article, I heard a knock on the front door and got up to answer it.

Behind the door stood Jackson holding a case of beer and Jade, Brooke, and Dallas beside him holding movies and junk food.

I smiled and asked, "What are you guys doing?"

"Dude, we texted you like hours ago," Jackson replied.

"Yeah, someone must like to ignore people," Jade

teased. I told them to come on in and closed the door behind them as we made our way to the living room.

"We felt like we all needed a movie night to wind down before another big week of school," Dallas said.

"Sorry, I guess I wasn't really looking at my phone," I told them. To be honest, I was glad they came over. It was nice to let my worrisome thoughts escape for awhile.

"My arms and legs are killing me," Dallas complained as he took a seat in a chair. He placed his legs up on a nearby ottoman and slumped into cushions.

"Is swimming still kicking your ass?" Brooke asked him.

"Hey, it's a lot harder in college. Like, you have to swim a lot more, and plus, I think when I landed on the beer pong table I messed up my leg."

"I know that Brooke was doing something with her legs the other night." Jackson grinned and kissed Brooke on the cheek as she slapped him in the chest. Jackson and Brooke Palmer had been dating since their freshman year of college, when they started helping each other in class and started talking. Even though Jackson could be a dumbass sometimes, he and Brooke were actually a pretty cute couple and seemed really happy together.

Sunlight always seemed to find Brooke. She had a

radiance like a summer's day—the sun needed her, not the other way around. Looks and good grades always came to her, and Brooke was a city girl stuck in a farmer's daughter's body, and she could not wait to move to a big city such as Los Angeles. Sometimes I would catch her valley girl accent, and that was all the proof I needed to know Brooke was meant for a city.

The others made their way in and got comfy in the spots they chose. Brooke sat on her legs, which I never understood how girls found that comfortable. She pulled out her phone to check her emails and messages before giving us her full attention. Jackson sat next to her with both his legs spread far apart. Jade followed me as we chose the other free couch

"You guys remember when we all went out for cross country freshman year and Coach would make us run all over town until no one would throw up anymore?" Dallas asked.

"Yes, and the three of us would run to the park and hide in the trees," Jackson added. "Remember that one time we were so far ahead of everyone, we hung out at the playground?"

"Why did you guys even go out, then?" Brooke asked as we laughed.

"We did the work and it paid off! We almost got first," I said.

"I bet the coach hated you," Jade said. We all laughed some more.

I nodded and said, "I mean, yeah, he did. That's why we went out for soccer."

Jade stood up. "So, what movie are we gonna watch? I brought a few horror ones and some Japanese horror film I found in my attic."

"Let's let the boys decide while we go make popcorn!" Brooke said. She got up and the two of them went to the kitchen to make some snacks. A few moments passed until we heard laughter and the sound of a wine bottle opening.

"We should do something for spring break" Jackson suggested. "We should go somewhere. Just the three of us and get away." He took out a steel flask and took a sip from it before passing it around to Dallas and I.

"My parents have a lake house in Florida, or we could fly to Cancun," Dallas said as he made a face from the whiskey. He finished taking a drink, then handed it to me.

"I don't care where we go, as long as I can get away from here for awhile," I told them. As the two of them continued to give out ideas, something else caught my attention. I finished my swig as I heard a faint sound like cracking ice, then saw frost make its way up the window next to the TV. The shape of a handprint made of ice, formed in the center of it as a coat of frost started to spread. Before I knew it, the window was covered in a thin, frosted layer of ice displaying markings of a hand, with thin lines of ice trailing up the window.

"Dude, what have you been looking up?" Jackson asked, stealing my attention from the vivid scene. I looked at him and saw he was on my laptop, and I realized I forgot to close out the pages I had been looking at. I quickly leaned over and grabbed it from him. I dropped the flask in his lap while I closed my computer.

"Just some articles on schizophrenia for my psychology class. I have a paper due this week and I was getting started on it before you guys came." I thought it was a pretty good lie.

Dallas grinned. "Smells like porn to me."

"I was just going to look up vacation spots for us to go to on break," Jackson replied, a little taken aback. I felt bad that I had taken it from him and didn't give it back, but it was perfect timing because Jade came back with popcorn, chips, and candy, which distracted all of us. Brooke was right behind with two wine glasses and a bottle of White Zinfandel. We popped in the movie and Jade and I started cuddling, with Brooke and Jackson doing the same. Dallas seemed snug on a chair, holding the popcorn bowl close. I glanced back at the window. The ice and handprint were gone, and I was the only one who seemed to notice the strange occurrence.

As the night continued, most everyone eventually fell asleep right where they were.

I was in a chair to myself, Jade was passed out on the futon, Dallas was on the floor snoring away, and Brooke and Jackson were tangled up together on the couch. I yawned as Jackson and I made eye contact. He untangled himself carefully from Brooke's grip and stood up. He walked over to his duffle bag and pulled out a bottle of whiskey. He raised his eyebrows mischievously.

"You and me. Backyard. Now," he whispered softly. He had the widest grin on his face, like he didn't have a care in the world.

I rolled my eyes and stood up. I followed him through my house until we made our way outside and onto the porch. We both sat down on the dewy chairs and got comfortable. The table and chairs set came from my parents. The table was a long rectangle that could seat up to six people. It had earthy shades inside each square that was placed on it. The chairs didn't have cushions and were made out of a sling fabric. My parents bought it the summer before my senior year and we only got to use it a couple times.

The night was brisk, but it was the perfect temperature where you almost—but didn't—need a sweatshirt. The last of the cicadas were buzzing away, warning us that winter was on its way.

A bottle of whiskey was always our drink when Jackson and I got together. We'd had countless nights of heart to hearts while taking pulls of it. We'd also had our countless times of throwing up. One of these nights was when my parents passed away and Jackson thought the best fix was to get drunk. So he stole a handle of whiskey from his parent's liquor cabinet and we got trashed.

Tonight the sky was clear of clouds and we could see every star we wanted to. It was almost a half moon and the light lit up my backyard and made the grass sparkle from the dew.

"What's your biggest fear? And go!" Jackson said as he twisted the cap off the bottle and slid it down the table to me.

I took a big pull and felt the harsh sting of the whiskey flood my mouth, burning my throat. I made a face the entire time until it was in my stomach. Instantly I felt a rush.

"My biggest fear is not knowing who I am anymore," I admitted. "I fear that I'll grow up without the proper guidance and I'll lose sight of who I am."

"All right." Jackson nodded in approval.

"What is your goal in life? And go!" I slid the bottle back to him.

He grabbed it mid-slide and took no time taking a big swig from it. He slammed it down as he wiped his mouth with the back of his hand. I made a face for him. "I honestly want to be successful in everything I do. I want to marry Brooke one day and have that dream job and travel the goddamn world."

"You think you want to settle down?" I asked him.

"Carter, I'm not the same douchebag I was in high school. Brooke has actually helped tone all of that down."

"I'm not judging, but I think it's funny, looking back at freshman year when I caught you at a house party the first night of school sleeping with two different girls."

He gave me a snarl and took another big gulp. He slid the bottle back down to me. The next pull didn't taste as lethal as the first, but I was already beginning to feel it.

"What's your biggest fear, Jackson?"

Believe it or not, Jackson King does not have any

fears. Although, junior year of high school I thought I wasn't going to be captain with you on the soccer team." Jackson grinned at me as he eagerly reached for the bottle, like a baby reaching for candy. I took another swig before giving it back.

"What are you thankful for, Carter?" Jackson asked as his speech began to slur. I was positive he missed the first few letters of my name.

"I'm thankful that you were the first person to see me right after I found out my parents were killed. I remember the only person I thought to call was you. Alex was visiting Emily's parents and you were the next closest person."

He slid the bottle back to me while I took more than just a few sips. "Carter, no matter where we end up and how successful we both become, I am always going to be there for you. We're brothers and anywhere you move, I move. Don't laugh,' cause I'm serious. Brooke will have to deal with it and if not, I'll go to another house party and take care of that problem."

I let out a small chuckle as I sensed one of Jackson's drunken rants coming on.

"Whether Jade works out or she doesn't, you are going to base your happiness solely around yourself. After college, Carter, we're finally adults and the real world is going to hold many opportunities. As your best friend, I want you to take as many of those as you can. If you have to, I want you to move far away from here, as long as you're happy. Life is shitty but if anyone can make something of themselves, it's you. I know you've been through a lot, but you're never alone and things do get better."

"Thank you, Jackson. But you know what's crazy?" My intoxicated mind started to wander away from the topic at hand. I looked at my back porch furniture and got to thinking. "I'm a homeowner at age twenty-one." I laughed to myself. "How fucked up is that? I guess wills can be a blessing and a curse." Once my parents died, Alex and I inherited their house but neither of us wanted it. It was placed on the market and sold within a month. I finished my senior year living in an apartment until I bought this house a year ago.

"Yeah, that's crazy. Did you know that Brooke wants a dog?" He squinted and leaned closer across the table. "I want a dog." Jackson stood up and swayed back and forth until he found his balance. He made his way down the four steps that led to the grass below. He walked to a nearby tree and I heard his zipper.

"I miss this, Jackson. I miss being young and being in

high school, except the high school part. And I miss being carefree with you and Dallas."

"You know me. I'm always down to hang out and get drunk with ya," he responded from the tree. "I would love a German shepherd." I assumed he was talking to himself. "You know, I mean this in the best way, but you're the one who's been distant." He zipped his pants back up and wobbled his way back up onto the porch. He dinked his hand on the grill and swore under his breath. He took a seat and made direct eye contact with me. "Carter, please don't shut me out again. It's fine if you need your time but it hurt when you didn't respond to my messages and phone calls. I mean you haven't seen Dallas since July. It's almost October. Don't get me wrong, I loved hanging out with Brooke and Dallas, but the person I really wanted to hear from was you."

"I know, and I apologize for that. I'm still working on some things. I'm not going to shut you out again."

"Dude, I get it." He let out an enormous yawn.

The screen door slid open and Dallas walked out in a white t-shirt and blue athletic shorts. His hair was disheveled while he scratched his head. He folded his arms to keep warm. "Are you guy's rallying without me?" He looked at the bottle of whiskey.

"You were asleep. We didn't want to wake you."
Jackson smiled as he slid the bottle Dallas's way. Dallas
walked over to the table and picked it up. He took a long
sip before setting the handle of whiskey down.

"How long have you guy's been out here?"

Jackson and I exchanged glances. "We couldn't tell
ya." I said while giggling.

"You guys want to start a fire?" Dallas pointed to my
fire pit.

"Even though it's late I'm down for one." Jackson said
while standing up. He swayed back and forth until he made
it to the fire pit.

"Sounds good to me." I followed the two of them off
the porch and helped set up a couple lawn chairs. I pulled
out the gasoline from my garage and poured some over the
wood. I was never good at starting fires with just paper and
a match. The guys always laughed at me but never
intervened. I lit a match and dropped it over the wood. A
blast of heat flew our way as the crackling fire ignited the
wood. We made a half circle with the chairs as we claimed
our seats. The welcoming flames felt good against my bare
legs.

Jackson sat down and began laughing hysterically. I
watched as his breath traveled through the air. "Remember

that one time we had a fire while my parents were gone?" He asked. "And we used gasoline for the first time."

"How old were you guys?" Dallas asked while taking another swig.

"Like twelve or thirteen." I answered. "Jackson poured the gasoline over an open flame that was on a piece of paper." I couldn't contain my laughter. "The fire followed the trail and lit the tip of the pour spout on fire. Jackson then threw the tank and gasoline spiraled in the air and landed on the grass."

"Flames were everywhere and we were surrounded in fire. I mean eventually the small flames died out but there were trails and trails of lit gasoline. I poured dirt on the tip of the spout and it died out before the fire met the inside of the tank."

"You guys could have died." Dallas said while he joined our laughter.

I sighed as the last of my laughter escaped my mouth. "Yeah, we could have."

"Hey did you ever hear back about you studying an abroad?" Jackson asked Dallas.

"Actually, yes! I got the email today. I was chosen along with fifteen other students to travel to Australia this spring!"

Jackson and I cheered. "Congrats, Dallas. You're going to have so much fun." I told him while grabbing the bottle from him.

"Oh shit, that means you'll be gone for spring break." Jackson said.

"We can always plan a trip to Florida this summer." Dallas added.

Jackson shook his head. "It'll be too hot then."

Dallas and I both looked at him and rolled our eyes. "Hey I saw you were talking to Ashley at your party. How is that going?" I asked Dallas.

He shrugged. "I'm not sure. She just got out of a relationship not too long ago. We don't text too much, but I did invite her to some of my swim meets."

"Ashley Mosher? What a babe." Jackson said.

"You guys want to make a drunk walk to the park, like old times?

I looked over at Jackson who was beginning to doze off in his chair. "I think we should call it a night. Who knows when the rest of them will get up. Right, Jackson?"

"Aw man, we just started this fire." Dallas said.

Jackson instantly opened his eyes. "I agree. We'll finish what's left of the handle for next time." He had no idea what he was agreeing to or what he was even doing.

He went to grab it off the ground for another sip, but halfway through he dropped his arm and retracted it slowly, realizing it was a bad idea. He looked like a kid who wanted more cookies but was too full.

I walked over to Jackson and helped him up. "You staying out here Dallas?"

"Just for a few more minutes. I know where the hose is to put out the fire." He looked up at me and smiled.

I nodded. Jackson and I made our way back onto the porch. Jackson bumped his way inside while I stayed behind looking at Dallas one more time. His eyes were hooked on the fire and he looked lost in his own world. I wasn't sure if it was from the alcohol or if Dallas was having a moment. The longer I stared the more I noticed the fire wasn't reflecting back in his eyes. I blinked a few more times to refocus my vision but Jackson made a loud thud in the kitchen. I looked at the screen door then back at Dallas and saw the flames were reflecting back. Shaking my head, I made my way inside the warm house.

Talking with Jackson and Dallas made me feel normal again, like my life hadn't changed. The comfort of having people over was even soothing. I could go to bed tonight knowing I had loving friends who I could always fall back on.

It was mid-morning when I woke up with a mild headache to the sight of my friends getting ready to go. When I looked at Jackson, I could tell I was in a lot better shape than he was. It was funny watching him try to hide his sweaty, clammy head and pea-green face from Brooke. It wasn't that we weren't allowed to drink, it was that Jackson didn't know when to stop when it came to the hard stuff. Dallas slowly started waking up on the floor. He was sprawled out the way I remembered him.

I was going to offer them breakfast when I remembered I didn't have enough eggs.

"Are you sure you don't want to come out for breakfast with us?" Jade asked me while going to the door.

"Yeah! Come get out of the house," Dallas added while standing up and collecting his things.

I shook my head and responded, "I would, but I need to finish up on some homework that's due at the end of the night."

"Which means you have all day to do it," Jackson commented.

"And I mean I need all day to do it." Jackson looked at me for a moment, reading me, then headed for the door as well. I knew he wouldn't have remembered a lot of our heart to heart, but I hoped it had changed his suspicions about me. Jade smiled, kissed me on the cheek, and told me she'd talk to me later. Jackson stayed a moment behind as everyone else headed for their cars.

"Dude, what is with you?"

"What? I have the right to say no every once and awhile," I responded.

"Yeah. But you never used to. What about our talk last night? You said you missed us and were going to work on some things. You used to always come out with us and do your schoolwork later and have a good time."

"I'm just busy right now with all this homework and dealing with what to do with my brother's things and all this stuff. Jackson, of course I want to get my life back to normal, but it takes time."

"What homework? That paper about schizophrenia and other weird stuff?" He gestured at my laptop and then back at me. "Correct me if I'm wrong, but didn't you already have a paper like that last year for intro to psych?"

"What business is it of yours? Is this built-up bullshit from my college work getting to you or the fact that I'm more of a homebody recently?"

He stared at me again in silence and then shook his head. "Good luck on your paper." He walked away and closed the door. I felt bad. It hurt me to know that he was hurt and that I couldn't tell my best friend what was going on in my life right now. It also sucked that I couldn't be as close to the girl I was into all because I didn't want to let her in to that part of my life, either. I shook those thoughts off and continued going through the box Alex had left at Emily's. I found a picture of them. I didn't know if she wanted it or if she even saw it in the box, but why would she give me a picture of the two of them?

I texted her and asked if her it was all right if I stopped by to give her something. As I waited, I got ready for the day, but still no response from her. Considering that she had showed up at my house without a text, I figured it would be all right if I did the same. I allowed a few more hours to pass before I decided to leave.

I grabbed the picture and drove to her place. As soon as I hopped out of the car, I noticed her front door was open. I ran in and was welcomed by the sound of an old, scratchy record playing some eerie, unknown song from the fifties. It felt as if I'd just stepped into a crime scene from a movie.

"Emily!" I called, but there was no response. I continued to make my way through her house. Her car was in the driveway and her place looked nice and neat, but something still wasn't right. I made my way down the hallway to her bedroom, but her bed was made and she wasn't in there. I was starting to get worried. I went from room to room calling out her name, but there was still no sign of her. I took out my cell phone and dialed her number. My heart stopped when I heard it ring inside the house. I followed the noise to her bathroom door. I slowly opened it, and my mouth fell at the sight.

Glass and blood covered the floor, and I saw the bathroom mirror was shattered. Emily lay crouched and bleeding in the corner, covering her ears. I ended the call and I could hear her whispering repeatedly, "Make it stop, make it stop."

"Emily, are you okay? What happened to you?" Her whole body trembled. When I kneeled down beside her, she looked up at me. She brought her hands away from her eyes and continued to shake. I saw fear in her eyes.

"Did someone do this to you?"

She shook her head and replied quietly, "No, I did it."

"Why?" Her hands and arms were cut up and bleeding. I couldn't tell where one wound started and where another ended. "We have to get you help. You're losing a lot of blood."

"If I don't see her, I'm fine . . ."

"See who?"

"That's why I shattered the mirror. I can't look at them. What I saw was . . . not okay . . ."

"Emily, what are you talking about? What did you see and what did you want to stop? Your record player?"

"I don't have a record player." My stomach knotted as I realized I hadn't heard the music since I found Emily. Goosebumps went up my arms and down my neck. Emily continued, "I figured if I covered my ears I would stop hearing the voices, and if I don't look at the mirror I'm not gonna see what I can't without it."

"Okay, come on, we need to get you help." I carefully grabbed her and tried to get her to stand up. As we started making our way out of her house, she looked at me and spoke.

"Do you smell that?"

"Smell what?

"Smell death. All I smell is rotting flesh. Whenever I lie down or am about to go to bed I smell decaying skin, as if the smell was from me. Carter, I don't think I'm safe anymore. For the past few days I've been seeing things and hearing things and I'm afraid I'm going down the exact same road as Alex."

"No, Emily, you're going to be okay, everything is going to be okay." I kept telling her that, but I was more scared than I'd ever been. I had no idea what was going on or what we were both seeing, but I kept hoping. I kept hoping that we'd all be okay.

Chapter 5

The doctors decided to keep Emily a few more days to run tests and watch her to see how she did. When she was admitted, she told them she slipped getting out of the shower, hit her head and broke some glass. Whether they believed it or not, I'm not sure. I stayed with her for the first two hours, but needed to run home and take care of some things. I told her I would come back around eight thirty that night.

When I got home, I gathered my brother's things and got on my laptop. Alex, Emily, and I were seeing things, but my friends weren't. I didn't understand what was going on, but I knew now I wasn't crazy. If Emily was going down the same road as my brother, then she would only be safe for so long. I had no idea how to stop this.

The sun started to set, and I remembered I had told Emily I would be back soon. I got up from the couch to go grab my laptop charger when I saw something out the window. I walked up to the glass and tried to see it, but it was out of my sight. Out of the corner of my eye, I saw it walk past another window. It was a human figure. It circled the house until it came back around and I got a good look at it. I almost had a heart attack. It was Emily in her hospital gown peeking through my window.

I rushed outside and ran to the side of the house, trying to catch her. I called out her name as I lost her again, but got no response. She wasn't supposed to leave yet, and how would she have gotten home?

"Emily, we need to get you back to the hospital," I called. "I told you I'd be right back." I saw the last bits of her gown disappear behind the house when my phone went off. It was her.

"Emily, what are you doing? We need to get you back."

"What are you talking about?" Emily asked. "I was calling to ask you to bring me some food that's better than the hospital's." The air seemed to get cold, and I choked on the lump in my throat as my mouth grew dry.

"You still there?"

"Yeah. I'll be back shortly." I hung up the phone and slowly started to make my way back inside the house. When I got back inside, I bumped into Jackson.

"Jesus, what are you doing here?" I asked him, my heart racing again.

"Carter, we've all been worried about you since Alex died. We'll always be here for you, but you have to let us in for us to help you."

"I know you guys are, but I don't need help. I don't need saving. I just need time."

"Carter, we've been best friends ever since we were little. I know everything about you and you know everything about me. But when it comes down to it, you're still not letting me know everything. I'm not one to keep pestering somebody, but just the other day you lied to my face once we all left your place. I could tell in your eyes, and after our drunken talk you still won't open up. Don't lie to me and don't deny anything, just talk to me. Talk to your best friend. I know something is on your mind, something that has your attention more than we do. Hell, do you want to start making Jade worry about you? Stop being selfish!"

"You wouldn't understand," I mumbled.

"That's bullshit," Jackson spat back.

"*I* don't even understand what is going on. I have no idea what is going on around me. All I know is that my brother wasn't crazy."

Jackson looked down at the floor and stayed silent for a couple of minutes. Carefully thinking about what to say next, Jackson opened his mouth. "Carter, I loved your brother. He was a great guy, but you can't keep chasing shadows. You can't sit in this house and think about all the what-ifs and all the facts and all the roads that point you in this sad, depressing state of mind you're in."

"You have no idea what you're talking about. You don't know anything."

"That's because you won't let me in!"

"Fine, you want in? You want to know what I've been dealing with for the past couple of months?" I stalked to the coffee table and threw my brother's journal at him. "That. That's what I've been dealing with. Whether he's dead in your eyes or not, he's still here in mine."

He skimmed the journal in silence. His face told me he was disturbed as much as he was intrigued. As he finished the last few entries, he set it back down on the coffee table and looked at me.

"Well, I can definitely tell you guys are related. Are you sure this is Alex's?" He gave me a wink, but it faded when he saw I was not amused by his flippant remark.

"What do you mean by that?"

"You guys both have that dinky-ass handwriting," he teased. "Could it get any smaller?"

"Jackson, I'm really not in the mood. That's fine if you don't believe me about the journal."

Jackson took another moment before responding carefully, "Your brother wasn't okay, and I'm sorry that he put you through all of this, but he needed help, Carter. There was nothing you could have done."

"No. You're wrong. He didn't kill himself and he wasn't crazy. It clearly states in there that something was after him. He found something and it got him."

"Don't you think this is all a little pretentious? What did he find? 'Cause whatever he found or whatever 'got' him, it's nowhere to be found. You expect me to believe this? Maybe he was schizophrenic, like you've been researching. We'll never know."

I became angrier from his ignorant, presumptuous remarks. "Whatever he found wants something and it obviously took it," I retorted. "It took my brother, Jackson. He is gone because of whatever he found, I know it."

"He's gone because he didn't get the help he needed. He didn't see a way out of it. What 'place' would he have gone to? What, he's just going to teleport somewhere and come back? Or did he drive someplace and get into a fight with an animal? Carter, there are no solid facts about what your brother saw, found, or what he was talking about. According to that article I saw on your laptop, the three signs of schizophrenia are delusions, hallucinations, and catatonic behavior. That logically explains every detail in that disturbed journal of his."

With pursed lips, I flatly responded, "What he found is with us in this world. You know Emily, Alex's ex? She's in the hospital because she's positive that she's seeing something and it's coming after her. She fears that she's going down the same path as my brother did. Explain that, Jackson."

"Explain what they 'found.' What did your brother and Emily see?"

"Emily saw something in the mirror that caused her to shatter it. Alex's mirror was shattered when he was found. Something has to be connected here, because I've been drawn to windows and I feel a presence when I'm near them."

"You just walk by every window and get a sense of not being alone?

"Yeah, as if I'm drawn to it."

He lowered his gaze and raised his eyebrows. "Every window?"

"You're missing the point."

"Carter, what is the point?" Jackson raised his arms in the air.

"All I'm trying to say is that Emily is becoming paranoid not because of what's in her head, but because of whatever is following her. You don't just go punching mirrors, and I don't just go up to windows for the hell of it. Something is trying to reach us."

"You know how crazy all of this sounds?"

I shook my head. "This is exactly why I haven't talked to anyone about this. You or anyone else won't understand. You are one of my best friends, Jackson, but I don't even understand what is going on around me. Alex's final words tell an unspoken truth that we can't quite see."

"You're so dramatic," Jackson said. "Why do you think that?"

"Because ever since my brother died, something feels like it's unfinished, and I feel like something's watching me. Why? All I know is that my brother wasn't crazy, and Emily is scared out of her ever-living mind."

Jackson looked away for a few moments and stared down at the journal. He took a seat and went through it once more. I couldn't quite tell if I was relieved that Jackson knew, or worried that telling him would somehow start a chain reaction of unfortunate events.

Breaking the silence, I said, "It says in there he found something and they're not human, that they lack humanity and they seem to follow him around every room. When we were at Dallas's party, I saw his parents in their bedroom when I went up to go to the bathroom."

Jackson spoke. "His parents weren't home yet."

"Exactly. Their eyes, just like my brother said, were as white as the moon. They didn't say anything to me, and they seemed to lack something."

Jackson shook his head and fought back. "Carter, that isn't possible. You're seeing things. Emily is in the hospital because accidents happen. Your brother was deranged and Emily is freaking out because she's alone, and so are you, but we're all here for you and it's going to be okay. If you don't think about it, all of this can go away."

"I am scared, Jackson. I am scared that I'm becoming just like my brother. I am scared that anything remotely positive in my life will be surrounded by darkness. Okay? Is that what you wanted to hear? You don't just wake up one day and tell yourself not to feel that way. Feelings aren't right or wrong. I'm having a hard time processing everything that has happened to me since our senior year."

"Carter, we don't shape events, events shape us. You have all the power to do what you want when things happen to you. Life is all about perspective, and it's okay to be scared. But don't let your fear control you; that's not living. Carter, live for once; live for yourself. Let go of all that wreckage inside your head. Enjoy college, enjoy your friends, and enjoy all the girls who will walk in and out of your life. Find that beacon of hope."

Laughing to myself about his rude girlfriend joke, I calmed my thoughts and said, "You're right, I need to stop this. It's all in my head. I'm sorry I've been distant lately, and now you know why."

"It's okay, Carter. I love you, dude, and everything is going to be okay." I nodded. "So come with me and the gang. Jade is working tonight and it's fifty-cent wings at Jersey's."

"I would, but I told Emily I would bring her back some food so she has something good to eat."

"I think she would love it if you brought her wings." Jackson smiled at me, and I couldn't help but smile back and tell him I'd go. Jackson and I hopped in his car and we drove off to go eat. During the drive I reflected on how unreasonable I was being and how the whole situation was unrealistic. Jackson was right: if I didn't think about it, everything would go away. The mind can be a strong thing, but I didn't want my brother's death to be in vain. Maybe deep down, the reason I'd made all this stuff up in my head was because it was the only way I didn't feel alone, like a part of me still thought he was here. It was a way for me to have closure.

Jackson pulled up to Jersey's Diner and we found

Dallas, Brooke, and Jade in our usual booth. Jade was in her work clothes and I presumed she had only taken a moment to come sit with us.

"Hey, you guys! We were just talking about what we should do for spring break," Dallas greeted us. "I obviously can't go but you guys should still go somewhere!"

"I think we should go to Florida," Brooke suggested.

"Yeah, that's what we were talking about the other day," Jackson said. I liked the idea, but as everyone else kept talking, I noticed Jade had been keeping her eye on me, which made me nervous. When our eyes met, she smiled at me.

She stood up suddenly and said, "I just got sat, one second." Jackson took her place in the booth and I made my way to Jade.

"Hey." That's all I could get out of my stupid mouth. Jackson got in my head about causing Jade to worry about me.

"Hi, Carter." Her voice was soft, but she knew I was feeling anxious.

"I have to tell you some things."

"Just give me a few minutes." She shot me a quick smile and walked off to greet her table. I turned and sat down next to Dallas to get back into their conversation. It wasn't much of one, considering Dallas was trying to get French fries into Jackson's mouth, and Brooke was on her phone taking sips of what was left of her shake. Starting to space out, my phone vibrated and I saw Emily was calling me.

"Hello?"

"Hey, Carter, the nurse told me visiting hours are over, but they're pretty sure I can come home tomorrow. The tests didn't take as long as they planned and I no longer need to be observed."

"I'm so sorry about not bringing you your food, I'm at the diner ordering some quick!"

"No, it's okay! The stale bread they gave me wasn't too bad." I could hear the smile in her voice. "But I was calling you to see if you were available to come pick me up later in the morning. I'd ask my parents but I haven't told them I'm here yet." She laughed uncomfortably.

"Yeah, I don't have class until one tomorrow anyway," I told her. The other end of the phone grew silent. "Everything all right, Emily?"

"Carter, last night . . . I, I woke up and I saw myself." Her speech was hesitant at first but then she began talking faster. "I saw myself staring at me through the window. And then today I got up to get x-rays and I saw myself at the end of the hall. Tell me I'm not going crazy and that I'm just creating these images in my head." Every word was said with longing hope.

"What were 'you' doing?" I tried to make it sound like a normal conversation so my friends wouldn't become curious or confused.

"I was just smiling at myself, and my eyes were all white. It's what I saw in the mirror. Carter, I'm scared. I don't want to be here, but I don't want to go home. I really have no idea what to do."

"I'll be there first thing in the morning. Everything is going to be okay, Emily. Just try to get some sleep and don't think about it."

She cleared her throat and sniffled and quietly said, "Okay." I hung up the phone and got back to my friends.

"How's Emily?" Jackson asked, but his question was more directed toward me. Jackson rested his elbow on the ledge behind him, taping his fingers with his other hand on the table.

"She's doing a lot better, and she thinks she can come home tomorrow."

"That's great! Is she worried about something?" Brooke asked.

"No, she just keeps thinking about her accident and

how she feels stupid and is tired of being in the hospital," I lied.

"Oh my God, if that table orders one goddamn more Coke I'm going to tell them that I'm not allowed to promote diabetes," Jade fumed as she came back to our table.

"What's wrong with your table?" I asked her. I tried ignoring how secretly turned on I was by her rage.

"They're just needy assholes who suck down their Cokes on purpose and make me run around for their every need just so they can see me in my little skirt. Also, I'm pretty sure my tip is on the center of the table, and each time I mess up they take a dollar away."

"That's messed up. Let's go over there and kick their asses," Dallas stated, standing up.

"Sit down, we're not getting Jade fired," Jackson told him.

"It's all good," Jade sighed. "I might just give my table to Doug. He's good at handling guys like that."

"Hey, Jade, I was thinking we should get our hands and feet done at Robbie's salon." Brooke said, changing the subject. "You know? Have a little girl's day. There's also this new store that opened in the mall last week and I haven't checked it out yet."

"You make it sound like she just moved here." Dallas inputted.

"Well, I just meant that . . ." Brooke trailed off.

"Oh my God, I forgot that that was a place, but yes, I'm down! Is that the place that almost got shut down due to rodents?"

"Hell no! That was City Nails. They're right next to Downtown Liquor on Third Street. Robbie's is in the nicer part of town."

"Oh, that's right." Jade said, but I could tell she still had no idea where Brooke was talking about.

Jackson turned to me with a big smile on his face. "Boy's, sounds like we're day drinking when that time comes."

Brooke lowered her gaze and made a face in disapproval. "Jackson, honey, don't you have a D in your sociology class followed by another D in your religion class?"

Jackson's eyes narrowed and he scowled at her and muttered under his breath before he came to terms that he should study. Before Jade got up again, I quickly talked to her.

"Hey, I wanted to let you know that I had a really great time with you at Dallas's. And even though my face looked completely shocked when you guys showed up, I was actually extremely happy to see you."

She gave me a puzzled look. "Carter, are you okay? You seem anxious and your eyes keep darting at me like I've been doing magic tricks every five seconds."

"Yeah, I just wanted to also apologize for not responding back to every text right away."

She smiled as reassurance. "You don't owe me anything. If you're busy you're busy. You're just making me paranoid because you look paranoid."

I gritted my teeth groaned at myself internally. I got inside my head and caused anxious thoughts and problems that were never there. I had to think of a quick save before she thinks I'm loony.

"No, I was wondering if you would like to go on a date with me tomorrow night?"

"So, that's why you keep apologizing, because you've been thinking about asking me out again. But a second date?" She smirked to indicate she was joking. "I don't know . . . I might have given my number to one of those guys over there."

"I knew you were the kind of girl who's into assholes."

"Which is exactly why I let you take me out once."

She smiled and I chuckled. "Pick me up at eight." She got

up and walked back to her other tables.

Jackson shook his head and gave me the biggest grin. "You two are perfect for each other. You're welcome."

"For what?"

"I totally told you she was into you and she left her number and the rest is history." I threw a fry at him and laughed quietly. "You want another shake, babe?" he asked Brooke, putting his arm around her shoulder.

"When have I ever had more than one shake a night?" Brooke asked him, surprised.

"I don't know, when have you ever came more than once?" Brooke slapped him in the chest and he coughed from the impact. "Babe, I'm just kidding!" he protested. Dallas and I chuckled and looked away.

"Tell me again what I liked about when you asked me out? I want to think of that feeling and then never feel that again." Brooke grumbled. Jackson leaned in and moved her blonde curls out of the way so he could kiss her neck. She shoved him playfully out of the way. "Stop!" She laughed as she tried to get away from him, then took some leftover whipped cream from her old shake, and rubbed it all over his face. He dropped his mouth and pulled her closer, Brooke squealing all the way.

"All right, you two, if I get a noise complaint I'm

kicking you guys out," Jade said as she made her way back over to us. She picked up a fry and threw it at them.

"He's being a dick," Brooke stated.

"When have I ever been a dick?" Jackson looked at me with a shocked expression. I gave him an eye roll and threw a remaining fry at him as well.

"I hate to be that guy, but I need to get going," Dallas said. "I have swim practice tomorrow at five in the morning." I moved out of the way for Dallas to get out. "It's funny, last time I checked, I thought Hitler died."

"Why did you ever want to do swimming in college?" I asked him.

"If it wasn't for my scholarship and my parents, I wouldn't have to." He rolled his eyes and left his tip money on the table. "I'll see you guys later. I hope you guys are considerate and choose Australia for spring break." He said goodbye and walked out of the diner.

"Doesn't he have a meet Thursday?" Jade asked us. Jackson stopped flirting with Brooke for a moment and he turned to us.

"Shit, I think he does. I think it's at like five." Jackson looked at me. "You're going, right?"

"Yes, Jackson. I'm going." I gave him a sarcastic smile and went back to sipping my drink. Despite my original plans, I was glad I was with my friends tonight. Maybe Jackson was right—if I didn't think about it, it would go away. Having a busy week ahead was going to help with that. As Jade continued sitting with us for a few minutes here and there, the more I realized how into her I really was. Sitting there with my friends, my heart yearned deep down for happiness and a new beginning. I hoped this new feeling would last. The pieces of my crazy life were fitting together better and better each day. And at that moment, there wasn't a part of me that was waiting for my life to go bad anymore.

Chapter 6

Nerves rushed through me like electricity, as my heart smiled. I drove down Jade's road to pick her up. I hadn't felt this way in a long time. Jesus, I hadn't had a girlfriend since sophomore year of high school. The way my heart raced, and my heartbeat in my throat, made me feel alive. Such a simple thing. I told myself to get a grip but then I was overwhelmed again. She was beautiful. She was incredible inside and out. If things continued to work out, Jackson was never going to let me live this down.

I pulled up to her apartment complex and sent her a text letting her know I had arrived. I rolled down the window, letting the brisk fall air dry the beads of sweat on my forehead. The smell took me to memories of bonfires and apple orchards with my family. It brought me back to the Friday night lights of football games with my friends. The smell was comforting and promising in its own way. Why was I so nervous? As soon as I wondered, I realized it was probably because this was our first real date. As I saw her open the building's door, I quickly reached in the middle console and sprayed on more cologne. I waved my hand around, trying to make the scent less intense, but I had no idea if it helped. I got out of the car and over to her side to open up her door. She smiled and thanked me as she hopped in. I walked back over to my side and got right in.

"Someone must be trying to smell good," Jade said when I got back in the car. She looked at me and smiled. "Would be a first, right?"

I nodded, feeling flushed. "And someone must be trying to look good? I didn't know you owned anything else." I gave her a big grin and started driving.

"So, Mr. Gray, where are we going tonight?"

"Well, if I would have known you were dressing as well as that, I would have picked a different place." I genuinely said. She wore a stunning white dress that stopped before it got to her knees. It had an open back with laced sleeves. Her hair was straight and she wore sparkly white high heels. Her lips shined from a chic pink lip gloss.

She let out a playful laugh and looked away. "I mean, I can go back and change into my work outfit."

"No. You look beautiful. When I told you to dress nice I just didn't picture . . . you like this." I reached my hand out to her for her to take. She smiled as she took it. "Now, don't get your hopes up, this won't be a fancy one star diner." I winked while I squeezed her hand.

She dropped her mouth while she tried taking her hand

out of my grip. I squeezed it tighter as I tried my best to focus on the road.

"I'm just kidding. We're going to one of my favorite places in town," I continued.

"Well, if it's anything like your compliments, I'm sure it's a great place." She laughed again and turned her attention back to the road. "Carter, you look very handsome. I love that powder blue button up." As soon as she complimented me, a lot of my nerves subsided. *I got this.* I was glad the blue button up with khakis was the right choice. A few minutes later, we arrived at the restaurant. "Ahh, so you like Italian," she commented as I helped her out of the car.

"Venice doesn't just have Italian food. It has some seafood dishes and chicken tenders if you're feeling adventurous."

"I guess you got lucky and knew what I liked."

I looked at her with a cocky grin, something I picked up from Jackson. "Well, duh." We went inside and were greeted by the aroma of seafood and Italian spices. We were seated on the lofted second floor, where we could look out at the lake behind the restaurant and the city's lights beyond. Venice was fine dining, with white tablecloths and candles on every table. A large chandelier hung from the ceiling and glistened like a million diamonds. Waterfalls were strategically placed to give off a soothing, peaceful oasis vibe. The expensive designer glasses and silverware twinkled and gleamed.

"Wow . . . it's beautiful." Jade's gaze was out the window at the view, while mine was on her. I smiled as turned back to look at me. "What, is something wrong?" Her hands quickly went to check her hair and then she looked down at her clothes.

"No. Just looking at you. I like this beautiful view." I gave her another smile and she looked down at the floor, trying not to blush, but she couldn't hide her smile. "So, tell me more about you."

"Well, I have an older sister, Claire, who lives in Oregon. She moved away from the Midwest around three years ago. She's twenty-six. My parents are still happily married in Detroit and are taking care of my cat, Charles."

I laughed. "Charles?"

"Excuse you, it is a perfect name for a cat. Or . . . a butler." We both broke out in laughter and she continued to speak. "So, anyway, I moved out here once I graduated and got a job at the diner my freshman year. I'm actually on scholarship for the university." She sat straight up in the chair while her hands were placed delicately on her lap.

She talked with confidence and I would have never known if she was nervous like I was.

"Jade, that's really awesome!"

"Thank you, but I hope you don't mean the diner part."

"I think all of your accomplishments are awesome." I winked. "So what else? What are your future plans?"

Our server, who was in his mid-thirties and dressed in a white button-up with black slacks, vest, and tie came over and asked us if we wanted to sample the spotlighted wine before taking our drink order. It was a Pinot Noir and a six-ounce glass was almost twenty dollars. I'm more of a moscato-type guy, but I didn't want to say no to free alcohol. We clanked our glasses together and tasted the dry sample. Smacking my lips together as the bitter liquid burned in my chest, I motioned for Jade to continue.

"Do I look fancy enough holding this wine glass?" Jade asked me while taking a sip. She gripped the stem near the bottom with two fingers.

"No, I think it needs to be more like this." I cupped the base of the glass in my palm with the stem in between my fingers. I smelled the glass while I talked, "I'm getting hints of earthy tones with some kind of wood. Mahogany maybe?"

"I think all you're missing is a mustache." We both

laughed at each other and finished the sample of wine. Jade continued, "I want to help people. I'm not entirely sure what field to go in, whether it's social work or being a dispatcher. I've thought about being an EMT, but I don't care for the hours. I love horror movies and puppies. I'm also a fan of mudding, and I fucking hate cauliflower." I laughed, and she continued. "I like reading, but I also like getting out of the house and doing anything. I love the beach and going on hikes. I can't wait to get a dog so we can go to breweries together. Is that weird? Once I graduate, I want to backpack through Europe. And I hate close-minded people, and I think that's about it. What about you?"

"Well, as you know, I lost my parents my senior year of high school and my older brother Alex just a few months ago. He was only twenty-five. I'm currently a teacher's assistant for a developmental psychology class. I'm a huge puppy fan, as well, I like a good horror movie every now and again, and I fucking hate pulp in my orange juice."

Jade busted out in laughter but then grew serious once more. "I'm sorry about your parents and your brother, Carter." She reached over and placed her hand on top of mine. "You're such a strong guy, and you have the biggest heart of anyone I know."

I gave her a sincere smile and moved my thumb so it sat comfortably on top of her hand. "I'm doing a lot better with everything. Time has helped, along with my friends and meeting you. I don't mean to make you feel uncomfortable, but meeting you has made me feel more alive in the past few weeks than I have in the past few months, so thank you for that."

"You don't need to thank me. But I am really glad I gave you my number. I almost didn't. Oh, God, I was scared."

I nodded toward her purse hanging over the back of her chair and said, "If you don't mind me asking, what's your one keychain about?"

Surprised but not embarrassed, she looked to her purse and noticed the metal keychain dangling on the side. "It says, 'My story has just begun,' and it's for suicide awareness. I got it from volunteering for the local suicide hotline."

"Oh, wow! I didn't know that. Are you still volunteering? How long have you done that?"

"It's been a little over four months now. I like it a lot. I only do it twice a week now because of school. It makes me feel great knowing that I have been there for someone when they thought no one else was."

I looked her in the eyes and said, "You're a really great person, Jade. I'm glad you gave me your number." We continued to talk and laugh together as our meals came, enjoying each other's company. As the night drew on a part of me wanted to open up to her and tell her more about what I'd been doing and why I'd been so distant, but my inhibitions told me not to. For once, Jackson was right: I needed to just leave it in the past.

"Thank you for tonight, Carter. It was perfect," Jade said as we pulled up to her apartment a couple hours later.

"Yeah, it was." I hopped out and opened the door for her, then walked her to the front door and stopped. I looked into her eyes, and leaned in to kiss her soft lips. All my thoughts disappeared again. After we pulled away, I stared at Jade Hamilton and pondered how I could ever deserve a girl like her.

Jade smiled and said, "I'll see you later." She went inside and shut the door behind her, and I was left with nothing but the taste of her lips and my heart beating as fast as it could. I shook my head and made my way back to my car. I couldn't help but think how things were slowly falling into place. I felt like I could finally be hopeful again. I was getting the girl, college was going well, and we were all going to go somewhere nice for spring break.

Sometimes when things are broken, you leave the pieces and start over with new ones.

I passed Emily's house on my way home, but something made me stop. I parked on the side of the road and started making my way over. The only sounds were my footsteps in the wet grass. Her car was parked in the driveway and all the lights were off, but that wasn't what got me. As I got closer to her house, I started to hear that old record music again: the raspy, crackly noises and the old 1940s tune. Why was I hearing this if it was all in my head?

I made it up to her house and realized what had made me stop. Every single window was covered in duct tape. It hadn't been like this when I dropped her off from the hospital this morning. There was no way for me to look in on her, and no way for her to look out. But then, I realized, that was exactly why she did it. I went up to her door and knocked, waiting. Moments went by with no response and I grew worried. I walked around the back of her house to see if I could get in any other way, but there was nothing.

Emily had lost it. I could see into the house through a few spots she missed with the tape and saw that she was in her bedroom lying down, with just a lamp on. As I started walking back around, something caught my eye in the living room. I went up to the window and saw Emily standing in the hallway, looking down it toward her bedroom. I quickly went back to the window in her room and saw she was still lying there. Chills went down my spine as I ran back to the living room, but if Emily was standing in the hallway, I couldn't see it. I could only see white. And then the hairs on my neck stood up and I felt goosebumps cover my arms and neck as I made the connection. I took a step back and remembered Dallas's "parents," with their eyes as white as the moon, same as what my brother said in his journal: "Those eyes, the color of the moon, so bright and white and mysterious, a simple but sinister glow to them."I stepped back and got away from the window, taking out my phone to call Emily. She sent me to voicemail three times and then the fourth time, she turned off her phone. Her lamp went off, and with no other light to illuminate the house, I was forced to go home.

This wasn't going away. Emily was in danger, and I didn't know how to stop it. No one would listen to me and Emily would probably never leave the house again. How do I help her? What the hell was I supposed to do? None of my friends had seen what I had except for Emily and Alex. Why was Emily after Emily? There weren't enough pieces to this puzzle and I felt like I was running out of time. What if Emily was forced into the same fate as my brother?

It didn't feel right of me to break into her house so I decided to call for a welfare check. Whatever was going on, maybe the police could help her. I was certain that once they saw the duct tape on the windows, they'd bust in and see what was going on. The police told me they would make their rounds sometime tonight. I was in a position where I didn't know if it was an emergency or not.

My heart felt like it was going to rip out of my chest, it was beating so hard. Right when I got home I grabbed a glass of water and lay down to take a breather. I calmed my thoughts and my nerves, slowly relaxing. Before I knew it, darkness consumed me and my thoughts and I blacked out.

***

I awoke mid-morning to crashing thunder that rattled the windows. Dark clouds covered the sky and water began to cover the ground. I immediately checked my phone to see I had zero notifications. I lay there and listened to the rain hit the window. *Should I call her? Was it a good thing I didn't hear anything from her?* I was starting to panic; something didn't feel right. I quickly shot her a message telling her to call me when she woke. The loud thunder couldn't drown out the thoughts that flooded my brain, but realizing I had class in thirty minutes, I figured I'd best be getting up and ready for the day. I had class at nine-thirty which gave me time to shower and shave. Once I was done getting ready I drove to school, forgetting to eat breakfast. Walking to the building, I checked my phone and saw I still had nothing from Emily. The idea of calling the police to hear an update ran through my mind.

All through my first class, I only thought about last night and what went on at Emily's. All I should have been thinking about was how well my date went. Annoyed with myself, I grabbed my things and headed out to my car as soon as class ended. As I walked to the parking lot, I bumped into Jackson.

"Hey, dude, how are you doing?" he asked me. His voice was softer than usual.

"I'm doing okay. Why?"

"I just didn't know how you were taking everything."

"What do you mean?"

He looked at me with a puzzled face and leaned in. "Carter, they found Emily's body this morning. The cops stopped by to check on her and found her in her bed."

I wanted to throw up. I was mad, confused, torn, dumbfounded. I felt like I wanted to die. I felt all the color leave my face.

"Are you okay?" Jackson asked. "I mean, you didn't

know? The town has been talking all morning. The neighbors and pedestrians were all concerned when they saw her windows and police cars there."

I looked at him blankly. "What?"

"They think it was an overdose and that she used sleeping pills prescribed to help her sleep at night, but they're not sure yet. I'm so sorry, Carter. Are you okay?"

"What? She's dead?"

"Yeah. Carter, I'm sorry, I thought you knew."

"It's fine, Jackson. I need to go." I walked past him and felt the rain touch my skin as I moved toward my car. I heard Jackson come after me as he trudged through puddles, but I ignored him and got in my car. He pounded on my window and I could hardly make out his words. I turned my car on and rolled down the wet glass.

"Carter, I know what you're thinking, but it wasn't your fault. There was nothing you could have done."

I shook my head. "You still don't get it, Jackson." The rain was pouring down now and Jackson's hair fell on his face, rain dripping off him. "It's not about that. I don't think it's my fault they're dead, nor do I blame myself for maybe not 'doing enough.' You're not going to get what I have to say because you didn't get it a few days ago when you were arguing with me."

"What are you saying? Do you know what happened to Emily, Carter?"

"No, I don't know what's going on or what happened to her, but I know for a fact that somehow her death and Alex's are related, and I'm going to figure this out." With that, I rolled up my window and drove out of the parking lot, leaving Jackson and what I knew behind.

This all seemed unreal, like a bad dream. I had just seen her and now she was gone. My head was spinning and I started feeling nauseous. I was mad that I couldn't do anything and I was mad that I didn't know what was going on, which made me even more mad. Everything was all fucked up and my friends knew none of it. Maybe they thought I was crazy. If that was the case, then I would be going down the same path as Alex and Emily.

As soon as I got home, I pulled out Alex's journal and leafed through the pages, trying to put more of it together. What did my brother discover that he kept going back to and wouldn't leave him alone? Emily saw more of what I couldn't see and it drove her crazy, and that's what my brother had been saying, too. Something with windows and mirrors; I saw more than just a reflection. All of a sudden I heard the front door close. I looked over and saw Jackson soaked and dripping wet.

"Carter, we need to talk." He stood in the doorway with his once suave hair, that was now a mangled mess.

"Yeah, you're flooding my place."

"No, we need to talk about what's going on with you and everything else."

"What is there to say, Jackson? Weren't you the one who told me if I didn't think about it, it would go away?"

"That's not fair. I just wanted to know what was going on and to see if you were okay. I want to hear what you have to tell me, that's why I skipped my next class. That and it was also my math class." Jackson took off his shoes and walked over to the couch.

I paced around the room running my fingers through my hair. My first initial thought was to just yell at him; to let out all of my emotions. But I knew that was on impulse, and Jackson didn't deserve that. I took in a few deep breaths before I cleared my head to tell him the story. "Last night I took Jade home after our date, and then I drove by Emily's house and saw that duct tape covered all of her windows," I began. "So I stopped, and then I looked through an open spot on her window and saw her lying in her bed. But then, as I was leaving, I saw Emily in the hallway staring toward her bedroom."

"I'm lost."

"There were two of her. I went back to Emily's room and she was still lying down. She never moved. I went back to the window and I was face to face with the other Emily."

"Carter, how can there be two of her? That's not possible."

"There were, Jackson, I don't know how or why. I saw the same thing at Dallas's with his parents, and their eyes were as white as the moon—and that's exactly how my brother worded it."

"So what are you saying?"

"I'm saying that somehow there were two of her and she saw something in her mirrors and windows, and she shattered her bathroom mirror so she wouldn't have to see it. She wasn't in the hospital from an accident, she was there because she was scared shitless. Jackson, I'm telling you, my brother found something and it didn't leave him alone, and Emily found the same thing and it got her. Ever since Alex died, I've been feeling weird things at the windows and seeing unexplainable things, too."

"What about mirrors, like Emily?"

"Only once after I got out of the shower. There was a handprint on the mirror, and it was warm and it didn't go away. It was weird. Also, the other night when everyone was over here, I saw a handprint made out of frost on my window."

"Why didn't you say anything?"

"What was I supposed to say? 'Oh hey, look guys, over there! I think I see a handprint.' I was having a hard time comprehending what I was seeing."

"Let's go." Jackson made his way toward my bathroom and I quickly followed. He turned on the shower to create a big cloud of steam. "Now we wait." A little irritated, I stood there and waited with him. When he was satisfied with the amount of steam, he turned off the shower and we stood there and watched the mirror. Condensation slowly reverted back into air. Jackson looked closely at the mirror as the last of the steam evaporated. "I don't see anything, do you?"

"No, but I'm not saying I see these things every time. Why are you so against this?"

"I'm not against it, but, Carter, this whole thing holds no logic. You're the only one who saw Dallas's parents, the only one who sees handprints on mirrors and windows, and the only one who saw Emily in two different spots at the same time."

"It wasn't Emily," I argued. "Just because you don't understand something doesn't mean it's illogical. Believing something is totally different. And just because you don't see or feel the same things as I do doesn't make me crazy."

He was silent for a moment, looking at me but not really knowing what to say. Beads of water dripped off his hair, creating tension in the quiet room. The orange pill containers caught his eye. He picked up a bottle and looked at me.

"You stopped taking these. Why?" He didn't have to say it; his eyes told me how disappointed he was in me.

"I've been fine, Jackson."

"No, you're not fine!" He raised his voice. "You're seeing things that aren't there and hearing things that don't exist! That doesn't sound 'fine' to me."

"I don't need those. And they're not for hallucinations, anyway. I know for a fact that something is happening all around us."

"Say there *is* something else, that the other Emily was not human. What would she be? Where did it come from? Say your brother did find something and it was after him, what did he find?" I led us out of the bathroom while I continued talking.

"That's just it, Jackson, I have no idea. All I have is this journal and what I saw. He said something found him, that he didn't go looking for it, and that he kept going back for more answers."

He shook his head in disbelief. He was still speechless. He took a seat while I picked up the picture that was on the coffee table. I handed Jackson the picture I had found underneath Alex's floorboard of me and him. "On the back he wrote, 'Keep the ones you love hidden,'" I said.

"Hidden from what?"

I took a moment to think about it. "I think he means hide from yourself."

"We're going back there," Jackson said.

"Back where?"

"To your brother's apartment."

Chapter 7

I hopped in Jackson's car and we drove off toward Alex's apartment. The storm continued to rage as water began flooding the streets. It was as if the sky was mourning. I leaned back, sinking into the plush seat and admiring how clean Jackson's car was. He'd gotten it from his parents as a graduation gift and had taken good care of it. Jackson's composure was calm and relaxed. He sat upright while he tapped his fingers on the wheel.

"Maybe your brother left more information or evidence behind," Jackson said, breaking the silence.

"I don't know. It was bare when I was last there, except for what the landlord brought in for tours. I cleaned everything out a few months ago, but we can see."

"Carter, if you're right about all of this, then we need to go where it all started." He pulled up to the apartment building and we hopped out. The sounds of gushing nearby storm drains roared. Rain drops splattered against my raincoat, the sound of them reminding me of the sound of rain on the tent when Alex and I camped in our backyard once during a storm. Jackson followed as I began climbing the fire escape up to his room. "This is so illegal."

"I know," I mumbled. I was almost to the window when my hand slipped on the ladder and I started losing my balance. My wet shoes squeaked as I tried to keep them on the step. I bit my tongue in the fall, and I couldn't tell if tears or the rain flooded my eyes.

"Carter!" Jackson yelled. I held tighter to the rail with my other hand, hanging over the edge. Jackson was below me. "Are you okay?" he asked. I hauled myself closer to the ladder and held on.

"Yeah. I just slipped is all." I waited for my heart to slow down before I continued climbing. I made it to the window and pushed it up, and we both entered the dark apartment. Once we were in I quickly shut the window. The grotesque smell hadn't changed, by the way Jackson was gagging. I tried turning on the light but the electricity was out, so we both used our phones as flashlights. The dark, dingy apartment didn't look any less creepy since the last time I was there. I already had a bad feeling, and the air was cold and musty. Our lights made the shadows dance, making the atmosphere more eerie. Jackson made his way over to one of the walls, which had the fresh coat of paint on it. The landlord must have added another layer because the bloody words were no longer visible.

"The landlord covered up what my brother wrote on

that wall. I believe he used his own blood and wrote out his thoughts."

"I'm sorry, Carter. This must have been hard for you," he said quietly.

Disregarding his comment, I stated, "I think he used three layers of paint on that fucking wall. The mirror in the bathroom used to be broken, like Emily's was when I found her that night I brought her to the hospital. The landlord fixed it, though." We walked into the bathroom to look at it. "This place was real beat up."

"It's like reliving a crime scene the more I know about this place. And if it took him three layers of paint that just sounds lazy to me." Jackson's eyes darted around the space as he took everything in.

"I don't know, maybe they don't plan on renting this out to anyone anymore." We walked out of the bathroom.

"Yeah, maybe. Where did you find the picture of you two? The one that was on your coffee table."

"In his bedroom." I led him to the bedroom and we looked around. "It was under a floorboard that seemed to be under where his bed used to be." We both knelt down and lifted the floorboard back up. My heart stopped.

"What's this?" Jackson asked. He grabbed a photo from the space and pulled it out. It was the picture of Emily and Alex that I found but gave back to her.

"I gave that to Emily just last week."

"Then why is it here?"

"She must have been here before she died."
Goosebumps crawled across my skin and I could see
Jackson was spooked, too. "How'd she know that the
floorboard was loose and that you could get in through the
window?" I asked out loud. As if perfectly on cue, we
heard the window in the other room slam down, making us
both jump. We quickly stood up and turned toward the
bedroom door.

"Didn't you shut that?" Jackson asked, trying to
reassure us both. We slowly crept out of the room and into
the living room to see the window was indeed shut.

"We need to get out of here," I whispered. The only
sound was the rain hitting the window. Lightning lit up the
apartment for only a second, but it felt as if a spotlight was
shined on us, giving us away. We went over to the window
and tried opening it. "It's not budging."

"This still doesn't explain anything," Jackson said as
he tried to open the window. "Goddamn it." As he
continued to work on the window, I heard the floorboards
creak. I looked behind us and sensed something in the
corner of the room. I slowly shined my light in that

direction and saw a pool of blood spilling over the floor. A figure moved toward my light." I guess we'll have to go through the front door."

"Jackson," I whispered, barely getting a sound out. He stopped what he was doing and turned around. We both watched in fear as we saw what appeared to be Emily emerge from the corner. Her eyes were all white and her hair was ratted. She had a wicked little smirk on her face. "Please tell me you see this."

"She's supposed to be dead . . ."

"I don't think that's her anymore," I said. "Come on, try to open the window!" Emily's arms bore stitches from the cuts she got when she broke her mirror, her face was sunken in, and she looked thinner. She slowly made her way to us. As she did, she dug into her arm and started ripping her stitches out. Dark blood and yellow pus started oozing out of her arms and dripping down her body. Jackson was still struggling to open the window as she came closer to us. I quickly grabbed a nearby lamp and smashed the window open, allowing us to crawl out.

Jackson started down the ladder first. My mind was in disbelief and I couldn't process any of my thoughts. About halfway down, I looked up and came face to face with my brother. His eyes were white just like Emily. Skin hung off his body and his bones protruded. I let out a horrified gasp and lost my grip on the ladder, falling to the ground. My body fell into Jackson as we both hit the wet cement with a loud thud. Groans escaped our mouths as we rolled around on the ground. The next thing I knew Jackson got up and made his way over to me. An instant headache formed as my brain rattled around. I had landed on my side, but the adrenaline was too intense for me to feel much pain.

"Carter, are you okay? Do we need to get you to the hospital? That was a long fall." A little dazed, he helped me up and we rushed back to his car. I looked back up toward the apartment, but Alex was gone and there was no proof of what we witnessed except for the broken window.

"I'm fine." We got in his car and sped off.

Out of breath Jackson asked, "Was that real? What the fuck did we just see?"

"I . . . I don't know if it was . . ." I said with the wind knocked out of me.

"What made you fall?"

"I saw my brother. We were inches apart, and it took me by surprise."

Jackson paused. "What the fuck is going on?" His hands shook as he held the wheel. I noticed only a few cuts on his hands.

"This is what I've been trying to tell you, Jackson. This is what I've been seeing for the past month. They're not human, and I have no idea where they came from. Alex is in the ground and Emily is in the morgue. "

"Okay, I have to be honest," Jackson said. He lowered his voice and swallowed hard, twice. He repositioned his hands on the steering wheel and straightened his back. "I didn't want to admit it at first, or bring life to my own imagination," he began. "I haven't been seeing what you have, but some nights when I'm up doing homework or lying in bed, I hear footsteps throughout my apartment. They always lead to my room but stop at my door. That's it. It's only happened a few times, but I thought it was just in my head. And now I understand that something is going on, and you're right, and I'm sorry"

"It's okay, Jackson." I clenched my jaw as pain ran up my shoulder. Raw skin scraped at the inside of my shirt through my jacket. I knew it was already bruising.

"So what do we do?" Jackson asked. "What do they want? I don't get it!"

"I don't know, Jackson, but my brother has the answers somewhere in his journal. He went somewhere, remember? So maybe we need to find that place or find something that tells us how this all began."

"This is just so fucked up. Do we tell the others?"

I shook my head. "No, not yet. We need to start figuring this out and if it involves them, then we'll let them know." I chewed on my fingernail, hoping my decision was the right one. Arriving back at my house, we hurried inside. We went straight to Alex's journal and started looking through it while sitting down.

"Do you think Emily went to where your brother went?"

"I'm not sure," I said. "She never talked about it. All she told me was that she heard things and saw things."

"It says in the journal that *it* found your brother, like you told me, and it kept coming back for him as your brother kept going back to that place. And once it found your brother, it wouldn't stop."

"Right. What are you getting at?" I asked.

"Well, did it find us? I know that was Emily in that room and you saw your brother, but—"

"No, Jackson, that wasn't them, it was those inhuman things Alex wrote about. They followed him and Emily back."

"Followed them back from where?" Anger and worry started to fill Jackson's voice. "This is going to drive us mad." He stood up.

"Jackson." I stood up with him. "I think my brother and Emily did the things they did to hide from themselves."

Jackson looked at me in confusion and walked toward the bathroom. He slammed the door and I let him be. I sat down and put my head in my hands, taking a moment to let everything sink in. For a moment, I was relieved that my best friend finally believed me and saw what I had been seeing, but that was shortly replaced with dread, because neither of us knew what was going on. I stood up and started making my way to the kitchen, but something stopped me. I looked down the hallway and noticed my reflection in the mirror. Something was different about it. I slowly made my way toward the mirror, captivated by my reflection. I stood a few feet away from it and saw myself. I looked like I hadn't gotten any sleep in a month, and my eyes looked sad. The only feature that looked somewhat presentable was my dark brown hair, which was gelled up. I had scrapes all over from my fall, and . . . I was smiling. I wasn't physically smiling, but my reflection was. It wasn't my smile; it was a smirk—an evil smirk. Something seemed dark and twisted with that face, a face that wasn't even mine.

Jackson

Come on, get it together, Jackson. It's going to be okay. What I saw was nothing but my imagination. What Carter saw was nothing but his. I cupped my hands under the running water and washed my face off. The scenes replayed in my head, and the look of Emily—or whatever that fucked-up thing was—stayed in my mind like a horrible movie. I turned off the water, reached for a towel and dried my face off. I took a deep breath, looked up, and turned to reach for the doorknob. I turned my head over my shoulder and looked into the mirror. As soon as I did, my heart stopped.

My reflection was still there, facing the sink, staring at me with a wicked smile and piercing glare. Chills went down my spine and I couldn't move. My body went cold, my mouth dropped open, and my palms grew sweaty. I couldn't tell if my body was going into shock or if this was what it was like to go mad. Was I going mad? My reflection's mouth opened and said, "Jackson."

The bathroom door swung open and Carter rushed in, saying my name. "Jackson, I think it found us."

Dallas

Something was off lately, and I didn't know if it was with me or this lonely house. When I was alone I didn't feel like it, though I complained about being lonely all the time to my friends.

Earlier today, I found out Emily Rawson died in her sleep from an overdose. I can only imagine what Carter is going through. I can't bear to think about how Carter deals with losses all around him. Thinking about Emily made me miss my parents. My heart yearned for them to come back home.

Ten o'clock hit and I decided to close my textbook and turn on the TV. Nothing but football highlights and car commercials were on. I double checked my phone to make sure my parents hadn't messaged or called me. The screen was blank, and even though I was right, it still hurt to see not even one notification from them.

I hated the thought of being alone. I was tempted to throw a last-minute party just so the house would be full and I'd have someone to talk to. Looking into the kitchen, I noticed I hadn't stocked up alcohol from the last one.

I rubbed my eyes and lie down on the couch. A yawn escaped my mouth as I relaxed. My eyes noticed a picture of my dog and I back when I was seven, which stood in a frame on the coffee table. He was a golden retriever named Finn. Finn was a birthday present and something to keep me company while my parents were gone.

I was ten years old when I lost him. It was a cloudy

day and it rained off and on. I was playing fetch with him inside the house when eventually my dad told me to go take Finn for a walk. Finn had the fluffiest golden fur. That kind of fur that makes a dog seem chunky. He had floppy ears that bounced on his head every time he moved. I loved being barefoot around him because I would put my feet on him while we lay on the couch together. Finn always reminded me of golden shag rug.

Finn loved to lie down while he ate or drank out of his food bowls. When he laid down his legs would sprawl out like butterfly wings. I never understood why. I also never understood why he always had his tongue out while he slept or even while he followed me around the house. It wasn't because he was panting, so I always thought his tongue was too big for his mouth.

I clipped the red leash onto his jet-black collar and took him outside. Right away Finn and I both stepped into a puddle that had formed on our front step. Finn immediately stuck his long tongue into the puddle and lapped up the rain water. His bright pink tongue reminded me of *Silly Putty* and it made me giggle each time I saw it.

I tugged on his leash and got the three year old dog to keep moving. Finn, LOVED walks. That dog was always eager to explore the vast outdoors and watch other animals adapt in their environment.

We only made it a few blocks away from my house when tragedy struck. The timing was off and as a ten year old you never understand why life can be cruel. Hell, even at twenty-two you still don't understand. I somehow had a rock in my shoe, so we both stopped while I bent over to take it out.

I must not have gripped the leash tight enough because I was focused on that damn rock. Simultaneously, there was a dog on the loose across the street and it took Finn no time to bolt away from me and run across the street. Surprised that the leash flew through my fingers, I watched as the white van drove down the road; in the blink of an eye, the front right of the van smacked right into the side of Finn.

I heard him yelp as I ran across the street to his aid. The other dog was already gone and the van pulled over a short ways down. I screamed and screamed in horror and sadness. Finn lied there like a mangled ball of fur. His once thick, fluffy fur was nothing more than a matted, dirty muck.

The driver came up to me and immediately knew who I was. He drove to my parents' house while I stayed with Finn's body. Within seconds, they were both there with me.

We took him to the emergency animal clinic to find out he had internal bleeding, a broken hip, three broken ribs, and a shattered paw.

My parents made the executive decision to put him down. They told me they'd get me another dog, but we moved later that month. The idea of a new dog was soon forgotten. Finn was there for me through thunderstorms, the lonely nights, and the long hot summers where he loved chomping at the water that came out of the hose. On those stormy nights, while my parents were gone, and the babysitter was asleep, I could always look at the end of my bed and count on him being there.

The wells in my eyes brought me back from my vision down memory lane. I blinked a few times and looked away from the picture. I promised myself that once I was on my own I would get another dog.

I rolled over to clear my thoughts. As I began to doze off, I heard something that jolted me wide awake. A little disoriented, I waited to hear it again. It sounded like a pebble being thrown at my window. I stood up and made my way toward the window, thinking it was one of the guys. I moved the blinds and peered out; didn't see anything, but a sense of not being alone rushed through my body.

Shaking my head, I chalked those thoughts up to paranoia. I let go of the blinds and made my way back to the couch, where I picked up the remote and turned off the TV. The only light illuminating the house now came from my bedroom. Remembering I still had laundry in the dryer, I made my way to the laundry room. I took my warm, clean clothes out and put them on top of the dryer, telling myself I'd fold them tomorrow. The soft, inviting smell of detergent took me back to when my mom did laundry and I would help her; it was how we bonded on Sundays when she got back from her trips. Leaving my memories behind, I went back upstairs to the bathroom and brushed my teeth, then noticed that I had a dark red stain on my shirt. I must have spilled punch on myself earlier. Rolling my eyes, I took it off and headed back to the laundry room. I laid it on top of the washer and sprayed some stain remover on it, but the stain was no longer there. I checked the entire shirt, but I still couldn't see the stain.

Ignoring my terrible eyes, I still sprayed the shirt and threw it in the washer with a few other dirty clothes, figuring I may as well start another load. I made my way out of the room and walked down the hall, but I noticed the whole house was completely dark. My bedroom light had turned off. I thought the storm took the power out, but the washer was still running.

"I need to go to bed," I said out loud, shaking my head. I was almost to my room when I heard heavy footsteps downstairs. I turned around but couldn't see anything out of the ordinary. I stood there in silence for a few moments, waiting to hear any noise again, but it was quiet.

I got into bed and started to close my eyes when I heard a little tapping at my bedroom window. I groaned as I rolled over and looked at it from my bed, but I saw no silhouette behind the curtains.

TAP TAP TAP

The noise haunted me, and the idea of someone actually behind my window was unnerving. Even scarier, the noise seemed to not only come from the window, but from inside my head, too. It was times like these that I wished I had a dog. Knowing he would be at the end of the bed would be comforting.

But as I lay there, it wasn't just the tapping that spooked me—it was the sound of a voice whispering on the other side of the glass, echoing the words, "tap, tap, tap." It was like someone was watching me from the window, someone wanting more than just to look.

Chapter 8

Carter

The next day looked like a scene out of a disaster movie. The sky was overcast, debris filled the streets, and a soft fall breeze swept through the air. Shingles from other houses filled the neighbors' yards while branches and limbs claimed the road.

Jackson and I parked our cars and walked into the diner to get a few cups of coffee. We had both skipped our first classes and came here instead. I knew Jade would be in class, and I was a little relieved. I don't think either Jackson or I got any sleep last night, so we needed something to wake us up. I'm not really a coffee drinker and I firmly believe the buzz we get from caffeine is just a placebo effect, but nonetheless I ordered a cup.

A server brought us our coffee and we both added cream and sugar, stirring our cups in silence. I looked out the window and saw Brooke pull up and get out of her car. I focused my attention on the clanking of our spoons.

"You invited Brooke?" I asked Jackson.

Just as confused as I was, he looked up and shook his head. "No. She knows I'm here, but I didn't invite her."

The door dinged as she walked in. Not seeing us, she went up to the counter and picked up her to-go order, then spotted us as she was leaving.

"Hey, babe, not going to your first class?" Brooke asked, reaching our table.

"No, I slept through half of it and I needed something to wake me up."

She moved her blonde hair behind one ear and smiled at him, then looked at me. "Are you guys gonna go to Dallas's swim meet today?"

I exchanged glances with Jackson. Looking up at her, I said, "To be honest, we forgot about it. What time does it start?" My face flushed from embarrassment.

"It starts at eleven and he swims shortly after that. I'm actually grabbing breakfast for Jade and I. We're getting ready at my place and then we were gonna go. It's at the REC center today."

"Did you skip your class this morning, too?" Jackson asked after taking a long sip from his dark roast. Jackson looked tired while he was hunched over. He brought his hand up to his left eye and rubbed it awake.

Brooke raised her eyebrows. "Jackson, you know I don't have morning classes on Thursdays. Are you guys all right?"

Speaking for the both of us, I said, "We're sorry, Brooke, we're just swamped with homework while preparing for midterms; we were up late last night studying." I smiled and told her, "We'll meet you guys there." She smiled at me, accepting my lie, and leaned in and kissed Jackson on the cheek. She said goodbye and walked out of the diner with her food. I looked over at Jackson, who was biting his nails and spacing out.

"Jackson, we have to talk about this." He nervously stirred his coffee and looked down at it. "We can't just pretend that that didn't happen. What we saw was real, and—"

He cut me off. "Carter, I literally have nothing to say about it. Your reflection isn't supposed to just stay there and look at you and you don't just see dead people in corners and have them come up to you and pull out their stitches. What happens next, we go mad? We die like the others?" He dropped his hand too hard on the table, making a loud thud and causing both our coffees to splash over the mugs. He cautiously looked around to make sure he didn't cause attention.

Silence followed as he realized what he said. I knew he didn't mean it, but it still touched a nerve and I didn't know what to say. Regret filled his eyes and his frustrated face softened.

"Carter, I didn't mean it like that . . ."

"My brother and Emily didn't die because they killed themselves; something found them and got them."

"Like the same thing that found us last night and was in those mirrors? That was *us*. Our reflections found us? Now what? How does anyone even explain that?"

"That's explained in my brother's journal. Not very well," I admitted, "but it's a start. Jackson, I know you don't understand this or want to believe it, but the only way we can get through this is if you do."

"Then what do we do now? What do *they* want? How do we get through this, Carter? Does your brother tell you that?"

I thought about that. I'd been trying to think of those answers and why, for a while, I saw what everyone else couldn't. The other Emily had stared down at the real Emily, getting closer to her, and she talked about how she saw and heard them. Just like what my brother wrote in his journal. They were drawing us to them.

"We just stay away from mirrors and windows," I told him. We simultaneously looked at the window we were next to. "We'll cover up our mirrors and not pay any attention to them."

"Carter, I'm not living in fear and staying hidden for the rest of my life. That is ridiculous. You know how many objects are reflective?" Jackson's anger started to rise, along with his voice. "Is the same thing going to happen to Brooke, or Jade, and Dallas?"

"I'm not sure, Jackson. I don't know what triggers what. I haven't seen anything peculiar in sunglasses yet. I'm just as frustrated and scared as you are."

Jackson stood up and left a few dollars on the table. With a cold, flat tone, he said, "Well, figure it out." With that, he walked on out of the diner and left me alone. The conversation was just as bitter as my coffee, and both left an unwanted taste in my mouth. Noticing the time and not wanting to be late to Dallas's swim meet, I left my money on the table and got up as well. I arrived at REC center before the others, so I got a seat and watched as the bleachers filled. I noticed Dallas talking to the coach before heading to the locker room to get changed, so I quickly decided to follow him.

"Hey, Dallas, I wanted to wish you good luck quick!" As if I scared the living daylights out of him, he jumped and turned and looked at me.

"Jesus!" He placed his hand over his heart and took a deep breath.

"I'm sorry, I didn't mean to scare you. I just wanted to catch you before you got too busy."

"No, you're good! I just didn't sleep the best last night and I've been on edge all morning. Coach has been on my ass, too." He pulled a razor from his locker and finished shaving a small patch of stubble on the center of his sculpted chest.

"I hear ya. I didn't sleep much, either," I admitted.

"But thank you for wishing me luck. I'll go kick some ass." We smiled and fist bumped. I started to walk out when he stopped me. "Hey, Carter, can I get your opinion on something?"

"For the hundredth time, Dallas, if any girl asks, I'll tell them you're a grower, not a shower, and that it's the cold water's fault," I joked.

"No, it's not that. It's actually about you," he said. "Through everything you've been through, how do you know you still have your sanity and grasp on things, even when they appear not to be real?"

"I'm not sure what you're asking." My statement was guarded as paranoia crossed my mind.

He shook his head and apologized. "Never mind, I'm out of it today. But anyway, I gotta change!" I accepted his shrug and headed out of the locker room and toward the bleachers.

Dallas

Carter walked out of the locker room and I quickly changed into my Speedo, feeling so stupid for my question. I wasn't thinking straight, which was frustrating, and Coach knew I wasn't on my game. But something was wrong. I didn't feel alone in my empty house. I was starting to see things, and oddly enough, I felt a weird sense behind every window and like something more than my reflection was looking back at me behind my mirror. I felt like I was losing it.

As my teammates came in and started changing I went into the bathroom, rested my hands on the sink, steadied my breathing, and looked at myself in the mirror. *You got this*, I told myself. I looked back down, and I could have sworn I heard my laugh. It sounded like my same exact chuckle, only it was a little deeper than usual. Knowing it didn't come from me, I looked out into the locker room to see if anyone was laughing, but there were only two other guys in sight and they were completely expressionless. *Is this what it feels like to lose your mind?* I shook it off and headed out to the pool.

My friends were in the bleachers, ready to cheer me on. Jackson looked like a crabapple, but the rest of them smiled when they saw me. I glanced quickly through the crowd, and my stomach dropped. My parents weren't there. They had only ever made it to one of my swim meets, and that was when I had to travel out of state and happened to be in the same city as them. I gave my friends a gracious smile back and started preparing myself, though I was distracted by my worries. *I don't know who I am anymore. My skin feels foreign, and all I want is for things to get back to normal,* I thought.

Standing on the platform, I stared down at the water and saw my reflection. I placed my goggles over my eyes, but saw that my reflection didn't. I quickly took them off and did a double take as I saw it still didn't mimic my actions. Captivated by my reflection, I continued to stare at it until the buzzer went off. Screams and cheers filled the room and I heard my opponents hit the water as I fumbled to put my goggles back on. I knew Coach was going to rip me a new one. Without another thought, I dove into the cool water.

***

I reached my arms out in this free style competition to quickly catch up. The familiar look and feel of the foam and bubbles tickled my vulnerable body and masked my vision. Before I knew it, I made it to the other end and turned around realizing I wasn't in last place. Feeling a little relieved I kept up on my strokes and continued forward. While I braced the wall and turned around I continued thinking about my reflection. It didn't make any sense and I knew for a fact what I saw was real. What I heard the other night at the window was real. Something was wrong with me.

Distracted, I saw that a couple of people were caught up to me. I'm statistically one of the fastest guys on the team but for the life of me I couldn't catch up and fix my mistakes. Water and screams kept filling my ears as the laps continued. I flipped over getting ready for the next lap when my chest began to burn. My lungs were more tired than usual and my body grew weak. I pushed through the pain but my head wasn't in the game.

I slowed down only to rest my sore arms. *Dallas, what are you doing? Suck it up and win this race.* I heard my coach scream my name, "Walker!" I gritted my teeth and bared the strains. I was letting more water into my mouth than usual. It was like every lesson and strategy I taught myself was thrown out the window. I started the final lap not knowing what place I was in. I pushed my thoughts away and continued giving it my all not caring who was by me. I swam harder, feeling my lungs burning with water entering my mouth, tasting the stingy chlorine. My arms were dead and my chest pounded so fast I thought it'd beat off rhythm. I saw the end as I was getting closer to the cement wall. I pushed towards while grinding my teeth and slammed my hand on the wall of the pool and looked up to see that I was in fourth place. Feeling a little disappointed, never getting fourth, I rested my arms on the pools ledge with my head down facing the water. The reflection of my arms alarmed me. It showed that blood was dripping down from a cut somewhere on my right arm. The dark red dribbled into the pool like rain as it slowly made the spot around me discolored. In shock, I withdrew my arm and anxiously looked at it. I couldn't find or feel any visible cuts and when I looked at the water it was no longer red. I put both my arms up like I was under arrest to get a good look at my reflection. Before anything could happen, the noise from the opponents getting out of the water captured my attention.

Hopping out, I shook my head. Fourth place was the worst I'd ever done in my college swimming career. Before this, my worst was second. Feeling discouraged, I made my way over to my coach.

"Walker, what the fuck were you doing in there? Where has your head been?"

"I don't know, Coach. I'm sorry."

"Hit the showers," Coach said, disgusted. His words stabbed into me like knives. My self esteem was shot and my face was flushed with anger and embarrassment. Walking away, I bumped into my friends.

"I think you did a great job! I've never seen a swim meet before." Jade said.

"It was so intense I got goosebumps." Brooke added

"Were you scared of the water for a second?" Jackson joked, slapping my back playfully.

"No, I just was out of it today. I swim again in about an hour, but I'm going to go relax before I swim again."

"You still did great, dude," Carter said. "You're going to do even better later. Everyone has their days." I smiled weakly, thanked them, and headed toward the locker room. Still dripping wet from the pool, I walked into the showers and turned one on. I let the hot water pour over my body, soothing me. I closed my eyes, letting the water and steam envelop me, hiding myself and my insecurities. I was trying not to let that race get the best of me, but I just couldn't shake off what I thought I saw. It seemed so real.

The steam and water felt refreshing, but that didn't stop the anger beginning to boil. *What is wrong with me? What the hell is going on?* I ran my hands through my hair and kept them on top of my head, trying to breathe. The only noise in the locker room was running water from my shower, but I thought I heard something else. I turned and looked behind me, but didn't see anything. I turned my attention back to my shower when I caught something in the corner of my eye. I turned, and through the steam I made out a figure in the corner. Thinking it was one of the guys, I turned my attention back to the wall. A little irritated at the feeling that the guy wasn't looking away, I asked, "Can I help you with something?" I turned and looked at him again, and through the steam I saw myself.

Taken aback, I blinked a few times. This was the first time I saw *him* in this world. *How is he here?* My double was still there, standing in the corner and smirking evilly at me. Its eyes were white. I was looking at myself, in the flesh! How could that be? I turned off the water and took a few steps back. It just stood there watching me, thick steam billowing around him.

I backed out of the shower, grabbed my towel and walked out of the locker room and back toward the pool. Looking over my shoulder as I dried off, trying to see if I walked out of the locker room, I bumped into my teammate.

"Dude, what is with you?" I quickly said sorry and got

out of his way. I was literally going insane. But I had to go back *there.* They kept taking me back *there,* but a part of me knew I should never go again.

Carter

"Do you think Dallas is all right?" Brooke asked us.

"I think he's just under a lot of pressure right now with the qualifier coming up, school, and what's been going on this week," I replied. I tried my best to shrug off Brooke's question. I knew there was something off with Dallas but I had no idea if it was related to what I've been experiencing.

"What time is Emily's funeral?" Jade asked.

"Tomorrow morning at eleven," I said softly.

"Can we all go together?" Jade asked.

"Yeah, we can." Jade and I turned our attention back to the races, and I noticed Jade shivered a few times.

"Are you okay, Jade?"

"Yeah." She nodded. "I just got the chills, is all."

I could hear Brooke and Jackson talking quietly behind us.

"Jackson, is everything okay with you?" she asked him.

"I'm fine, Brooke."

"It's just that you haven't been saying much all morning and you were short in your texts today, and that's not like you. Is there a reason you're being monosyllabic?"

"I don't even know what that means. Do we have to do this here? I'm seriously fine, so let it go." I couldn't help but feel uncomfortable. Brooke was upset, and Jackson was being ruder and more blunt than usual, which made things worse. "I'm gonna get some fresh air. And that's *not* an invitation." He got up and stalked outside. Brooke watched him go, then sat next me.

"Do you know what's going on with him?"

I wanted to tell her everything, but what was I supposed to say? *Oh, by the way, your boyfriend and I saw Emily and Alex last night while we broke into his old apartment. We've also been seeing and hearing weird things, but other than that, things are fine.* "Instead, I said, "I know he hasn't been getting enough sleep lately. He's been irritated and short with me, too."

"I don't know," Brooke said. "He's been acting different today. Yesterday he was off, too, and I don't know if I did something."

"No, oh God, no. You're completely fine, Brooke, you didn't do anything. Jackson probably just needs some air, like he said."

146

She still looked hurt and puzzled. "I hate thinking that it's just me, but things feel weird lately. I know midterms are coming up, but Dallas and Jackson aren't the kind of guys who let school get to them."

Jade put her hand on Brooke's leg for comfort and was about to say something when Brooke's phone dinged. Brooke's already-sad face got even more upset.

"Everything okay, Brooke?" I asked her.

"Yeah. I mean, no, not really." She sighed. "It's my mother. She's been battling liver cancer for a few years now." I knew this, but figured she was filling Jade in. Brooke continued, "The chemo takes care of it, but the tumors come right back. She was in remission for about four months of our freshman year, and then it slowly returned." Brooke spun a strand of hair around her finger while she reread the text.

"Aww . . . Brooke, I am so sorry," Jade said, rubbing Brooke's arm.

"Thank you. She texted me telling me she's feeling worse today, and that Dad is taking her to the hospital to do some vitals."

I knew Brooke wanted nothing more than for her mom to be at her college graduation and wedding. It scared her deep down that her mom might not get to see her graduate.

I knew that feeling.

"She's a fighter, though, and as long as it doesn't spread to any nearby organs, she has a chance," Brooke finished.

We all noticed Jackson was coming back up to us. Growing silent, we all let our old conversation go and tried sparking up a new one. Despite Jackson's pugnacious attitude the tension between everyone slowly lifted.

I wished everything would just stop. It seemed like everything was going by so fast, and I couldn't wrap my head around it. I didn't know what to do, or where to turn. Whatever was going on was eating away at all of us, slowly but surely, and I don't know who was going to snap next.

***

I picked Jade up the next morning for Emily's funeral. My stomach was in knots, and a huge lump formed in my throat. Just like that, she was gone. Everything felt so unreal. Jade kept her hand on my leg as I drove to the cemetery, and we tried to talk about anything but the funeral.

"Brooke stayed over last night," Jade said. "She and Jackson got into a little fight. Do you know what's gotten into him?"

"No, we haven't really been talking to each other," I

told her.

"I just want to know what's going on with you guys. Even Dallas is being aloof. "

I gripped the steering wheel a little tighter. It was killing me not opening up to her. It was killing me that my friends were going crazy and no one knew what was going on. It was killing me that I kept losing the people I love. It was killing me that whatever got Emily and my brother was after us and I didn't know how to stop it.

I looked at Jade and give her the most sincere smile I could without giving myself away. "I know."

We pulled up and parked, making our way into the cemetery to find our friends. Brooke and Jackson seemed to be getting along a little better, but Dallas wasn't there yet. My friends weren't close with Emily, but their support meant everything. I felt as if I had lost the last person who kind of linked me to my brother, and now she was gone.

It was a small ceremony, but Emily's family filled the first few rows of seats. I recognized a few of them, and told myself that I should probably go say hi. Maxine, Emily's mother, looked as if she hadn't slept in days. Emily's father, Dave, looked ten years older than when I had last seen him, and his face seemed sunken in. Her older sister, looked torn to shreds, destroyed. My heart went out to the family.

As soon as they saw me, they stood up and each greeted me with a big, welcoming hug. Maxine lost it when she embraced me, and my shirt started sticking to my shoulder from her tears. I patted her back, trying to comfort her. Through her tears, she thanked me for coming, and I hugged the others.

Maxine pulled me aside and asked me a couple questions. "Emily told us that she visited you the other day to give you some old things of Alex's. Did she seem or look depressed? Sad even?"

Her deep ocean blue eyes stuck on me like glue. She longed for an answer to bring closure that I could never provide.

I shook my head. "I'm sorry Maxine. She was happy when she saw me and she looked bubbly as always. We caught up and talked about Alex and college."

She wanted more. "What happened when you went over to her place and found her all cut up? What was she like?" Her mouth began to tremble.

My mind immediately went to that day but that image quickly turned into the one of her ripping out her stitches. That was such a loaded question I didn't know how to answer it. "She was scared from all the blood and was stunned from the accident."

Maxine shook her head in disbelief as her hand went to her mouth. "We live out of state you know and I'm thankful you . . . were there to help her." Her speech trailed off.

I didn't help her at all. I gritted my teeth, trying not to cry.

Maxine moved some stray hairs out of her face before continuing. "My girl was always so happy. Your brother made her so happy. She loved him." Tears strolled down her cheeks as she choked on her words. "I just keep asking myself what happened in her final moments. Why did she feel the need to take her own life? That wasn't Emily." Anger, guilt and sadness ran across her face in that entire speech. "We would have been there for her. I don't under—"

Her husband stepped in and held her while a flood of tears came pouring out. Every word hit close to home. I went through the exact same thing with Alex. I walked up to her and gave her a long hug.

I gave them my condolences while they thanked me for coming. Feeling numb, I walked back to my seat.

As I made my way back to my friends, I saw Dallas by a tree. The tree was behind the seats closer to our parked cars. Dark circles surrounded his eyes and he looked afraid. I walked over to him, and for a second I was a little freaked out. His eyes were bloodshot, dark red and purple veins covering the whites of his eyes. It looked like he let salt sit on them for days, they seemed so agitated. I didn't believe he'd gotten sleep anytime recently.

"Dallas, are you okay?"

He looked at me like I was crazy. It felt like he hardly recognized me.

"Carter, I'm scared out of my mind. I'm constantly in fear. I haven't slept in days, I haven't been swimming well, and my mind has a mind of its own. I feel sick."

"What do you mean, sick?"

"Well, just the other day I took a bite out of a sandwich and it tasted almost foreign. As if it wasn't a sandwich. It was bland. Kind of like how a cold starts, when you can't taste anything. And last night I took a scorching hot shower, but I couldn't get warm and the water still felt cold."

Shocked, I said, "Earlier, Dallas, you told me you were afraid. Afraid of what?"

Before he answered, he turned around and lifted the back of his button-up to show me his blistered, raw back. "I'm afraid of myself." He looked terrified, lost. I'd never seen him like this.

"Oh my God, Dallas, we need to get you to the doctor. Was that from the shower? Doesn't that hurt?"

"The blisters only hurt when he is near. They were made as a gateway to feel me. He wants me to feel him. So I took a hot shower to help him imprint with me. I'm afraid because of what I hear, what I feel, and what I see. It's as if I'm not me, that by night I'm someone else. Not only that, but I'm afraid of myself and how I run after myself in the late hours of the night. I'm chased all through my house until I disappear."

My blood ran cold and my stomach churned. Dallas looked sad and exhausted, but I saw the fear in his eyes. He was screaming for help, even if he wasn't screaming at me.

"What else do you—"

Jackson interrupted us, startling me with his presence."Dallas, are you okay?"

"I'm doing all right . . ."

"Well, are you two gonna come sit with us or have your own special gathering? The funeral's about to start." He began to walk away and I followed him. I looked back at Dallas.

"Are you coming?"

He shook his head. "I have to go back." Before I got

another word out, he turned around and started to leave. Jackson and I sat back down and I looked around for Dallas, but he was gone. Brooke and Jade appeared fine, but I knew Jackson hadn't looked through a window or in a mirror since that night we broke into Alex's apartment. He was just as scared as I was, but he wouldn't admit it. He wouldn't talk about it, wouldn't face it. He was letting it destroy him on the inside, just like Dallas was.

I spaced off as the service started. Emily looked so peaceful in her casket, but that didn't mean she was at peace. Something was off about her carcass. It looked like her, but also didn't. A dark aura covered her body, like the shitty makeup that covered her face and her scars. Maybe it was because we just saw her pull out her stitches and come after me and Jackson, or maybe it was because I'd gone mad. Everything about this was maddening. It's all dark and sinister. Some people have already lost it in this world, they've gone mad, but aren't we all a little mad?

Chapter 9

Dallas

I just needed one good night of sleep. One was all I asked for; maybe a little prayer before bed would help. I wanted to hear my own voice and not the other ones that drowned out my thoughts. I wished my parents were home. I would love it if they could read me a bedtime story and put me to sleep, like when I was little. But no, here I was all alone in this house with all the lights on because I didn't like what I couldn't see. Then again, what I did see was no better.

I was so cold; always so cold. It felt as if my heart was made of ice and I was slowly freezing from the inside out. I trembled, as if I'd just lain down on a pile of snow. I yearned for heat, begging for something to make me feel alive. I looked at a picture of Jackson, Carter, and I from a frat party a year ago and remembered the old us. I saw the Dallas that I remembered, not the one I was today.

I set the picture down and stood up. Looking at the clock and seeing it was almost midnight, I knew I needed to go to bed. I was exhausted, but I couldn't sleep. My friends had been trying to call me all day. I lied and told them I was feeling sick. Carter knew something was up. I didn't know what was going on with me. I was scared out of my fucking mind and didn't know how to tell anyone.

As I started away from the couch to head to my room, the lights began to flicker and the air turned frigid. *It's happening again.* I didn't want to see it. I didn't want to hear it, either, but it began. A deep hum mimicked the lullaby my parents sang to me when I was a child. The hairs stood up on my arms and I started to walk toward the stairs. My breath fogged in the air while I shivered on the hardwood floor. The door to the basement slowly creaked open, and the humming got louder. The noise came from behind it. I stopped in fear and peered into the dark crack. In that moment, I knew I was no longer lone. Tears filled my eyes as fear stopped my voice.

Time froze, and the house was filled with tension. The lights went out and I was left alone in the dark, listening to the humming tune. The air got even colder, and abruptly the humming stopped. I kept looking through the crack and the door creaked open even more. I listened to my heart pounding in my chest. Then the door burst open and I saw myself run out of the dark toward me. Those eyes were not mine; the bright beams dug into me like claws as he ran my way. The smirk on his face grew, and everything seemed to go into slow motion.

A scream of help and fear escaped my mouth. I turned and ran up the step that led to my bedroom, but it felt like I was running in a dream, where you're going as fast as you can but you can't seem to make any progress. My adrenaline was pumping as I continued to climb up the staircase, waiting for his hands to reach out and grab me. I made it to the top, petrified, and looked behind and saw him following. I ran to my room and heard his heavy footsteps right behind me as I went to slam my door, but his arm got in the way.

"Get away from me!"

I heard him cackle in a sinister, deep tone as I pushed on the door harder. I kept increasing my force until I finally closed the door and locked it. I pulled up a chair and placed it under the doorknob to secure it as he rattled the knob, trying to make his way to me.

The rattling went on for half a minute, then the noise abruptly stopped. I was forced to listen to the sound of my heartbeat and my heavy breathing. I didn't know what I'd been seeing, but almost every night I ran away from myself, and he seemed to be getting faster and stronger and closer to me. I didn't know what to do, or who to talk to.

I jumped into my bed and pulled the covers over

myself so only my eyes were showing. It was as if I was five years old again, scared of what lurked under my bed and in the dark corners of my room. But I wasn't five and what lurked under my bed was real. The thought of *it* getting in here or being under my bed waiting to grab my feet played over and over in my mind. Time dragged on until I caught a white light coming through my door's keyhole.

I swallowed hard. I wanted that to be the welcoming light from the hallway, as if my parents had just walked in the door. But it wasn't. It was from that evil thing's eye. It was an eerie shade of white, one that made me uncomfortable. The light went away, but only for a second. It came straight back, as if *it* repositioned itself to get a better look at me. He, if you'd even call it a *he*, never took his eye off me. That vile, loathsome eye watched me. It was waiting for me. Craving me.

That place I went to, it wasn't like any other place. It was dark and mysterious, but it held something awfully familiar, something human. It found me. If only I hid better. If only I was more careful, everything would be different. I didn't know how much more time I had left. I didn't know how much time my friends had, either.

Carter

158

I couldn't sit still anymore. I was going crazy sitting here and doing nothing. My best friend wanted nothing to do with me, it seemed like Jackson and Brooke were falling apart, and him and I were the only ones who saw Alex and Emily. And I was the only one who saw handprints but still, here I was with no explanations. Dallas was losing his mind, Emily was dead, and all I seemed to be left with was the destruction around me. None of us had really talked to one another since Emily's funeral, two days earlier. They say things get worse before they get better, but right now it was just getting worse.

I was dozing off and on. It was almost one in the morning when my phone lit up and I saw I had a missed call and a voicemail from Dallas and a few other notifications. He sounded petrified. "Carter, I'm scared," he said, "I don't know what has happened to me in the past few weeks, but—" His voice cut off, and then I heard a different voice through the phone, more harsh and raspy than Dallas's, though it still kind of sounded like him. "I'm getting closer to what I need . . ." I heard him lick his lips and breathe heavily as he continued. "And what I need is the warmth of your blood, your beating heart. I want to make that warm blood cold, so cold that it feels exactly like home." His voice got raspier as he started to cough, and the message ended.

I jumped out of bed, grabbed my keys and headed toward the door. On my way out I saw myself in a mirror. My hazel eyes still looked human, but I wore a smirk. I watched as my reflection slowly started taking off my jacket, while mine stayed on. My reflection then began taking off my shirt, followed by my pants. My smirk grew wider as I watched my reflection grab a knife. He took the knife and brought it up to my chest, running the blade across it, drawing blood.

I peered inside my shirt to make sure I wasn't actually bleeding. I wasn't cut, but my reflection continued to toy with me like I was some kind of prey. Before I knew what was going on I noticed myself getting closer to the mirror, caught in his gaze. My reflection let the blood run down my body and drip onto my leg. I watched the droplets of red run down them like water running down a window. My reflection touched the wound and brought his fingers up to what looked like the glass, leaving his hand there. A voice in my mind asked, "Aren't you scared?" But I wasn't; I didn't even know what was going on. I slowly brought my hand up to the mirror. Looking deep into my reflection, time seemed to slow down and nothing else existed. I watched the blood run down the mirror, but I couldn't touch it. All I needed to do was touch my hand.

"Carter, what the hell are you doing?"

I spun around and saw Jackson standing there with Brooke. I turned back around and saw that my reflection was back to normal, but somehow my jacket was on the floor. I must have started taking off my clothes as I got closer to the mirror.

Brooke looked confused and Jackson looked worried as hell. I picked up my jacket and walked toward them.

"What's going on?"

"It's Jade," Jackson told me. "She's been trying to contact you. She texted Brooke instead."

My heartbeat quickened and my whole body tensed up. "What? What's going on? Is she all right?"

"She didn't say, but she needs us to come to the diner," Jackson said. Brooke looked just as worried as he did, and I felt the same. I put my jacket on and we all headed out the door to the diner.

"I don't understand why life is being a dick right now." Jackson said while he drove. Brooke placed her hand on his leg trying to comfort him. She was waiting for him to take her hand but he never did.

As I sat in the backseat I went through the two texts Jade had sent me. "Hey, I don't know if you're up or not but I'm at the diner if you'd like to come see me!" The other one read, "I don't know if it's because it's so late but I'm seeing things, Carter. Text me when you can."

"Guys, if we have time we should go see if Dallas is alright." I said.

Jackson looked at me through the rearview mirror. We were both thinking the same thing about Dallas.

When we arrived, we found Jade in her uniform, sitting with her hands wrapped around a steaming cup of coffee. She looked shaken up. The diner wasn't too busy, the booths taken up by truckers and college kids studying for tests. We walked in and sat down with her. She looked out the window, evading our faces, looking embarrassed and scared. This was a side of her I hadn't seen.

I scooted next to her and placed my hand on hers, letting her know I was here for her. We all sat in awkward silence until one of Jade's coworkers, the one with brown-sugar-colored hair, told her she just got sat. I scooted out of the booth and she got up to go greet her new table.

"What do you think is going on?" Brooke asked out loud.

"I don't know. And Dallas isn't responding to me," Jackson commented. *Shit, we should have picked Dallas up.* I didn't even know if he was okay, or what happened.

This was all a mess. My palms began to sweat.

Jade came back with a worried look and glanced down at the table. "I guess I don't really know where to begin," she said. "And you guys are going to think I'm crazy, but I'm seeing people that I shouldn't be seeing." She sat back down next to me.

"Like who?" I asked, knowing already what she was going to say.

Her eyes narrowed, and she paused for a second before answering. "I saw Emily and Alex. I recognized him from that picture you showed me." My ears roared and time froze. My stomach dropped, and I knew she wasn't seeing things. Jackson and I exchanged glances and then looked away.

"Now, I know what you're thinking and I know that they're not with us anymore, but I swear I saw them. An hour ago I was at table twenty-seven and for a split second I saw Emily sitting there, looking normal except for her eyes. She had no pupils. And then I saw Alex walking around the diner outside, just looking through the windows. When I looked back at the table, Emily was gone and no one was there anymore." Her hands trembled while they brought the coffee cup up to her mouth.

"It's okay, Jade, this is all okay," Brooke reassured

her.

"What is? Seeing dead people? Something is wrong, something doesn't feel right," Jade said, frantic. Brooke backed off and I could see that she felt a little stupid. I looked at Jackson again, and I could tell we were both thinking whether we should say something. I wanted to tell her, but figured it would freak her and Brooke out even more, and what good was that?

As the other two tried to comfort her, I spaced off and looked at the other patrons. I rubbed her back and kept her to close to me. In the back of the restaurant, I saw Dallas sitting at a table. I perked up and stared at him. He looked so different, scared, even a little worse than he did a few days ago. Dallas turned and looked at me from across the room, and for the first time I hardly recognized his face. A few people got up and blocked my line of sight, but when they left, Dallas was gone. Even then, I knew that wasn't Dallas.

"Is that the first time you saw them?" Jackson asked Jade.

"Yes, but lately I've been sensing weird things, like I'm not the only one in the room. I don't know if I'm over thinking this, and . . ." she put her head in her hands and trailed off. I then embraced her with both my arms and kissed the side of her head.

"No, it's okay, Jade!" Brooke reassured her. "I've been feeling weird things, too, and not sleeping so well. I think all of us are going through the same things."

"You've been sleeping next to me; I hope you've been sleeping well," Jackson joked. He pulled her closer and she gave him a smile.

"Jade, everything is going to be okay, with all of us," I said while rubbing her leg and thinking if I believed the lie I just told."We all just need to take some time and breathe and not let fear control our lives. We have to keep moving forward. With the funeral of Emily fresh in our minds I think it's safe to say we're all a little spooked." I was trying to find the right words but I didn't know where to draw the line. "Jade, I still see Alex sometimes. In public when I pass strangers I swear I think some of them are him. But the closer I get I see that it was never Alex." Brooke and Jade deserved to know everything. I opened my mouth to say what I've been going through when Jade accidently spilled her coffee.

The hot brown liquid oozed over the table and started spilling off the sides. We all dodged it while I stood up.

"I am so sorry you guys." Jade said while reaching for napkins.

"I'll go ask for a rag." I said while walking away.

"We should all do something this weekend," Brooke said while helping Jade clean up the mess.

I kept trying to see if Dallas was anywhere in the diner, but he was nowhere to be seen. Something was wrong. Everyone was now seeing or and feeling something, and Dallas was in a lot of trouble. I needed to stop thinking this was all going to go away. This was all real.

Dallas

My skin burned. Blood matted my hair where I had clawed at my arm to stop it from burning. I stopped hiding in my bed but now I was under it, for I didn't want to me to find myself. I hadn't slept in God knows how long, but if there was a God I wouldn't be like how I am today. Those harsh whispers of all hours of the night, the whispers telling me how I needed to feed my demons.

But I was done. Tonight was the night I would fight back; I needed to finish this once and for all. The little bit of what I had left of my humanity would hopefully suffice for my survival. My eyes were just as eager as my ears, listening, watching, and waiting for me to emerge from the shadows.

I inched my way out from underneath my bed and

carefully crept out of my room. I turned on the bathroom light and stared at myself one last time. I saw purple veins run up my face like vines on a tree. The blood vessels in my eyes pumped vigorously, almost to a point where I could feel them. The whites of my eyes were speckled with black, and my iris looked like it was beginning to fade.

I turned off the light and went back into my bedroom, looking out the window to the quiet, secluded area around me. I was about to look away when I noticed something. Down the dirt road in front of my house, I saw my parallel self run toward me. He came from nowhere out of the shadows and was running in a way I'd never seen a human run. He was fast, but something was off with his form. It looked as if he wasn't in control of his movements, like something else was making him run.

Every object around him cast a shadow, but he didn't have one. My mouth grew dry and my heartbeat quickened. As if knowing exactly where I stood, his eyes stared directly at mine through the window. His look pierced my soul and shook me to the core. He smiled big and his eyes said it all: "I'm coming for you." His gaze didn't leave mine until he went around the edge of the house. Within seconds, I heard the front door open and slam shut, and I knew this was it.

I quietly walked through the dark house. I had to be the one to find him first. Right away, I saw me in the doorway to the kitchen. The moonlight from a nearby window gave off just enough light for me to make out the silhouette and see the smirk on his face.

Tonight it had been keeping its distance, for normally it was almost right next to me. It got closer to me moment by moment, feeding off what humanity I had left. But I prepared for this. The house was ready; I was ready. I grabbed one of the bottles that I had hidden in a careful spot and inched closer. The smirk on his face, those white eyes, how they taunted me. *Well, I'll show him. I'll show everyone.*

I took out the lighter, started the wet cloth on fire and threw the Molotov cocktail straight at him. I watched as the whole doorway burst into flames, filling my eyes and the room with light. It was nice to feel the heat against what it felt like my cold, dead skin. I heard the screech as he ran away, but I had more bottles prepared.

I continued to throw them at all the main doorways so he couldn't escape. It was genius, and it was working. The house was soon a sweltering oven, the flames making their way through the house.

"You're not going take me, you're going to burn! You

hear me?" I lost sight of him, but I knew there was no escape for him. I ran to the kitchen and grabbed a large steak knife, bracing myself for when he would strike.

The ringing of the smoke detectors was more satisfying than displeasing, music to my ears for a job well done. I didn't even know what was left of me anymore, and my burning house was a great example of that. It's hard to control reality when your fantasies are stronger. But I knew I needed to get out before the flames enveloped me. I dodged the angry embers, burning drapes, and smoldering ashes on the floor. I darted across the room and toward my exit. I slammed the door behind me, threw one more bottle at the front door and walked away, smiling as I watched it all go up in flames. Relief washed over me. Beads of sweat trickled down my face and my breathing steadied. No more running away in fear. No more hiding and no more being alone in that house with that demon. A tear slid down my face as I could finally breathe again.

I was caught up in my head when I almost missed it. It was a familiar sound that made me feel like I was ten again. I heard Finn's barking from inside the house. He was afraid and in trouble. I had to go help him!

I started my way back towards the house when a gust of heat and power came crashing through the living room's windows. Flames latched onto the house like tendrils and devoured the once wholesome house it used to be.

"Finn!" I yelled in desperation. Anger and heartache filled my body while I listened to my whimpering dog burn to death. I couldn't make it inside the house, I would die.

The sound of a car door woke me from my reverie, and paranoia consumed my mind.

"Dallas! What happened? Are you okay?" It was the sound of my mom, with my father's footsteps quickly behind. How could it be them? They were never home; they were never there for me. Anger rushed through my veins. I felt Mom touch my shoulder, and Dad touched the other one. This wasn't real, none of this was real. All of this was just my imagination, the things I'd seen, what I'd been though. I don't have a dog, not anymore. I have nothing. The anger kept building and my head was pounding and before I knew it I heard another voice.

"Dallas! What have you done?" It was Carter's voice, but he wasn't alone. I felt the knife drop out of my hand and heard it hit the cement with a sharp clank. Warm blood oozed down my fingers, like I had squeezed rotten fruit with my hands. The scary part was that deep down, I liked it. I liked feeling other people's blood. I turned around and saw my parents bleeding out on the ground. My dad's neck was slit open and my mom had a stab wound right by her heart. My heart stopped. Vomit poured out of my mouth and I covered the grass with bile and half-digested food. I dropped to my knees, and my eyes burned in agony as I wept. Everything hurt.

"I had to . . ." I said between sobs. "I had to finish it. I didn't think they were gonna be home for me."

They were all near me, rubbing my back and holding me. That was when I knew this was real. This wasn't me; the old me left a long time ago. I killed my parents and I set my house on fire all because I tried to kill myself, the one person I couldn't stand to look at, the one person I knew was still alive inside me, waiting for me to go to the dark place again. A sinister voice echoed in my head while I watched the roaring flames, *Sometimes being mad can be a beautiful thing.*

Chapter 10

Carter

Dallas was on the ground crying next to his dead parents, and my heart ached for him. I had no idea what had just happened or what he went through, but I was too late. I should have done something as soon as Dallas sent me that strange voicemail. No, I should have done something when I saw him at Emily's funeral.

The house was being swallowed in crackling hot flames. Jackson helped me pick up Dallas and move him away from the knife, away from his house, and away from his dead parents. The girls were trying hard not to cry, but we were all heartbroken and scared.

"I didn't mean to . . . I didn't think it was . . . actually them . . ." Dallas cried. I pulled him close and held onto him tightly as Jackson stepped away to call the cops. Dallas's tears and his parents' blood covered my jacket. My guilt for not stepping in earlier made me feel almost like I was the one who killed them.

"Dallas, it's going to be okay," I said soothingly.

"I had to finish it . . ." Dallas kept whispering things that didn't make sense between sobs. "I just want them

172

back. I'm sorry . . . I'm so sorry . . ."

"Shhh, shhh, it's all right, Dallas, you're okay now."
His eyes were so bloodshot that his irises were no longer
brown. Honest to God, he looked crazy. I didn't know what
was going to happen. This all felt like a dream within a
dream.

I heard sirens in the distance and felt relieved, but at
the same time, I was scared for Dallas. The fire trucks
showed up and the firefighters hopped out and began to try
to extinguish the blaze. The house was going to be long
gone by the time they put out the fire. A few moments later,
three cop cars showed up, along with two ambulances. The
EMTs rushed to Dallas's parents and checked to see if
either of them were still breathing, but they had both bled
out. The cops swarmed us, and we were left to keep a
secret, hidden in a story no one else would believe.

Dallas was in no state to talk to the cops, so the four of
us were left to tell them what we thought we knew. The
cops put caution tape around the fence and sidewalk, while
his parents were placed in body bags, lifted on stretchers,
and put into an ambulance. Within time, the cops managed
to get Dallas to talk, and he admitted to killing his parents
but said he didn't remember it. Dallas had a few cuts on his
hands and on his face. He was checked out by an EMT and

placed into a second ambulance to go to the hospital to get tested for any vital injuries and to evaluate his mental health. We wouldn't be allowed to visit him until tomorrow, if they even let us then. A police officer would accompany him but they told us they'd know more tomorrow.

The cops told us we were good to go, so we left Dallas's and headed to Jackson's place. Everything felt surreal. None of us knew what to say; we were all sad and distraught, and honestly, I felt like the worst person in the world. I knew something was going on with him but I just let it go, and now Dallas had finally lost it.

"I don't understand," Brooke said. "Why did he set his house on fire and . . . do the things he did?"

"I just wish he reached out to us. I feel so awful," Jade added as we walked up the stairs to Jackson's apartment.

Jackson looked at me. "It's none of our faults. Dallas decided to keep it from us."

"How can you say that like it's his fault?" I asked, getting a little angry.

"He didn't open up to us about it and he kept it a secret."

"Well, wouldn't you? Because I hardly think that anyone who accidently kills his parents or feels crazy wants to open up and tell people," I retorted.

"Guys, please stop," Jade said. "This isn't helping. If I were Dallas, I know I wouldn't want my friends arguing over what we think happened and what we actually know, because as far as I'm concerned, we know nothing."

When Jackson unlocked his door, I saw clutter claimed the space. Jackson had left video game cases spread all across the floor, crumbs were left in chip bags on the coffee table, and I couldn't tell which of the clothes draped on and around the suede couch were clean or dirty. Brooke tried her best to keep up with the place when she stayed over, but clearly Jackson's bad habits overruled. Jackson wasn't necessarily a messy or a lazy guy, he just took more care of his looks than his actual home. The scent of teakwood from a wax melter on the edge of an end table permeated the apartment with a soothing, masculine smell.

Jackson lived in a penthouse-type apartment, thanks to his mother, who was an interior designer and got a discount from designing most of the apartments in the building. The polished gray oak floors brought out the stainless-steel appliances, while the beautifully polished granite counters circled around the open kitchen with a small island in the middle. His parents told him if he stayed on the Dean's list, they'd pay for his rent until he graduated; thanks to Brooke, so far he had.

Jade's words played on in my head while we all sat in silence. I wanted to throw up, and the thought that Dallas killed his parents and was now being tested in the ER made my stomach turn.

I got up from one of the clean couches. "I need some fresh air," I said, opening the screen door and stepping outside onto the balcony. I put my hands on the railing and breathed deeply, looking out at the city lights below. The sound of leaves scraped against the balcony's floor, and I heard soft footsteps behind me as Jade came up next to me.

"I feel like I'm going crazy, Jade," I admitted. "I feel like I failed my best friend, and I lost Emily and Alex and my parents. What the hell is going on? What's next?"

"I don't know what's going on, but none of it is your fault or anyone else's." Jade placed her hand on my shoulder, and her touch helped soothe wounds that weren't even there. A soft breeze blew her beautiful brown hair around as she looked at me. "Carter, I am so sorry for what you and your friends are going through."

Kissing her on the forehead and hugging her tightly one more time, I took a step back and said, "There's something I didn't tell you. I never really knew how to, if I'm being honest."

Concern filled her eyes as she stood up straight.

"About what?"

"Jackson and I went to my brother's apartment earlier this week—"

"Hey, Jade, what kind of topping do you like for pizza?" Brooke asked, sliding open the door. "You should come here and look at all these kinds we can get! You too, Carter!"

Jade and I looked at each other and walked back in, leaving the conversation where it was. We ordered in pizza and then, realizing it was almost two in the morning and we were all stressed out and run down, we began passing out on the floor and on the couch.

About four in the morning, I started to get restless. I was cuddling Jade on the couch and Jackson must have moved to the chair and Brooke to his room. The apartment was freezing, and I couldn't recall if Jackson opened a window before bed. Goosebumps covered my body and the stone-cold wooden floor made my toes curl. I carefully got up to go to the bathroom when I met Brooke coming out of Jackson's bedroom. She gave a big yawn and smiled at me.

"Did you and Jackson have a fight?" I whispered.

"No, why do you ask?" she replied, crossing her arms trying to keep herself warm.

"Well, why is he on the chair?"

She looked really confused and said, "He's not. He's sleeping with me in his bed." Behind me, I heard a dry cackle that sent more chills down my spine. The lamp by the chair began to flicker and I saw Dallas slowly make his way from the chair over to us. My heart stopped and I pushed Brooke behind me. Dallas had almost no color left in his eyes, and his face was all scratched up like he had been clawing at it. His once perfectly well-nourished brown hair was now a disheveled, matted mess. He looked like he belonged on *America's Most Wanted*. He didn't look like my friend anymore.

"You guys left me there." He was smiling. "You let me kill my parents and you let me suffer the same fate as your brother."

"Dallas, what are you doing here?" I asked.

He stepped closer. "Did they not tell you, Brooke, did they not tell you what's been going on here?" He cackled again, only this time it didn't sound like Dallas.

I whispered to Brooke, "Go into Jackson's room, lock the door, and wake Jackson up." Brooke quickly ran into his room and locked the door. Jade was still asleep on the floor, and I was afraid Dallas might do something to her. My heart was beating so loudly I thought surely Dallas would hear it.

"Don't you get it, Carter? We're all dead and cold on the inside. That's why you left me to suffer, and Emily, and your brother." Dallas pulled out a knife. "Everyone left me—my parents, my friends—and all I had left was myself. It's always myself. If only you knew the countless times I hid in fear while the other me tried looking for me. So I had to do it. I had to burn it all down. Something is out there making us pay for all our sins as we face our demons alone. Why does life seem like hell at times; because we live in the hell that we create. We were born into sin and sin is what we do. Something is here with us, waiting for us to sin again; to remind us that we're all human and human is what we are."

The lights continued to flicker as he got closer. "And the funny thing is, I liked burning it down to the ground." With that, the lights turned off, and before I knew it he had me pushed up against the wall with the knife to my throat.

His breath smelled rotten and his eyes were bright and colorless. He titled his head and kept his smirk. I grabbed his arm and tried to keep the blade off my neck as he kept me pinned on the wall.

"Dallas, stop, you don't want to do this." I could see dark veins latch around his arms and move up to his throat.

"Just let it happen, Carter. Let it in, let it all in. I did."

He was strong and the grip was tight. The cold blade started to hurt as it got close to tearing through my skin. In a blink of an eye, Jackson ripped him off of me, but Dallas spun and stabbed Jackson in the shoulder. He then pushed Brooke up against the wall, smiling at her. Without thinking, I tackled him to the ground. At this point, Jade was wide awake and distraught at the scene.

"Dallas, stop!" I yelled. His skin was cold to the touch. He was fighting me, trying to push me off. Dark veins like tendrils ran up his neck and his face, as if they had a mind of their own, and he let out another cackle.

"They're all going to find you in the end." His voice was deep and dry. He pushed me off of him and got on top of me, beginning to choke me. His bony fingers wrapped around my throat, like talons latched onto prey. Jackson grabbed his lamp and whacked Dallas across the face with it, sending him flying off of me and blood into the air. Dallas slowly got up, grabbed a shard of the broken light bulb and charged at Jackson, sending them both through the glass door and onto the balcony. Glass went everywhere as they tumbled out and continued to fight one another.

"Dallas, what is your problem?" Jackson asked, trying to hold him down. Veins protruded around his neck in anger and exertion. Dallas dug his finger into Jackson's wound, causing him to yell in pain and allowing Dallas to throw him off. Dallas picked up a shard of glass and slowly went back after Jackson.

"Dallas, this isn't you," I called, stepping onto the balcony. "Please put the glass down."

He turned and looked at me, his eyes as bright as the moon and holding no other color. Dark circles surrounded his eyes and a mad smile grew upon his lips. It didn't look like him at all. It was the same exact eye I had looked into at Emily's. *They all get this way,* I realized, *like my brother said.*

"I don't know how to feel anymore," Dallas said in a deep voice, dropping his smile. Blood ran down the sides of his face and his hand shook uncontrollably, still holding the shard of glass. "I can't go back anymore; it's too late for me to be saved." He tilted his head and looked at me nearly sideways. The wind picked up, blowing leaves around us. "Those beautiful eyes of yours can't see."

"What are you talking about?"

Dallas's smirk grew back. "It's all around you, Carter, everywhere you go. It's always been there. When you see it, when it becomes you, when you feel it, that's when you know you're home."

Still confused, and before I could say anything else, I watched as Dallas ran the piece of glass across his throat, tearing open his skin and letting the blood pour down. His eyes never left mine as he choked on his blood and fell to his knees. Brooke and Jade screamed as Jackson and I both ran to help Dallas, but it was too late. He fell over, closing his eyes, and lay in his puddle of blood.

Jackson's eyes filled with tears, as did mine as we kneeled down beside our best friend, his blood covering us. Everything was catching up to me, to all of us; so much death in so little time. Something sinister was going on, something that held the same fate for all of us. Dallas was right: there was something out there I didn't see yet, that we didn't understand. What I'd been dealing with for months had always been around me, and it found all of us. I didn't know what it was or what it wanted, but I couldn't help but think that the only person after us was ourselves.

Chapter 11

We were all quiet in disbelief while we waited for the police and ambulance to arrive. The four of us were taken to the sheriff's office to be questioned, since we were also at the scene of Dallas's house burning.

They separated us, and, one by one, took us into a private room and asked us what we saw and knew about tonight and how well we knew Dallas. The small office was like one of those you see on TV. The room wasn't too big but held filing cabinet after filing cabinet, with a large wooden desk centered in the far back. The only windows in the room led to the hallway, but blinds covered them up. A lamp on the edge of the desk illuminated the room.

Deputy Riley looked to be only a few years older than me. His five o'clock shadow matched his jet-black hair, which was parted cleanly on the side of his head. The rest of his short hair was gelled up. Small freckles painted his nose like a speckled egg.

I took a sip of my water and continued my story. "No, we just got to his place when we saw his parents on the ground."

"Can you tell me more about what Dallas was like, Mr.

Gray?" the deputy asked. His hazel eyes never left mine.

"He was on his knees and in sorrow and disbelief. He was terrified by what he did."

"Tell me more about his home life. You said you guys have been friends for years and hung out as much as you could. What would give him a motive to kill his parents?"

I narrowed my eyes and clenched my teeth as anger boiled in my blood at his questions. It wasn't because of the way he asked it was because I didn't have an answer myself. "Dallas's parents were never home; they were business partners and always on the road. Dallas was a busy and active student, but it ate at him. But he didn't kill his parents just to do it. He loved his parents and they loved him. Dallas wasn't like that."

"What was he like?"

I rubbed my shaky fingertips back and forth across my brow. "He . . . wasn't himself in the end. He was troubled during his swim meets, and Emily Rawson's funeral was really when we noticed he was different."

The deputy scribbled down some notes and continued. "So Dallas Walker escaped the hospital and made his way to your friend Jackson's place about two hours ago, attacking you and your friends there. And then he tackled Jackson onto the balcony, on which shortly after Dallas took his own life with a piece of glass?"

I looked away, as if that helped not to relive the memory, but it was just as gruesome hearing it summed up as it was to watch it. "Correct," I mumbled. "You have my witness report."

"I understand, Carter, but I need to ask follow-up questions to help get to the bottom of this."

"Dallas is dead." The words tasted bitter as they rolled off my tongue.

"I understand. Did he say anything before he took his own life?" Deputy Riley's tone seemed patronizing and condescending, nonetheless.

"He told us he was finally home." The comment hung in air, as eerie now as when Dallas said it.

"Do you know what he would have meant by that?"

Thinking about it again and still not understanding it, I shook my head.

"It's strange to think about how Dallas killed his parents, then wanted to kill you guys."

"He didn't want to kill us. He came to Jackson's place to tell us how pissed he was."

"But you told me he held a knife to your throat and then stabbed it into Jackson King's shoulder," Deputy Riley said. "Is that not correct?"

"No, it is," I confessed.

"Was Dallas ever bullied in high school or college?"

"Not that I was aware of."

"Did Dallas have any animosity or anger toward Jackson or any of you in the friend group?"

"No. Dallas was never an angry person. He was well liked and successful."

"Dallas wasn't on any un-prescribed medications or steroids to help his performances?"

"No," I said, exhausted. "With all due respect, every question you ask me will be answered with a 'no.'"

"This sounds just like your brother," the cop mumbled.

"What?"

"I said, it's hard to lose someone like that. Are you sure, Mr. Gray, that you're all right?"

"Why do you ask?"

"You keep looking around the room like something is here with us."

"Sorry, I have a lot on my mind. I've been losing everyone around me lately."

"What do you mean by that?"

I laughed, harsh and mocking. I was done with this conversation. I couldn't wait to be released so I could head over to the liquor store and drown in bottles of booze."I don't know if you know this or not, Deputy Riley, but I lost my parents and my brother as well. My parents were killed in a car accident and my brother lost a battle for his life. Dallas and my brother were not suicidal, I can tell you that much."

He was silent for a few moments. His eyes softened, as if he realized he needed to take a different approach. He tried hiding his concern, but the silence made me feel like I was crazy. I opened up to this prick about my family and here he was looking at me like I was delusional. "Are you inferring that someone told them to do it?" he asked me.

"That's up to you guys to figure out."

"Do you know something we don't?"

"I wish I did so I could help everyone out, but I don't know anything more than you guys. Now, can I please be done?"

"Yes, that is all. Thank you very much, Carter. You and your friends are free to go." We both got up and he led me to the lobby, where I was reunited with my friends before we were brought back home. Since Jackson's place was now a crime scene, we all went to my place and crashed.

In the distance, we could see the light of the rising sun. It was comforting to know that we got to see another day, even when everything else got bad. But it was bittersweet that other people didn't.

"I don't even know if I can sleep anymore . . ." Jackson quietly said after the police officers dropped us off.

"I feel like I'm living in a nightmare and I can't wake up," Brooke added while hugging a pillow.

"I can't even fathom what happened tonight. I don't get it. This isn't right . . ." Jade commented.

"We all need to get some sleep," I told them. We all looked and acted like zombies. I wanted my brain to put me in a different nightmare for awhile, somewhere that didn't feel so real. Somewhere where I could scream, someplace where I could let it all out, some other world where I had a family and wasn't alone.

***

I woke up before anyone else, a little after ten. I could feel the bags under my eyes, even if I couldn't see them. Guilt and dread washed over me as the memory of last night burned in the back of my head. What became of Dallas consumed him, Emily, and my brother.

I poured myself a glass of water, gulped that down and started refilling it. I don't think I ever fell asleep last night. My head pounded like I had drank a whole bottle of vodka by myself. Jade walked into the kitchen, her long, curly brown locks of hair falling gracefully on one side. She walked up to the island and set down a book. It was my brother's journal.

"What is this, Carter? Is this yours?" She looked disturbed.

I shook my head. "No, it was Alex's."

"I see why you kept this a secret . . ." She looked away. "You knew about Dallas, didn't you?"

"As far as what?" I diverted her accusation.

"Don't play stupid with me, Carter. At the swim meet, you knew what was going on, and at Emily's funeral, you knew he was in trouble." She looked hurt.

"What are you saying? It's my fault because you think I knew something was wrong with Dallas?"

"Well, didn't you?"

"Jade, we all knew something was wrong with him. It's not like I didn't try to help him. As you could tell last night, that wasn't Dallas."

"What do you mean?" She folded her arms.

"It's all in that journal. Everything I know, everything my brother found and what happened to him is in there." I lifted my hand in a weak gesture. I didn't feel like fighting. Not today, and not with her. Brooke and Jackson made their way into the kitchen, looking like we had just woken them up.

"So you're telling me your brother and Dallas went through the same things," Jade said. "Why didn't you tell me about any of this? And now I feel like I'm losing my mind, too, and none of this makes sense."

"Jade, what was I supposed to tell you? That journal doesn't hold every answer we need. Was I supposed to say, 'Oh, by the way, I found my dead brother's journal and it seems like Emily and Dallas are all suffering through what he did'? Then what, Jade? I can't tell you what they went through, because I don't know. I know they needed help, but that doesn't mean I knew how to give it to them, and worrying you or Brooke was not in my plan. I don't have any answers to any of this. I am on a road of recovery from my past. When I lost my family I felt lost, in the dark, and helpless. I spent most nights alone. Away from Jackson, I let my dreary thoughts convince me I was going crazy. It was one thing after another and I blamed myself until my therapist taught me how not to. I thought I was doing well and recovering fully until I found Alex's journal. I read it and began to question everything, and that was when I started to hear and see things. I felt crazy and alone again, and that last thing I wanted was to tell all of you and have you look at me like I actually was crazy."

The three of them didn't know what to say after my rant. Jade looked hurt and I could tell she felt bad. Her tired eyes became soft again. My words came off harsher than I intended and I didn't mean to hurt anyone, though I felt slightly relieved to have gotten those things off my chest.

"Carter . . ."

"It's fine, Jade. I'm sorry. I'm sorry for trying to hide things from you, all of you. I thought I had this under control, but it's bigger than me. I wish I was there for all of them. Maybe they'd still be here."

"Wait, so you're saying your brother, Emily, and Dallas's deaths were all connected?" Brooke asked. "How can that be?"

I scooted the journal closer to Brooke so she could look through it. Jackson made his way over to my coffeepot and began brewing some coffee. "Last night, I started to tell Jade that Jackson and I went back to my brother's apartment the other night."

"Why?" Brooke asked, beginning to page through the journal.

"To see if there were any more clues to what happened to him. But Jackson and I saw Alex and Emily, just like you did at the diner, Jade. Emily was ripping out her stitches and my brother was coming after us."

"I don't get what makes all of this connected," Brooke said. "Carter, can I be frank? Could this maybe a confirmation bias?"

"A what?" Jackson asked.

"A confirmation bias, when person searches for information, or recalls information selectively to confirm or 'prove' one's beliefs," Brooke answered.

"No, but I had considered it—until last night. I know this all sounds ludicrous, but this goes farther than just trying to prove that this is real. In the journal, it says 'something' found my brother. Later, Emily started seeing it, too, and before I knew it, Dallas was experiencing the same things. Then the same night Jackson and I went to my brother's place—"

"Carter and I saw our reflections," Jackson finished. "But they weren't just reflections. I didn't want to believe it at first, so I was distant with everyone. After Emily's funeral, I knew Dallas was far more into this than we were, and that scared me."

"But what do you mean they weren't just reflections?" Jade asked. She pulled a stool out and sat at the island.

"They didn't move the way we did. Something was off about them and then they started doing things on their own, their own kind of actions and movements," Jackson explained.

"So Alex, Emily, and Dallas all saw what we are now experiencing?" Brooke asked.

"We're pretty sure," I replied.

"Sounds like *folie à deux* to me," Brooke suggested.

"Folie a who?" Jackson echoed back.

"Shared psychosis," I muttered. "Brooke, I understand that this is a lot to take in right now, but I can guarantee that's far from what this is. I mean—"

"Wait, wait, wait, so you're saying you think that Alex went off the deep end and Emily and Dallas eventually followed him?" Jackson interrupted.

"I'm not saying anyone went off anything," Brooke said defensively. "I'm only suggesting that maybe all of Alex's symptoms were transmitted to everyone else. It makes sense that you're feeling and seeing things that your brother was, Carter, and Emily dated him for a long time, which is why shared psychosis is relevant."

"Oh, so like schizophrenia?" Jackson asked.

"My brother wasn't schizophrenic, I know that for a fact. And besides, you know how rare shared psychosis is? I'm not taking on any mental illness or symptoms of anyone else. There's no way in hell that shared psychosis can go through so many people so fast. I know that there's something out there; I'm not going crazy. There is something behind our reflections. I swear by that."

"So our reflections are after us?" Jade asked.

I shook my head. "No, it's not our reflections. It's ourselves. And for some reason, at least after Alex and Emily died, they still seem to exist in our world." hard to fully explain. Each question made it easier for me to understand, but for the others, I wasn't so sure.

"What do you mean 'our world'?" Jade asked.

"I think my brother discovered a parallel universe," I said slowly. I hadn't explained my theory to anyone yet. "His reflection helped him find it. His journal stated that *it* found him and he kept going back *there* for some reason. It found him one day and it didn't stop until it got what it wanted."

"What do they want?" Brooke asked.

"They're going to follow us and they won't stop until they become us. They want *us*," I explained. The room was silent as we took it all in.

"Our parallel selves live in another dimension. Like it says in Alex's journal, maybe we were all born with four arms and four legs, but were split in half to be rid of our sins and demons, and they were put away in another world," Jackson said while pouring his first cup of coffee

194

and taking a sip.

"And I think once they see us, and find us, they're going to continue to get closer to us until we become one, the way it started," I added.

"Is this figuratively or literally? How do we stop them?" Brooke asked, terrified.

I looked down at the floor and grew silent for a moment. "It's a myth so I assume figuratively, and I'm not sure."

"What causes this to happen? Our demons just decide when to find us?" Brooke asked.

"Vulnerability? I don't know," I admitted. "Dallas mentioned something about sin. And how something is out there waiting for us to sin. He said 'we're human, it's what we do.'"

"So they're just going to follow us around through mirrors until we become insane? I mean, this just all seems a little stretched. We're going to go off of what your, no offense, but what your dead brother's journal says?" Jade asked.

"No," I replied. "One night after I dropped you off, I drove down Emily's street and noticed duct tape all over her windows. Through a crack, I saw her lying in her bed, but in another room I saw her looking down the hallway into her bedroom. And same with Dallas; he burned his house down because he was trying to trap himself in his house. I know all of this seems crazy and all of the pieces still don't fit, but I do believe Alex's journal can help us lead to answers and solace. Maybe to even where my brother went to."

"Somehow the bond between our parallel selves and us becomes stronger," Jackson added.

"So, the stronger the bond, the closer they get to us," Brooke said, catching on.

"What makes it stronger?" Jade asked. Everyone looked at me.

"I don't know. I still don't know how my brother got to the parallel universe. But for awhile now I've been sensing things near windows and mirrors. It's like a presence and a feeling that I'm being watched and they want me to get closer. Or the other way around."

"We need to figure out how to stop this," Jackson said.

"Well then, saying there really is another world where our demons go . . . what if the entrance to this parallel world is through the mirrors and windows? I mean, you guys were just talking about how your reflections don't move the same way as you and how you feel a presence at the windows," Brooke suggested.

"That could be a good theory, but I don't know how we would be able to go through a window or a mirror," I stated.

"But neither one of you have seen your parallel self in the mirror?" Jackson asked the girls.

"No, I just saw Alex and Emily at the diner and that's it," Jade responded.

"But that doesn't mean anything," Brooke added. "So all we gotta do is find this parallel universe and go in."

"But then what?" Jade asked. "I mean, say there is a parallel universe, but what if it's only our minds making it up and it's not an actual place? Yeah, we have that journal, but there's still no proof of a different world even existing."

"She's right," Jackson said. "So as of right now, if anything weird happens or if we sense anything, we contact each other and get the fuck out of there. And if entering that world is as easy as going through a mirror, we don't go in alone."

"What if the only way to enter it is if we have to be alone?" I asked. Silence followed my question as my friends looked away. "If this place involves my sin or whatever, then it makes sense that it's only meant for me. And vice versa."

"I can't believe this is all happening. I mean, just last

month we were all living normal lives, and now we're trying to survive against ourselves," Brooke said. She looked to Jackson for comfort. She then left the kitchen going to grab something.

"Welcome to my life," I mumbled.

"Shit," Jade said, looking at her phone. "I just got called into work. The first lunch server didn't show up."

"Say your friend just died," I told her. "Besides, you're always working."

She looked away for a moment and then back. "I have to pay for college and my other bills and expenses, Carter. It's not that I don't want to not work, it's because I have to."

"But, Jade, you've been doing just fine working the hours that were originally in your schedule." She took my arm and pulled me into the other room so the others couldn't hear us.

"Carter, there's a few things I didn't tell you when we went out to eat," she began. "Years ago, when I was little, when my father came home from the bar, he would hit me. Not every night, but he would handle me roughly and take his anger out on me for Mom leaving us. Fear consumed me. I was awake every night, just waiting for him to come into my room. I prayed to God so many times, and finally I got enough courage to send him to jail. For years I felt bad. I didn't talk to my mom, I put my father away, and I felt like everything was my fault, but it wasn't. My dad needed help and my mom was a coward. It drove me crazy not having anyone. My mom never came back into my life. She and I don't talk. My sister really is in Oregon, but she and I had a falling out awhile back when I told her I didn't like how her boyfriend treats her. I'm still afraid my father will find me again, but I don't let it consume my life or make me live in fear."

"Jade, I'm so sorry." I had no words.

"It's okay. I don't tell that side of me to just anyone." She let out a small sigh. "I'll admit, the day you and I met helped me with my fear. With you, I feel protected, and I can finally be myself again."

A part of me wanted to tell her, *you shouldn't feel protected around me, because death follows me everywhere. There is not one good thing I can provide for you, Jade. You don't know anything about me, and I don't know anything about myself. I'm anxious all the time and some days I can't control my dark thoughts and want to be left alone. I don't think I can be there for you. I was too late for my brother, I was too late for Emily, and I was too late for Dallas.*

"His final words to me were, 'Once I get out of here, you'll never be safe again. I'll be coming for you, daughter of mine.' Those kinds of words said to you by your own father don't sit well growing up."

"Jade, I'm not going to let anything happen to you," I promised, not only for her but for myself. I pulled her close and kissed her softly on her forehead.

"I'm afraid he's going to hurt my mom first once he gets out. He's not mentally stable, Carter. Even though I'm older now I'm still terrified of him."

"He's still in jail, Jade. He's not going to lay one finger on you."

Her silence was her response and I hoped I made everything better for her, at least temporarily. "Wait, does that mean you don't have a cat named Charles?" I joked.

She looked up at me and smiled. "We used to. We got him when I was one, but he later died from old age." She thought for a moment. "My father could be released at any moment. So I set up an extra savings account in case I need to pack up and leave."

"You'd leave me behind?" I teased.

"I don't want you to get hurt and I don't want him to find me."

"Jade, no one is going to hurt you."

"Everything I went through when I was a child, Carter . . . I don't want to go back there." Tears started to well up in her eyes, so I pulled her closer.

"I'm going to make sure no one will ever hurt you again, I promise."

"That means more than you know, but I really have to go to work. I'll text you once I'm off." She kissed me softly and quickly on the lips and grabbed her things. She told the others goodbye and walked out.

"Dallas needed us," Jackson mumbled as I stepped back into the kitchen. "We ignored him, Carter. We ignored all the signs and all the cries for help, like he told us last night." Jackson's voice trembled with rage and fear.

"You guys didn't know what to do. None of us did," Brooke said while coming in with a granola bar. She tore open the wrapper and began nibbling on the end.

"Before he killed himself, he told me he couldn't go back *there* and that it was too late. I don't think he meant it was too late for his sanity, but that it was literally too late for him to go back for some reason," I stated. "He told me the other him had been looking for him and that he'd chased himself through the house. So, Jackson, why aren't you and I doing that yet? Emily told me the same thing, and I saw two Emilys at once."

"Then it's not just our mind, but an actual place," Jackson responded. "They entered our world at some point. And Emily and Alex must still be in it."

"What if you didn't see two Emilys at once, but they were really one whole person? Aren't one of the bodies buried?" Brooke asked.

"Are they?" I asked. They both looked at me like I was crazy. "Think about it: if our sins and demons live in another world, that makes them an entity, and an entity feasts on living things so they can inhabit our bodies."

"I'm not following," Jackson stated.

"Well, since they're all dead, where would that entity go? It's not gonna go back where it came from," I said.

"The law of conservation and mass," Brooke added. "Neither energy or matter can be created or destroyed. If we were all born with four arms and four legs, then split, that matter and energy would be converted and still exist, but in a different form. And if that theory is true about us once being one with our demons, then this is really happening. For there to be two of us at once is a bit of a stretch. What if you saw Emily right before she died, and somehow it was during the moments of the two coming together?"

"That could be an accurate theory," I stated.

"So, if the energy which is now an entity can't go back to its world once it's here, it must find a host, which is our bodies," Jackson said in a questioning tone.

"That's what I'm thinking," I replied. "Because they still have that connection with a body. They need that body, that safety net of existing in our world, hence why I'm still seeing Emily and my brother. Two Emilys and two Alexs can't coexist."

"Which means their bodies can't be six feet underground if we're seeing them walking around today." Brooke finished.

"So all we have to do is not let it inhabit our bodies," Jackson said. "Somehow we need to stop it from within the parallel universe."

"Yeah, but if energy and mass can't be destroyed, where do *we* go once they get to us?"

"I guess that's the age-old question of what happens after death," Jackson replied.

"I mean, all of this is still such a stretch. We have little to no proof and we're just pulling things out of our asses here," Brooke remarked. "We do know that an evil entity is out there—we can't deny that anymore—but we don't know where it lives and we don't know how to stop it. I'm afraid we can't go *there* unless *they* want us to."

I watched as Brooke twirled her blonde hair around her fingers, something I noticed she did whenever she was anxious. During finals week, that was all she would do while she studied.

"You have a good point, babe," Jackson said.

"I'll go to the campus's library tomorrow and see if there's anything I can find that can help us," Brooke said. "As much as I don't want to believe it, I do think the only way to stop all of this is from the source."

I looked at the both of them. "And once we find it and go in *there* . . . we're going to have to get really brave."

Brooke

My head had been swimming with all the new thoughts and fears all weekend, along with the stress of midterms coming up. I had a test tomorrow and that was the last thing on my mind. A test was never the last thing on my mind. Dallas was gone and I found out our parallel selves were after us and all I wanted to do was get my life back to normal. This all seemed like a dream; a terrible, terrible dream.

While trying to study to get my mind off things, Jackson reached over and closed my textbook, pulling me closer to his shirtless chest. My eyes swept over the parts of his body that showed he'd put thousands of hours in at the gym, and I practically drooled.

"Babe, I really need to study," I pled as I tried to get out of his tight grasp.

"It's getting late, give yourself a break," he told me as he kissed my forehead. I knew he wanted attention. A certain kind of attention.

"I feel like my normal life has completely flipped. If I'm being honest, Jackson, my mind is still trying to make sense of it all. But it doesn't make any sense, and the scary thing is, we can't get answers from a book."

"Let's not think about it," he told me as he started to kiss his way down my body.

"Jackson, this isn't going to go away. It's—"

"Hey." He stopped me. He put his lips on mine and started kissing down my body again, pausing between kisses to say, "You still have your wonderful boyfriend, who is going to make you feel wonderful in about ten seconds."

His whiskers tickled my stomach, sending chills all over and a smile across my face. I squirmed on top of the sheets as he hit all my ticklish spots. A laugh escaped my mouth and I started to relax for the first time in awhile. Before he got too low, I stopped him,

"Wait, babe, I need to go the bathroom quick." I squirmed out of his grasp as he groaned playfully. Washing my hands, I took a moment to look at myself. I couldn't help but feel dread and guilt wash over me like waves crashing on a shore. The past can be such an ugly thing. I took off my shirt and threw it on the floor, then grabbed my hairbrush and began the painful journey of untangling my messy hair. I took my free hand and fluffed up the neat blonde locks.

I quickly finished and set the brush down, but noticed my reflection was still brushing her hair. Her face was blank, and she continued to brush for a few moments, set the brush down, and slowly turned her head to stare at me with a smirk. Vertigo hit me harder than ever before as her eyes met mine for the very first time. I felt like I'd known this thing for as long as I could remember, but I also didn't recognize it at all.

My heart raced and fear filled me as my reflection went back to normal. I made a few new movements to see if it followed. My reflection continued to match, so I slowly and cautiously grabbed my toothbrush and started brushing my teeth. The more I brushed, the more I felt the presence once more behind the mirror, staring at me with sinister eyes. I could feel that it never left. That it was waiting for me, watching for me. Those eyes didn't look like mine. I quickly bent over the sink, spitting out the minty toothpaste, and looked back up into the mirror to see Dallas right behind me, his eyes glowing an ominous white.

I screamed and turned around, but he was nowhere to be seen, and he was no longer in the mirror when I looked again. *What was I really looking at? What is going on with me? Am I next?* I wondered.

"Babe! Are you okay?" Jackson called. I stared intently into the mirror waiting for anything else to happen. When nothing did, I turned off the lights and made my way out. As I was almost out of the doorway I heard a knock from behind the mirror, and it sent chills down my spine. I knew something was behind it, something that wanted to be on my side of the mirror.

***

I tossed and turned all night while sick dreams toyed with my mind. It felt like every hour I woke up gasping, heart racing. Almost every dream I had was about Dallas. In one of the dreams it was dark all around us and he was chasing me, yelling my name. In the dream I knew it wasn't him, but I was still scared. He told me he had to tell me something, but I knew all he wanted was to catch me. I was terrified to look back at him because his voice didn't match his face. It was a much darker voice. In another dream we were at the town park, swinging. It seemed normal except for the fact it was late at night and I was the only one swinging. Dallas sat stationary on his swing, looking out into the woods before us. I said, "Dallas, come on! Let's see how high you can get!"

"Aren't you scared?" he responded.

"Scared of what?"

He abruptly stood up and continued to face the woods. I couldn't see his face, but I could sense he was expressionless.

"Scared of who you are."

He then began whistling a tune that I had never heard before, but sounded like something from the 1940s. There was an eerie vibe to it that started to give me goosebumps. "Dallas, where did you hear that song?" I asked, slowing down on the swing.

"I was getting ready for bed one night and all of a sudden I heard the noise. At first it was familiar but the noise eventually turned into an unfamiliar tune. I didn't know where it was coming from, so I checked all over the house. I even placed my ears to the walls to see if it was coming from inside them, but it wasn't. I walked around my street and went through my yard and when that wasn't enough I walked over to my neighbors and peeked through their windows. Eventually, I realized it was coming from inside my head."

Dallas then began walking over to the trees. Without turning to face me, he said, "Come on. I want you to learn how to whistle the song, too."

"Aren't you scared?"

He took a few steps into the timber before replying. I hopped off the swing and slowly made my way over to Dallas.

"Not anymore."

It had to be past midnight when I woke up for what felt like the tenth time. I rolled onto my side and looked at Jackson, who was fast asleep and still trying to reach me with his hand. I turned back on my other side and grabbed my glass of water on the nightstand. The lukewarm water soothed my dry, cracked throat as I swallowed a couple of times. I set the glass down and lay back down on the bed. A few moments after I closed my eyes, I thought I heard a voice.

I opened them wide, but stayed lying down. Jackson talked in his sleep from time to time so I waited to make sure it was him. I was almost back asleep when I heard Jackson saying my name.

"Brooke!" It was almost a soft shout.

My heart raced as I sat up and looked at Jackson. He seemed to still be asleep.

All those bad dreams must have really gotten to me. *Come on, Brooke, get it together.* I took a deep breath and pulled the covers back over me as I lay down. Another minute went by and I found myself sitting straight up once more.

"Brooke, listen to me." It was Jackson's voice again, only it wasn't coming from him. It sounded like an urgent command.

I had never been petrified than I was that night. My breathing was coming in shallow gasps and my heart continued to race.

"Brooke . . . everything is going to be fine with your test . . ." Jackson mumbled as he rolled over to face the other side of the bed. This time the voice did come from him.

"Brooke, that's not Jackson. Come on, we need to get you out of there!" It was Jackson's voice again, only it was coming from outside the bedroom. Our door was opened a crack, and it sounded as if the other person was right behind it.

The hairs on my arms and the back of my neck stood

straight up and my blood instantly ran cold. I had no idea what to do. If this was a dream, I wanted nothing more than to wake up.

"Brooke, walk over to the door so I can make sure you're okay," the voice ordered.

I was paralyzed by utter shock and fear. I couldn't fathom what was happening. I looked over at Jackson, and he was sound asleep. My mind was screaming at me to wake him up, but my body wouldn't follow.

"Brooke, listen to me," Jackson's voice said again. "Something isn't right. We have to get out of here. Are you coming with me?

My tightened lungs had to remind me to breathe and my eyes grew dry as I forgot to blink. I knew this wasn't a dream.

"Okay, Brooke, that's it. I'm coming in there to get you."

My heart skipped a beat.

"Ready?"

Tears filled up my eyes and my hands began to shake. My stomach was uneasy and the lump in my throat started to burn. I watched in horror as the door to our bedroom slowly swung open straight ahead of me.

"Jackson, wake up!" I loudly whispered, shaking him

awake. He mumbled as he stirred.

"*Jackson!*" He finally jolted up and looked at me dazed and confused.

"Brooke, what is your deal tonight?" he asked, looking at me like I was crazy. He sat up and reached over to turn on the lamp. When he got a good look at me, he could see how terrified I was. "Was it another bad dream?"

I didn't take my eyes off the door. It was still opened a few inches, and I knew that whoever was talking to me from behind that door was not Jackson.

"Brooke, I don't mean to be an asshole, but is there anything we can talk about right now that will help you sleep better?" Jackson scooted closer to me and looked me in the eyes with his still half shut. "Because I think we both need some sleep."

My heart was still racing and my head was beginning to throb, but I still turned and looked at him. "I'm sorry, Jackson. It's just been bad dream after bad dream. Nothing is wrong. I love you."

"I love you, too," he mumbled as he kissed me on the forehead and lay back down, half asleep.

I lied to him and I lied to myself. I wasn't fine. I wanted to sleep more than anything, but knowing that something was here with me, something dark, I wouldn't be able to. I didn't dare get out of bed to close the door. I'd rather lie in this bed and have my paranoid thoughts and the eerie whispers run me to sleep.

Chapter 12

Carter

Tomorrow was Dallas's funeral. For thoughtful reasons they decided to have it separate from his parents'. The whole thing was tragic and left me with a dark, empty feeling. Every minute I felt a different emotion—anger for not knowing any answers to the important questions and for losing friends to this god-awful fate; sorrow for losing not only friends recently but family, too, and knowing I was left alone with nowhere to go; and dread, not knowing what was going to happen to any of us, or when. I felt trapped, and not even hiding in the shadows was safe.

When the tub had filled, I turned the water off and stepped into the almost-sweltering bath. I lowered myself, straightened my legs, and slowly lay down, letting the hot water surround me. Steam filled the room and rose from the water, enveloping me like a blanket.

I held my breath and submerged, letting the water cover me. With my eyes closed, I tried to relax and drown out all my thoughts and fears. My chest began to hurt with the loss of oxygen, but I went past the pain. My mind could finally breathe.

I opened my eyes and my whole perspective changed. I looked up at what should have been the ceiling, but instead I saw myself in the bathtub under the water. My reflection opened its eyes, looked up at me and smiled. I felt myself slipping, falling forward out of the bathtub, which now seemed to be on the ceiling. I lost my grip and fell straight toward the tub below me. I felt the water follow behind me as I landed in the tub. The water splashed all over the room, like a big wave crashing into the shore. I quickly pulled myself out of the water, gagging and spitting up water.

I jumped out of the tub like a wet cat would and grabbed a towel to dry off. It took me no time to put my clothes on. Water covered the whole floor, and barely any was left in the tub. I didn't know what had just happened. I grabbed more towels and started drying the floor. I left them there and didn't bother to look at the mirror as I opened the door and walked out of the bathroom.

The house remained dark, though moonlight illuminated some of the rooms. Something felt weird and dark. I walked down the hall and into the living room. I turned on a lamp, but something was still off.

I peered down the hallway and noticed it. My head started to spin and the hairs stood up on the back on my neck. The light from the lamp wasn't reflecting off the mirror. In fact, the mirror wasn't a mirror. My reflection wasn't looking back at me, but instead I was looking into my house. I was in Parallel.

"Welcome home, Carter." I turned around and saw my father and mother smirking, their eyes white. They both let out deep, dry cackles and titled their heads. They turned off the lamp and I looked at what used to be the mirror as the lamp turned on in the other universe. I turned back around and my parents were gone. None of this made any sense. They pulled me in here, but I didn't understand why. I looked around and saw the white curtains dancing from the wind. My eye caught a glimpse of what appeared to look like myself standing behind the curtain.

The main door to the house opened, as if it were a sign to go outside. I watched as the parallel me walked behind curtain to curtain, staring at me until it disappeared through the door. I carefully followed and walked toward the door and looked outside.

A few inches away stood my brother. His back was toward me, and it sounded like he was crying.

"I didn't mean to," he mumbled through sobs. It was dark, but it wasn't nighttime; it was like the sun was blocked by hundreds of clouds, and dreary shades of gray and dark blue filled the sky.

"It's all my fault, but I can make this right. Yes, that's what I'll do. It'll all be okay again." He continued to sob, his head in his hands.

"Alex . . ." I said. As if my voice held the control of all noise and sound here, everything else seemed to be silenced. It was like one big dream. Alex immediately stopped crying and slowly lifted his head up. My heart raced and all I could hear was my quiet, heavy breathing. Time seemed to go by slowly, if there even was time here.

He slowly started turning his head until he faced me, and I could hear bones start to crack and pop out of place the farther he turned his neck. I grabbed the door, getting ready to close it if he charged at me.

"Don't close the door," he said firmly. His voice was very deep and dry. He turned all the way around, completely facing me. His eyes were white, but I could see a little color left in his irises. What looked like black blood leaked from his eyes and dripped down his body. A few blood vessels remained in his eyes, covering them like spider webs.

"Set me free, Carter. I need to be punished." I heard the pitter-patter of the black blood hit the porch as it fell off his face. I looked past him and saw human figures walk around the streets, seemingly with no direction. Some had no faces, and others were expressionless. They looked like humans, but I knew they weren't. One looked like my old neighbor Rodger, but my attention was taken elsewhere as another stopped walking and turned and looked at me, noticing me. A smirk developed as he started to make his way to the house. Everyone else near us stopped walking and looked at me. I quickly slammed the door as my brother yelled, "No!"

I locked the door and took a few steps back. *What is this place?* I was quiet for a few moments, listening to see if I could hear anything. I cautiously placed my ear on the door. All I could hear was mumbling and murmuring from my brother, words that didn't make sense.

Goosebumps ran down my body as I heard my mom's voice scolding from behind me, "You never listen." Her voice wasn't hers; it was taken by something else. I turned around and saw her walking down the stairs. I was in the house I grew up in. Why was I back here? She was wearing the long, white silk dress that she was buried in, but it was all ripped and tattered. The dress was stained with blood below the center of her waistline. My mind immediately went to the time my mom had a miscarriage. It was before I was born but after Alex. It was only brought up once and it was something we never brought up again. All I remember was that it was supposed to be a boy. *Why would Parallel show me this?*

"Your brother was trying to tell you something." That was my father's voice. I turned the other way and he was sitting in the chair he always used to sit in. He stood up.

"Tell me what?" I sputtered.

"I wish you were in the car with us the night of the accident," my mom said in a soothing tone, while cackling.

"Honey, that would ruin all the fun we're having today," my father chimed in. The two walked closer to me until they were side by side. Once they stopped moving, everything grew silent. All I could hear was the sound of my heartbeat. They locked eyes on me and I felt trapped. I had to get out of this hell. Those weren't my parents.

All of a sudden, I heard Alex mumble, as if he was right behind me, "Don't close the door" in a demonic voice. I looked behind me, and to my amazement, I didn't see him. The door was still closed. I waited for a couple moments to make sure nothing else happened. Time slowed down and the door swung open, making all the windows shatter and sending the door and I flying backward. It felt like I had stepped on a landmine. Glass flew through the air and everything was a blur as I was sent through the mirror and back into my own bathroom.

My arms were cut open and glass littered the floor around me, but the mirror was fine. Parallel had answers. That had to be why everyone kept going back there. Nowhere in my right mind wanted to go back, but for some reason, I didn't care. I was a little frightened, because *I wanted to.*

Brooke

I parked my car and quickly made my way to the library before it closed at ten. Jackson was passed out and I couldn't sleep with the thought of Dallas on my mind.

The whole idea of having another world that we didn't even know about where our past and demons lived was too unnerving. I didn't blame Carter for not telling us sooner. We had no idea what we were messing with. The realistic part of my brain told me that none of this was possible. It was hard for me to believe, let alone go along with the old mythology. That's why they called it *mythology*: it wasn't supposed to be real. But facts don't lie. Everything I saw and heard only further proved this was as real as it got.

I went up the stairs and walked inside the dimly lit library. The smell always reminded me of a Barnes & Noble, where the smell of coffee and fresh new books was always in the air. Memories came to mind of when I would help Dallas study for big tests and homework that he didn't fully understand. He was on the swim team by scholarship, which stressed him out. He would show up with coffee for the both of us, and we'd spend the next few hours studying together.

Those times were when he and I really bonded. We used that time to vent about Jackson, and when Dallas would vent to me about his parents. He told me he was really happy to be in college because even if his parents moved, he wouldn't have to follow. Dallas was so funny. A lot of the times we wouldn't get anything done because he would just make me laugh. He was easy to teach because he wanted to learn. We almost always got kicked out for laughing too loud. Mrs. Crawford, the librarian, would let me have pocket full of warnings because she loved how studious I was.

I relished in the memories while climbing the stairs. As I made my way up to the second floor, more memories filled my mind. The oldest table in the building was where everyone always wanted to sit, as it was believed whoever sat there before a test would do well. I shook my head as I remembered Jackson trying to get there before anyone else, and being a complete dick to anyone who was there before him.

The library contained just a few students sporadically spread throughout, which was nice and quiet but also made it a little eerie. I looked around at all the bookshelves, feeling a little overwhelmed and not really knowing where to start.

"Brooke, it's always nice to get to see you." A soft voice made me to turn around and I came face to face with Mrs. Crawford. We'd always been close, and sometimes she would let me stay past closing time.

I gave a warm smile back and said, "Yeah, I've been so busy with other things I haven't had time to come study here."

"Oh, I bet! So, what brings you to come study tonight?"

"Umm . . . well . . ." Still not entirely sure what to look for, I wasn't ready for her question. "I guess I was wondering what area I would be able to find books about demonic entities and possessions."

"Oh!" She seemed a little taken aback by my response, but not judgmental. She smiled and commanded me to follow her by crooking her index finger. Long and thin wrinkles sprawled out on the sides of her eyes. I noticed her long, gray hair had more gray in it than the last time I'd seen her. Her thin, bony arms stayed stiffly by her sides as she walked down rows and rows of books. She stopped, glanced up a section on a shelf and pulled a book out.

"Here you are. This is a really good book about entities, possessions, and a few other supernatural topics. I'm sure this is for a very interesting class. Unfortunately our selections on these books are scarce."

I nodded as I took the book from her and stared at it. "Yeah, it's a very challenging class."

"Well, you're smart, so I'm sure you'll figure out whatever answers you need to know. I'll let you be, dear. Let me know if you need anything else and I'll leave the key in my office if you have to stay late."

"Thank you so much, Mrs. Crawford."

"It's Dallas now."

My heart skipped a beat. "I'm sorry, what?"

"I said, Jackson not around?"

"Oh, no. He had other plans tonight." I lied.

"All right, dear. You enjoy your time. If you come across anything interesting I'd love to hear it." She smiled again and started walking away. Before she got to the stairs she turned and looked at me. "Please . . . don't let your demons become your present," she said. After she spoke, she went down the stairs and out of my sight. I brushed it off and turned my attention back to the bookshelf.

My phone went off and just about gave me a heart attack. I forgot I had left the ringer on loud. Embarrassed, I took my phone out of my purse and saw that my older sister was calling me. I sheepishly looked around and got irritated looks from nearby students. I set my things down at a table and answered the phone.

"Vanessa, how are you?" I quietly asked.

"Brooke! Hi! I'm doing well. I've been putting in about sixty hours a week at the hospital. I'm still waiting for you to get a job here." I heard the eagerness in her voice.

"I know, I just still don't know if I want to stay around here forever."

"Around here? What do you mean? The hospital is two hours away, and you'd be closer to me!"

Vanessa is three years older than me. We grew up on a farm together, until our parents lost it to the bank and we had to move in with our grandparents. We were only there for about five months, with Mom supporting all of us until Dad got a job at a factory. He hated that job, but it definitely made us financially stable again. When they could, our parents bought a house right outside of the city. They couldn't farm there, but they didn't care. All they wanted was to live in the country with few neighbors.

Vanessa went to college right in the heart of downtown and got her own apartment. I, however, got accepted to the university two hours away and I'd been here ever since.

"I know I would. I'm still figuring everything out. I have a lot of schooling left!" I responded.

"I just know you're going to be the best cardiovascular surgeon ever." I could hear the smile in her voice. "But I was calling for a couple of things. How are you doing with everything? I'm so sorry to hear about your loss. His name was Dallas, right?"

"Yeah, it was."

"Brooke, I'm so sorry that you had to go through all of that. I knew Mom and Dad were worried about your safety. I'm glad that you weren't hurt."

"It's okay, V. Thank you, though."

"And I know we haven't seen each other for a couple of months, but I can take some vacation days and come down there and stay with you. I miss you, Brooke."

"I miss you, too. I would really like that, but I just don't know when would be a good time yet."

"I totally understand," Vanessa said. "How's Jackson taking everything?"

"He doesn't show it, but I know he's hurting and that he thinks about it every day. Dallas and he got really close freshman year of college. It's just crazy to think that just the other day, we were watching him swim for one of his meets."

"It's just awful," she replied. "Are *you* doing okay?"

I hesitated. She and I told each other everything. What I wanted to tell her was, "*No, not really. I'm just at the library looking up rifts and entity possessions because I strongly believe there's a parallel universe where our demons lie. Oh, and that's also why Dallas died. He became his demons and it killed him. But it's okay, V, because my homework and studying helps distract me from losing my mind, even though I hear weird things and see things that shouldn't be there.*"

"Are you there, Brooke?"

"Yeah . . .Yeah, sorry, I'm doing okay. Some days are better than others, but it's not an easy thing to lose a friend at a young age.

My heart was crippled by pain and the ugly truth that I couldn't share with the closest person to me. She would never understand, and that wasn't a can of worms I'd like to open up with her.

"I know." Silence followed, and all I heard was static for a few moments. "I don't mean to make matters worse, but Mom isn't doing too well. Her liver is starting to fail."

Her voice cracked. "And . . . they're grouping it T4, wh . . .which means . . ."

"Which means it's growing into a nearby organ," I finished for her.

I felt like I'd been struck by a truck. I was almost tempted to grab my things and drive the two hours just to see my mom. My chest grew tight and a lump formed in my throat. My mouth was dry and I felt light headed.

"We have to stay positive, Brooke," Vanessa started. She sniffled. "It's really bad, but the doctors and Mom are still fighting. She has a chance, Brooke."

"Did the cancer start to spread to the pancreas?"

"Yes. It's just one small pea-sized tumor, though. They're doing more chemo, then waiting to see if that helps. Once she's done with her cycle they'll do surgery if they need to."

"They can get to the one on the pancreas?" I asked.

"Yeah." She took a deep breath. "Like I said, Brooke, everything will be okay. Mom's a fighter and we're not giving up hope."

"How's Dad?"

"Oh, Brooke, he's a mess," Vanessa admitted. "He doesn't sleep, and the factory won't let him pick up any overtime hours because of payroll. He refuses to ask me for

help with the bills, but he told me he has it under control."
A few more sobs followed.

"V, it's okay. Like you said, this is all going to be okay. I can make next weekend work and I'll drive down there and come see you guys." I fought back a wave of tears and bit my lip to help keep my mouth from trembling.

"You're right. It's just hard news to process. She's been fighting for so long now. My heart hurts for her. Anyway, Brooke, I'll let you get back to studying or however you're spending your evening. I'll keep you posted on Mom. So, see you next weekend?"

"See you next weekend. And, V, if there is anything you need or if you just want to talk, call me whenever you want."

"Of course, and same goes for you. I love you, Brooke."

"I love you, too. Tell Zach I say hi and that I'm going to kick his butt at Scrabble again."

I got a small laugh out of her and she told me she'd tell her boyfriend. We finished saying goodbye and I hung up. I set my phone down and let the words settle. The news felt like a raw wound. My lower lip trembled as my composure crumbled. Tears stung my eyes and made their way down my cheeks. I was tired of crying. I placed both of my hands over my mouth and tried calming myself down.

A few seconds went by and I lost the fight to my stability. I placed both my hands on the table and hunched over. My hair shielded my eyes as the river of tears came rushing out. My body trembled with each sob and all my fear and stress came out. It felt great to cry, almost like I was shedding old skin. I gave myself a few more minutes before I stopped. I didn't want to think anymore negative thoughts. I had to compose myself and keep moving forward. Crying wouldn't solve any of my problems.

I reached into my purse and pulled out a Kleenex. I blew my nose into the white tissue, wiped my tears with the back of my hands, then rubbed my eyes for a few moments. *Okay, you can do this, Brooke.*

I walked over to the aisle Mrs. Crawford had directed me toward and pulled out a few other books that looked like they could help me. I made my way over to the table and sat down, then opened the first book she gave me and began skimming through it. "The root of the word comes from Latin; an entity is a thing with an independent existence," I read. "An entity develops power from a living object and can become a solid state by attaching itself onto something that is more or less alive. If the living body dies with the entity attached, it shall all become one. An entity needs a living thing on which to stay attached, and if the original host is destroyed, the entity will not survive. It has been said that this world is home to yet another world. Where there is life, there is death, and there can't be life without death."

I continued to mumble along with the words I read as I turned more and more pages. A part of me almost didn't want to believe this, but it was all starting to add up and all come together. If it was true that our sins and demons were split from us figuratively, then that old part of us had to have gone somewhere, and if it was true that there couldn't be more than one physical state to exist in a world at any given time, then only one could cease to exist.

They were trying to cause a rift into our world. They needed a void, which was us, and once they became us, we would die but our body remained. *So how do we get rid of something that is attached to what used to be us? You would have to destroy the body,* I thought.

A noise came from down an aisle nearby. I lifted my head but all I was able to see were long red locks disappearing behind the shelves. Dismissing it, I went back to reading. Moments of silence went by until the sound of someone vomiting disrupted my focus. I quickly stood up and walked away from my table. The noises continued as I walked toward the aisle. Nearby students looked at me but then looked away.

I walked up to the aisle and saw a woman my age hunched over, puking. Expecting to see a pile of vomit before her; I was shocked to find a puddle of black bile. The woman turned her head to make eye contact with me as long strands of black ooze, like snot, hung from her mouth. I was shocked to see that it was Sarah Windsfield. Dark veins wrapped around her like a cobweb. Her irises were almost void of green as she looked at me in complete horror.

"Let me get you help, Sarah."

"You can't help me. It's too late." Black liquid slid down the sides of her eyes and stained her cheeks. She began to crawl my way while more bile gushed out of her mouth.

"Brooke, is everything all right?" One of the students asked me from a nearby table. I turned and looked at her and noticed my mouth was wide open. I turned my attention back to Sarah and saw she was gone along with the pile of black ooze.

I closed my mouth and nodded in response. I did a final glance before returning to my table and took a deep breath. My heart raced as I comprehended what I saw. It made me wonder back to Dallas's party and when I saw her. She was going through what we all are now. She needed help but for her it was too late.

Shaking it off, I grabbed another book from my pile and started flipping through pages, many of which contained passages of old Greek mythology. It showed gruesome depictions of what looked like the splitting of the bodies in half, removing their double arms and legs to free themselves of their sins and demons. *People really believed in this?*

"I brought you your coffee. Double shot of espresso, all black."

I quickly looked up and saw Dallas standing next to me holding a Styrofoam cup. His eyes were as white as the moon and his skin was as pale as snow. I noticed his grip on the cup was really tight, and dark veins were prominent on his hands. I watched as his fingers poked holes through the cup, sending scorching hot coffee down onto my leg. I screamed in pain as the coffee singed my leg through my pants. I quickly wiped off the remaining coffee and looked back up to see that Dallas had disappeared.

I lifted my pant leg and saw that there was a burn mark, but not from liquid. It looked like a handprint, but the thing that made me want to throw up was the fact that the handprint was coming from the opposite way than I expected, like something was trying to make its way out of me.

Jade

It was a quarter past nine and my shift at the suicide hotline was over in an hour. The night was slow for me, as I had few calls. I kept telling myself to quit yawning. I stared at the small mirror in my cubicle and glared at the bags underneath my eyes. I looked as tired as I felt. We weren't allowed to rest our heads on our arms or hands while we were here. I normally didn't have a problem following those guidelines, but tonight tested me.

I pushed down on the hand sanitizer pump and lathered the clear goop around my hands until it was all absorbed into my skin. The sanitizer burned a few cuts on my fingers from the hangnails I had ripped off. As I took another sip from my coffee, I grabbed a Kleenex and wiped up the excess goop that fell on my table.

My heart jumped and my mind felt wide awake as my hotline phone went off. I cleared my throat, inhaled, exhaled, and picked up the phone. Before I could get the first word out, a deep, gruff voice stopped me.

"Is this the suicide hotline?" The voice sounded scared

and panicked.

"Yes, it is. How may I—"

"I don't think you can help me." The voice sounded like an older man, maybe in his mid-forties.

"What are you feeling right now?"

"I feel scared and alone." I began documenting while the man talked to me.

"What has caused you to feel like this?"

"Why don't you tell me?"

I was taken aback by his response, but I changed topics. "Are you having thoughts about suicide?"

"I wouldn't say suicide."

"Do you feel depressed?"

"I feel cold."

"Where are you at right now? Are you safe?"

"I don't know where I'm at. It's dark."

"Do—"

He was quick to cut me off. "Can we go back to when you asked me about suicide?"

"Of course."

"I don't feel like hurting myself. I feel the need to hurt someone else."

My chest tightened and my palms grew sweaty. You would think the more phone calls I took would help with each new call, but each case was different. I didn't know how to fully respond to this type of call. I wondered if my supervisor had tuned into this one. A part of me was hoping she did.

"Why do you feel like that?" The line grew silent and static buzzed my ears. "Are you there?"

"Aren't you going to ask me who I feel like hurting?"

My mouth went dry and the tension in the air rose like heat in a furnace. I licked my lips nervously and pulled my fallen bangs back over my ear. My eyes darted around the building to make sure I wasn't alone, even though I knew I wasn't.

"Who do you feel like hurting?"

I pushed my ears harder against the phone once as he started murmuring. It was difficult to make out what he was saying, and the static had gotten worse. In a quiet, eerie tone right above a whisper, I heard him say, "Something is here with me."

"I'm sorry, sir, but I'm having a hard time understanding what you're saying."

Seconds went by with no response, and I was beginning to get worried.

"Remember when you asked me where I was? I'm sitting on cement. It's hard and cold. Four walls are around me. You put me here, Jade. You put me away to rot."

My blood ran cold as goosebumps covered my skin. At first I thought it was a sick joke, but I could hear my father's tone within the voice. I had the right to hang up but I waited it out.

"You there, Jade?" He let out a short, sadistic laugh. "I feel like hurting *you*. I can't wait to get out from behind these four cold walls and cut open your chest to your cold, empty heart." I immediately tried flagging down my supervisor but she was on another call. My hands trembled while I continued documenting this call.

Tears from fear filled my eyes while my hand struggled to keep the phone held up to my ear. *This isn't real. This can't be happening. How did he find me?*

"You can't hide from me. Daddy knows best." His voice started to get lower.

"This isn't funny. Who is this?" I gritted my teeth and felt my chin tremble.

"I'm coming home." He began to laugh uncontrollably now. His voice sounded no longer like his; it sounded demonic.

I quickly hung up and slid my chair away from my desk. I stood up and looked around in despair. My heart felt like it was beating out of my chest and my throat began to tighten. I felt like I was about to have a panic attack. I needed to call Carter right away. I needed to leave.

I grabbed my belongings once I finished up the documentation and headed to my boss's office. She believed my made-up emergency and I headed back to my place. My hands wouldn't stop shaking while I held the steering wheel. I contemplated calling Carter numerous times, but eventually decided against it. I didn't want to get him or the others involved. It was best to keep this my secret.

That wasn't my father. That was something else, something that knew who I was and how to make me afraid. I didn't feel safe going home, but I had to keep telling myself that my father was still locked up. I pulled out my phone and called Carter. It went straight to voicemail but I didn't leave one.

I got to my apartment and locked every door and window before laying down in my bed. I let out a deep breath and tried to calm myself down. *Everything is going to be okay. I'm not going crazy.* I wanted all of this to go away.

I rolled over and looked at the window, and for a second it looked like I wasn't really looking outside, but at something else. Ignoring it, I got up and walked toward my closet to change into shorts and a tank top. I checked myself out in the mirror, and noticed I had a few bruises underneath my right eye. I quickly pressed my fingertips on them, but they didn't hurt, so I went to go look at myself in the bathroom mirror instead. The bruises were gone from that eye, but I had a gash underneath my left one. I put my fingers to the blood, but it wasn't there. *What is going on?* I quickly walked out of the bathroom and went to find my phone so I could call the others.

As I got into my room and grabbed my phone, I heard a noise similar to nails on a chalkboard coming from my window. I looked over and saw a message written on the glass. My mouth dropped open as I walked closer to it, reading the message.

"Where's Mommy?" The words looked like they were written with the sharp end of a nail. My heart skipped a beat as those two words brought back many memories from my childhood. Memories I didn't want to remember.

I slowly walked up to the window and traced the words with my fingers. The words felt warm, while the rest of window was ice cold. I walked away, but I noticed something in the mirror behind my door. Looking at myself in the mirror, I saw a blood stain start to form on my stomach, making its way up my shirt. I frantically lifted up my tank top and saw that there was no open wound, only a scar of where one used to be.

I opened my door all the way so I didn't have to see the mirror and started to dial Carter's number again while grabbing my car keys. As I was dialing, my door slammed shut, scaring me enough to drop the phone and car keys. I heard the playful sound of a girl's giggle and the sound of a disturbed man's chuckle.

I walked over to the door once more and firmly gripped the knob, getting ready to open it. I took a deep breath, and with my heart in my hand, pulled the door open. I was no longer staring down my hallway; I was staring at the front of the house I grew up in. I looked behind me, but all I saw was a road and more houses.

Fog drifted down the empty street and masked the eerie house that held the memories of a disturbed past. *I don't want to do this.* I had no choice but to go inside the house. It was like I opened my door to the past and time traveled, but something told me I was where fear thrives.

Why am I back here? I shouldn't be back here. I want out of here, I thought. Nevertheless, I continued to walk up the steps and onto the front porch. I hadn't been back to this house for at least ten years. I went to my aunt's place after the whole thing went down with my dad and I. I opened the door and walked into the dark house. The house smelled like it had been locked up for decades. The floor creaked as I walked across the floorboards, and the smell of must filled my nose. The brown couch was exactly where we left it, the leather chair on its right. Nothing looked like it'd been touched.

I finished walking through the living room and into the kitchen. Fog rolled even into the house, hiding my feet and half my legs. The moon shined through the windows, but there was still hardly enough light to see. I rifled through a cupboard and found some matches, grabbed the candle from the dining table and lit the wick.

My father's empty and half-drank bottles of alcohol collected dust on the counters and near his liquor cabinet. Cigarette butts were left all around the floor and tables, like confetti.

Dirty dishes were still in the sink and were a home to mold and dust. The once-colorful plates my mom used were nothing more than old, rotten circles. It was like the house was still aging as how it would be today. Everything felt familiar but foreign at the same time. This was my home, but it wasn't.

Memories started to flashback at me, all the good and bad. I remembered where I stood for the first day of school, and where I stood when my mom left my dad and me.

Our pictures still hung up on the fridge, the ones where we were a happy family. One was from when I was about four years old. It was the day I rode a bike with training wheels for the first time. The slamming of a door jolted me, and I felt all the blood leave my face.

"Well, well, well, look who decided to finally come home." It was my father's voice. At first I thought he was talking to me, but then I heard my voice.

"I'll be right there, Daddy."

"Where were you?"

I slowly crept to the doorway, still holding the candle, and peeked around the corner and into the living room. My father was on the stairs looking down at the other me, who was taking off her shoes. He had an almost empty bottle of vodka in his hand and an empty bottle of whiskey next to the stairs. Why did this feel familiar?

My dad's eyes and those of my double were white and glowing. They were showing me something in Parallel, I realized. "Your mother isn't coming back. She didn't leave just me, she left you, too." He took another swig of his vodka and then let it fall down the stairs.

"Where were you?" he asked again, taking another step down the stairs. His voice was deeper, foreign. I noticed that my parallel self had bruises underneath her eyes. I remembered he hit me a few nights before this incident. This was the night I left him, when I called the cops and sent him away. When it happened I was younger than this, but for some reason I looked the same age I was now. I quickly hid as I saw my other self come into the kitchen. I was still able to peek around the corner and watched as my dad stumbled down the steps and went to the door and locked it. I looked back and I was searching for my phone to call my friend Ashley, who had just dropped me off.

"You're just like your mother, such a fucking slut." I looked back and saw my dad standing in the doorway. "You can't hide, Jade; you can't keep running away from Daddy." My heart was beating fast, and I covered the flame as best as I could so he wouldn't notice it. He walked by me and into the kitchen.

I watched as he pulled steak knife from a drawer and followed me into the other room. I quietly stood up and crept around so I could see where he was going. I saw that I ran to the front door, but it was locked.

"You gonna leave me, too?" A path of blood trickled down his arms from the needles he had poked into them. The fog helped hide me as I continued to follow them. He let out a dry cackle and fiddled with the knife.

"Dad, stop!" the other me cried out as he got closer.

"Don't be afraid, Daddy's here . . ."

He got closer to me and threw me down. I watched as my stomach ran into the corner of an end table, hitting stitches from the wound he had given me a few nights earlier. I grimaced in pain as the other me fell to the floor, clutching her abdomen.

I started crawling away from him as he laughed and said, "Where's Mommy?" I quickly got up and started running for the stairs, clutching my re-ripped open stomach. My father smirked and started chasing me up them. I screamed in terror as I slammed my bedroom door shut, and he began banging on my door. Caught up in the moment, I realized I was at the top of the stairs with them.

He was banging on my door, yelling at me to let him in. Tears fell from my eyes as the pain and fear all came back from the past—how scared I was of him, how my mom left me, how they both got into drugs. Not being able to watch anymore, I took a step back, which caused the floorboards to creak. My father stopped banging and turned his head to the right and stared at me.

In a deep, sinister voice, he said, "YOU!" I quickly took a step back but I tumbled down the stairs, which put the flame out. All I was left with was his glowing eyes in the dark. I heard him come down the steps and in the faint moonlight, saw a smirk grow back on his face. I painfully got up and headed toward the door. It was still locked, and I couldn't see how to unlock it. I felt beads of sweat run down my forehead while I frantically tried to get the door open. All I could think was, *He can't hurt me. This isn't real. OPEN THE DOOR, JADE!*

My father chuckled as he made his way down the steps. "You can't hide from me forever." I shook the knob and fiddled with the latches and locks, but nothing was working and I started to panic. I banged on the door and screamed and cried as my deepest fear came back to haunt me.

I turned around and saw he was now at the bottom of the steps, only a few feet away from me. I looked around to see if there was anywhere I could go, when an idea quickly entered my mind and I went for it. I ran over and jumped through the window in the living room, sending shards of glass everywhere as I not only fell from the window in my old house, but broke through the window in my current bedroom. Pain shot through my arms and I saw they were lacerated and glass stuck out of them. I was back home.

I got up, opened my bedroom door and ran to the kitchen to wrap paper towels around my arms. Once I got the bleeding under control, I had to find a way to pick up the glass. It was embedded into the carpet but that was the least of my worries. My apartment was a little more dark than usual, and as I walked through the living room I saw my dad standing in the corner with his back toward me.

"Dad?" He didn't move or say anything, just stood there and looked at the corner. I was trembling and my blood was beginning to soak thorough the paper towels. All I could hear was my blood hitting against the floor, like water dripping from a broken sink. I slowly started to make my way toward him. *He can't be here,* I reassured myself. *I locked him away, and he will never find me.*

I kept walking, watching him and noticing how he didn't even move a muscle. He looked still as stone and cold as ice. There was no humanity left to him. My arms shook and adrenaline pumped through my veins. I felt as if I was going to have a heart attack. I got closer and closer until I was close enough to reach my hand out and touch him. I inched toward his shoulder. Even though I was near him, it still felt as if I were miles away. I didn't know why I hadn't turned away and ran outside yet, but something pulled me in. My hand was almost to his back when the sound of glass shattering screeched across the room.

I jumped back at least two feet and looked in the

direction of the noise. When I looked back, my father was gone and I was left alone in the room once more. I walked down the hall and peered into my bedroom, where glass from the mirror on the back of my door was scattered across the floor. I went in and saw that no one was in there, but my mirror was completely shattered.

A cool breeze from my broken window touched my open wounds and reminded me I needed to go get help. I grabbed my things and hopped in my car, not realizing that my tank top bore the exact same blood stain it did in Parallel.

Carter

I got a call from Jade saying she was heading to the hospital after going through her window. She told me she would let Brooke and Jackson know and that they didn't need to come, but she wanted me to be there. I got to the emergency room in a panic and walked quickly to the reception desk.

"You said Jade Hamilton?" The eighteen-year-old-looking receptionist asked me. I nodded in confirmation as he looked for her information. This experience matched up with Emily's, filling me with dread. I hated being here. Hospitals had always reminded me of death, and I hated the obnoxious scent of disinfect ant and rubber gloves. Deep down, I knew I didn't have much time to save my friends.

"Mr. Gray?" the receptionist asked to get my attention, pulling me away from my thoughts.

"Uh . . .yeah, sorry."

"Room 306."

I headed for the elevator and in no time I found Jade lying down on a hospital bed with gauze and bandages wrapped all around her arms. She had a few stitches on her forehead, too. The nurse was letting her rest as the painkillers took effect.

"Oh my God, Jade, are you okay?" I ran up to her and gave her a careful hug. She looked terrified and drained.

"Carter, I don't think I'm safe anymore."

"What do you mean?"

"Somehow they took me into Parallel and my father was there. He was after the parallel me and he spotted the real me and ran after me. But the thing is, it took me back to the night I called the cops and finally put him away. I was reliving that night."

"And then what? How did you get away?"

"My only way out was the window because he'd locked the door, so I jumped through it and ended up back here."

I hugged her again. "I'm glad you're okay, Jade."

"Carter, that's not all of it. I told you I don't feel safe anymore. My father followed me back and he was in my living room, then I heard a noise and the mirror in my bedroom shattered. The same mirror I went through to get to Parallel. My dad, he found me."

Her voice cracked and tears formed in her eyes. I squeezed her tighter and told her everything was going to be all right, even though I had no idea how. "No one is going to hurt you," I said. But I couldn't help but ask, "Why would your mirror shatter if you fell through the window?"

"Did yours once you came back?" she asked me.

"No . . ."

"I'm sorry, sir, but visiting hours are over unless you're family," a short red-headed nurse said, entering the room and interrupting us. "Jade should be released tomorrow. We just need to do some x-rays and a few more tests while she's with us overnight."

"Yeah, no, I totally understand," I said. I gave Jade another hug and told her everything was going to be all right. Jade gave me a reassuring smile and followed the nurse out of the room. I started to make my way out of the hospital when I heard that old 1940s tune again. I couldn't put my finger on where I had heard it before. Something didn't feel right. The atmosphere changed drastically as I continued toward the lobby. The last time I heard an old record tune was when I was with Emily in her bathroom . . . after her mirror shattered.

I turned around and ran back to the elevator. When the doors opened on the third floor I ran back to her room, but she was still gone doing tests. The anticipation was killing me as I waited there for her to come back. Finally, I peeked my head out of the doorway and saw she was down the hall, going into another room.

"Jade! Wait!" I called, but she was already gone. I quickly ran down the hall after her and reached the room she was in. I peered through the little glass window and looked around for her, but she was nowhere to be found.

A creepy whisper haunted through the air like a cold, fall breeze. The whisper said, "Where's Mommy?" A deep chuckle followed, and I looked back down the hall and saw Jade, blood covering her whole body, being pulled by who I guessed was her father. A blood trail that looked like smeared red paint stained the white tile floor.

I started to go down the hall after her when a nurse stopped me. "Sir, you can't be in here. I'm going to have to have to ask you to leave."

"But you don't understand, my girlfriend is—"

"Carter? What are you still doing here?" Jade asked from behind me, about to go into the room I thought she was already in.

"Sir, I'm going to have to call security if you don't leave now," the nurse kept telling me.

"I'm going to be okay. I'll see you tomorrow," Jade reassured me with a kiss and smile, but her smile was a mask. She walked into the room before I could say anything else. As the nurse pulled me away, Jade bent over to take off her shoes and I saw the parallel her behind her, staring at me with a smirk and white eyes. Before I could do anything, I was taken away.

Chapter 13

Carter

The following morning I met up with Jackson on campus. We had some time in between classes, so we sat down on a bench and caught up. The fall breeze was soft while the muggy heat stuck to us like sweat. Radiant colored leaves fell through the air and painted the sidewalks and grass. Jackson took his backpack and hung it over the side of the bench.

"Jackson, I think we're dealing with something much more sinister than we thought," I said.

"I know. Brooke heard knocking on her mirror and saw Dallas last night." He paused before continuing. He ran his fingers through his hair and exhaled. "While I was asleep, she heard my voice coming down the hall. It was trying to convince her that the voice was me and that the me she was sleeping next to, wasn't. And now Jade said something about falling through her window, I think." The soft breeze played with Jackson's athletic shorts and moved them up his thighs. He bit his nails while listening.

I nodded. "She's in the hospital until later this

morning; I took her there last night. I don't have much time. I need to get back to Jade but I wanted to catch you up on everything. I saw Jade's dad pulling her body across the floor. Jade told me she got a weird call from him last night, too," I told him.

He looked at me puzzled. "Why was her father there? Was it actually him?"

I shook my head. "Jade sent her father away when she was younger; for child abuse. He was a deranged alcoholic. She fears that he'll come back for her and kill her and her mom. I saw him pull her dead body away but it wasn't real. Something is very wrong with all of this."

"It gets worse," Jackson started. "I noticed bloody handprints on Brooke's side of the bed, like something was crawling toward her. Whatever this thing is, it's getting closer to all of us. Carter, we have to figure this out."

"I know. Last night, I realized something that could maybe help us," I began. "Before Emily died, the night she went to the hospital, her mirror was shattered, just like Jade's."

"But Jade fell through her window," Jackson said.

"Right, but later, her mirror shattered apparently on its own. I just assumed Emily broke her mirror because she couldn't stand looking at her parallel self anymore, and that was why she duct taped her windows, too. But she wasn't afraid of her reflection anymore. She was trying to keep something *in*. Her mirror broke, and then later that week I started seeing her parallel self in our world. She was following me around and following Emily around, like that night when I saw the parallel her looking at Emily while she slept."

"Oh my God . . ." Jackson said, catching on.

"Once the mirror breaks, the barrier between our world and theirs is broken, allowing them to come out of Parallel."

"Jade's in trouble, then," Jackson said.

"We only have so much time before it gets her."

"So, Parallel, it's a trap to get us to go in there?"

"No." I shook my head. "I don't think it's a trap at all. In fact, I think it holds answers we need. I think Parallel is where it all begins and we need to go in there, again and again. Parallel, is telling us a story, our own story. It doesn't show us the whole thing until we continue going back. We shouldn't go back there but we don't have a choice. It shows us our sins. Look, the demons made their imprint on me somehow," I showed him the scratch on my wrist, "but they did that to my brother as well. They are longing to get to us and get inside us. There is a divide between our world and theirs. We are the void, and once they consume us, they can live in our world, but only when that barrier is broken."

"Then why the hell would we go back there? This is insane, Carter!"

"Alex was in my Parallel, and he was crying about how something was all his fault. The more times I go in there I think the more answers I'll get, which could lead us to stopping them."

"How come your mirror didn't break but Jade's did?" Jackson asked.

I held onto his question before I answered. I knew what it meant but I didn't want to say it out loud. Tears formed in my eyes as I rubbed my legs in stress. "I think that Jade's broke because her story about her sins was finished. I think Parallel showed her all they needed to in order to break her barrier." I bit my cheek trying my best not to cry.

"Emily died shortly after her mirror broke and same with Dallas." Jackson continued. "How do we stop them once they're in our world? How do we save Jade?"

I shook my head back and forth. "I don't know . . ."

Brooke

My last class of the day got cancelled and I decided to go meet Jade, who had been discharged in the morning, for coffee. I pulled up, parked my car, and got ready to go in. I checked my hair one last time and for a split second, I thought I saw Dallas and his split-open neck in the rearview mirror. Startled, I quickly glanced to the back seat, but he was nowhere to be seen. I shook it off and headed into the coffee shop.

Jackson called me earlier to catch me up on Jade's past and the mysterious phone call from her Dad. He also mentioned we needed to keep a close eye on her because her barrier was broken. It worried all of us because we were running out of time. Before I had arrived I made a few stops and found what I was looking for.

The smell of rich coffee woke me up. My mouth began to water as I tried to decide what to get. Brew Beginnings was not only the best coffee spot on campus, but critically acclaimed state-wide. No matter what day and time it was, this place was never empty. It had a bubbly, trendy vibe that ensured even non-coffee drinkers felt welcomed. You'd always hear the baristas on campus brag about their tips, which was kind of annoying but also eye opening. The walls were painted a dark cream, and earthy colors complemented the dark oak tables and bar. Single light bulbs dangled from the ceiling, giving it a rustic, trendy look. All their house drinks were served in mason jars, which I always found to be cute. Every month the owners selected five art students to showcase their work, and a new, vibrant painting in the far back caught my attention.

Jade sat underneath the new painting at a small, round table. Textbooks surrounded her and her coffee, but also provided privacy. She was secluded in a corner, minding what was hers. I was taken aback by the gauze and wounds covering her head and her arms. She looked exhausted, and her eyes held pain which I guessed wasn't only from her accident.

I took a seat and gave her a welcoming smile, and she gave me a quick, forced one back. She stirred her coffee, looking down at the circling spoon.

"How are you feeling?" I asked.

"Better, it just hurts a little as it's trying to scab. Just like any other wound trying to heal. It has to get worse before it gets better."

A bit concerned, I nodded. "Yeah, I understand. I'm going to go get some coffee quick." I stood up and made my way to the counter to order. "One medium iced white chocolate mocha, please." For only a second did the decadent croissants and freshly baked cookies catch my eye. Whenever I'd bring Jackson here, he'd always get the chocolate-glazed croissants and double chocolate chip cookies. Somehow the cookies always remained soft and moist, and the gooey chocolate would melt and cover your teeth. *Okay, Brooke, that's enough.* As the barista made my drink, I looked back over at Jade, and what I saw added to my worry. She started to peel off one of the gauzes on her arms, which seemed almost grafted to her skin and took the beginnings of a scab along with it.

Blood dripped down her arm and stained her other gauzes a dark crimson. She started to scratch at her skin. Blood started to fall onto the table, and she robotically took her finger and swirled it around in the small puddle.

Horrified, I grabbed my drink after tipping the man and rushed over to the table. "Jade, stop doing that!" I lifted her arm away from the blood and she looked up at me with confusion. My eyes darted around to make sure no one saw what she was doing.

"It burns, Brooke. I feel like they're scratching from underneath the surface. If I open the wound, maybe they can get out." Her lips were chapped and dead skin began lifting up off of them. Sometimes her teeth would trip on the skin while she talked.

"Who? Who are you talking about?" I sat back down.

"My dad's back and he's not leaving until he takes me. He always finds me, and the scariest part is, I can't wait until he finds me again. I'm ready." I looked down at Jade's coffee mug and noticed some of her blood had dipped into it. I grabbed some napkins and handed them to her.

"Here, apply pressure and keep it covered until the wounds are clotted. We should really get you back to the hospital."

"It's okay, Brooke; I have home remedies for stitches." She let the napkin soak up the blood while she grabbed her coffee.

"Jade don't! Your blood's in that!" I lifted my hand, trying to stop her from drinking it.

She took a long, hard, sip anyway. Steam came off the surface of the drink, but neither the blood nor the heat bothered her, for she drank the coffee until it was almost gone.

I was uncomfortable, and my mind was running a mile a minute. Jade looked like Jade, but I didn't recognize her anymore. I could tell she knew I was unsettled, and for whatever reason, she loved it. I quickly pulled a newspaper article from my purse and placed it on the table. "Jade, I found this. Your father died in jail. He's not back, he can't be."

"How did he die?"she asked with no emotion in her voice. She wasn't even fazed from the news. And if I didn't know any better, I'd say she hadn't even blinked since I got here.

"He hung himself with shoelaces that he got from someone," I said."He died a couple of weeks ago. Jade, I'm so, so sorry, but he can't hurt you anymore."

She looked up at me with a wicked stare, something that didn't look like Jade.

"I know he's dead. That shitty prison called me two weeks ago. But he's alive, Brooke; he chased me around the hospital all night. He pulled me off my bed and dragged me down the hall. The past always catches up with you. I mean, look at Dallas, and look at his parents."

"Jade, stop," I said, as if even hearing Dallas's name took me back to him butchering his parents and then slicing his neck.

"And Emily, she couldn't stand how crazy Alex became, so she dumped him. What's your nasty little secret, Brooke?" She gave me another smile and stirred the little coffee she had left.

"I actually have to go make up a test," I lied. "I totally forgot about it. I'll talk to you after. Just be safe, Jade."

"Brooke, you'd make a great doctor one day," she said in a normal tone. "Too bad you won't be alive to be one."

I stood up, shaking her comment off, and began walking away. I could sense her eyes digging holes in my back, not leaving until I drove out of sight. Something had gotten into Jade. When I got home, I shot both Carter and Jackson a text about what happened and waited for their replies.

As I lay down in my living room to do some homework, I heard a knock at my window. My heart began to race, for I was on the third floor. I got up and made my way to the window, no one was behind it. I looked down to see if anyone had thrown a rock at it, but no one was in sight. I opened the window, stuck my head out and looked to my left and right, but no one was there, either.

I brought my head back in and closed the window. I turned around and found myself no longer in my apartment. Darkness surrounded me as I looked around and tried to see where I was. As my eyes started to focus, I realized I was in Dallas's house. *Oh my God, I'm in Parallel.*

I quickly turned back toward the window, but found only darkness behind me. Realizing I had to go forward, I started to take a few steps but abruptly stopped when I saw myself and Dallas come laughing and stumbling through the front door.

It was the parallel us. I stayed hidden in the darkness and watched them make their way to the couch. *Why was I brought here?* I wondered.

"I told you, I have to go home," I told Dallas, still giggling.

"I know, but we're way too drunk to drive and Jackson would be here, too, if he wasn't on his family vacation," Dallas told her.

My heart started to race and dread washed over me as memories of this night came flooding back.

"Would you like another drink?" he offered.

"It's already after two, holy shit."

"Come on, we have to celebrate your acceptance to your summer internship. Soon–to–be Dr." He gave me another smile.

"Dallas, you are such a bad friend," I told him. "But sure, I'll take another." I watched as he went into his kitchen to fetch me another beer. I wanted to leave.

"Are you a Bud kind of girl?" he called out.

"Sure! I'm drunk enough for one." I giggled again as he brought me a bottle of Bud Light and sat down next to me. I twisted off the top, took a big swig, and leaned back on the couch and sighed.

"What's wrong?" Dallas asked.

"Just Jackson. He didn't want me to take this internship because I leave a few days after he gets back, and our one year is almost here, and just all of this stuff that's leading us to fight."

"You still want to go through with pre-med?"

"That's the other thing. I want nothing more than to do that, but Jackson is making a big deal about how much homework I'll have. And we already don't see each other that much now. He stresses me out, Dallas, but I love him."

"He should be more supportive and understanding," Dallas stated. "But that's just Jackson, a hot head."

I watched as I saw myself try to stand up but fell right onto Dallas. Our dark, deep laughs filled the dimly lit room as I rolled around, trying to get up, and ended up in his lap.

"I'm soooo sorry," I said drunkenly as I noticed I had spilled my beer on him. I helped him take his sodden shirt off. "Wow, Dallas, swimming has really made you less scrawny." I watched as I touched his abs and laughed again. Dallas then grabbed my hand and brought it up to his mouth, passionately kissing it. *Stop. Stop. STOP.*

I continued to watch as he laid me down and started to kiss me. We both smiled and laughed as the foreplay continued. He then took my shirt off, and I was left with just my bra and shorts on. He started kissing down my body, working his hands down my sides until he got to my shorts. He began to unbutton them. Veins wrapped and sprawled up and down his toned arms. Everything was sun-kissed on Dallas, from his freckled shoulders to his light brown hair.

I watched as he wiggled me out of my shorts and threw them on the floor. *Please stop.* Guilt and pain rushed through me as I pulled him down and started to take off his belt as we locked lips. The tan lines on his waist took my eyes to an even lower part of his body. He was well endowed. *I didn't mean for this to happen . . .* I frantically ran my hand through my hair and looked away. I covered my ears as the moaning and giggles continued. *What kind of person was I? Who was I back then to do that to Jackson, and who was I now to hide it from him?* The shell of my identity felt cracked and the reflection I had of myself felt worse than this memory.

Stop. Stop. "STOP!" I caught myself yelling, my voice filling the room. Dallas and the other me looked up from the couch and stared straight at me, their white eyes piercing through me. My parallel self stood up, pushing Dallas, who was now naked, away, and he disappeared. She walked over to me.

263

"What's wrong, Brooke? Don't you like what you see? You did back then." She let out a sinister cackle and tilted her head and looked at me. "Did you not feel special or pretty enough while your boyfriend was away? You had to get your attention from someone else?"

"It didn't mean anything." Tears formed in my eyes as I backed up while she continued to get closer to me.

"You're sad, Brooke. Now let me have a taste of your boyfriend since your other one is dead." I kept stepping backward until she stopped and smiled at me. It was freezing. I could now see my breath as the temperature dropped drastically. The stinging cold froze my blood, and I stayed right where I was. It kept getting darker and darker around us. Goosebumps covered my body and silence filled the air. Before I knew it, she threw her head back, let out a deep cackle and ran toward me. I screamed bloody murder as my heart about jumped right out of my chest. I turned around and started running into the darkness.

The smell of fresh-cut hay filled my nose, instantly taking my mind back to our farmhouse. Memories of vibrant sunrises and long, hot summer days painted a picture in my mind as if I were ten again, herding cows to get milked. Straight ahead stood my mother, and behind her stood the house I grew up in. Darkness surrounded us like a cold winter's night.

"Mom?"

She looked weak from all the chemotherapy. Her skin had lost its pigment, and dark liver spots covered her arms. My brave, stoic role model was now unrecognizable, decrepit. She was my mother, but wasn't. Her platinum-blonde hair was now a washed-out dirty blonde. Her lips were a dark blue, and locks of her hair slowly fell out. She looked battered and bruised, with a sinister glow. She pursued her lips tightly.

"Brooke, look at you. I'm dying and all you care about is fucking," she said scornfully. I followed her eyes past me and turned to notice Dallas standing a few feet behind me. He was still naked and his face was expressionless.

Tears filled my eyes. I knew it wasn't actually her, but the pain felt as real as it would if she found out what I did. "You don't visit me. You don't even call. You're just a slut. The cancer will kill me, but it will be you who has to live with the disease and scum of what you did."

"Mom, please stop." My lips trembled as I felt ten again. The nostalgic scent of hay turned into a repugnant odor of a rotting carcass.

"I can't wait for you to rot like me." She cackled as I put my hands over my ears and closed my eyes.

"STOP!" I screamed with everything I had. I opened my eyes and the vision was gone.

The terror didn't end there. The parallel me taunted me once more as I was left alone in the dark. I refused to look behind me, as I could feel her rotting, warm breath run down my neck. I started to run again and heard her behind me, laughing like she'd lost her mind. My breath was no longer visible as Parallel got darker, but the cold was just as sharp. I kept running and running and before I knew it I fell right through my mirror in my bathroom, shattering the glass and falling to the floor.

I hit the ground and shards of glass punctured the hardwood floor right next to my head. My hands were a little scraped, but other than that I wasn't injured as badly as I thought I was. I quickly got up, and all I could hear was the parallel me laughing. The evil laugh was all around me, but it sounded like it was coming from inside my head.

"Just another taste . . ." It was Dallas's voice, but he was nowhere to be seen. I ran out of the bathroom, grabbed my purse and car keys, and got ready to leave. I opened the front door to find Jade standing behind it.

Her eyes were losing color, and a few thin purple and red veins remained in the whites as she stared at me.

"I thought you had to make up a test." Her voice was a

few octaves lower than normal. Her wounds were ripped back open and I saw scratch marks all over her arms and face.

"Jade, you need to get help . . ."

"They watch me sleep. They roam my house, feeding off me. The shadows in my rooms are real. I hear everything: their cries for help, the cackles at all hours of the night, the sound of an old record player, the smell of their burning flesh, everything."

"Jade, we need to get you to a doctor."

"After awhile, you don't feel what they do to you anymore."

I quickly slammed the door shut and locked it, trying to find another way out. As I fumbled with getting my cell phone out of my purse, I saw the parallel me come out of the bathroom holding a piece of glass, walking toward me.

I took a few steps back and as I did, the front door swung open and Jade started to come in. I screamed and ran over to the window.

"Come on," I muttered, quickly trying to open it as they got closer to me. I got it unlocked and pushed it up. I heard them run at me and before I could think about it, I jumped the three stories toward the ground below.

Chapter 14

Carter

My brother was right: him and I were similar. I needed to keep going back to Parallel. It had the answers. It was showing us certain parts of our lives for some reason. I feared I didn't have much time. I thought I used to fear a lot of things, but before I found Parallel I didn't know what fear was.

I picked up my phone and noticed Brooke had sent me a text and called an hour ago. The text read, *"Something is wrong with Jade, we need to do something now. Text me after class!"* I swore my phone didn't go off for every phone call. I was about to call her back when my phone started vibrating. It was a private number so I hesitated picking up, but against my better judgment I finally hit "answer" and brought the phone up to my ear.

"Hello?"

"Hello?" All I heard was my voice echoing.

"Who is this?"

"Who is this?"

"I think you have the wrong number."

"I think you have the wrong number."

"I'm hanging up now."

"I wouldn't." The voice was again mine, but deeper and sinister.

Goosebumps ran down my spine.

"What do you want?" I firmly asked.

I heard only static, but I was still not alone.

"When it's said and done you'll be dead." After he spoke, he dropped his voice down to a whisper and said, "Like your brother." His maniacal laugh pounded my ear as his voice grew louder and deeper with each cackle. Tears formed in my eyes from anger and fear as my head filled up with his laugh. All of a sudden, his cackles no longer came through the phone but from inside my house, right behind me.

I quickly turned around and saw myself down the hall in the mirror. My reflection was normal as I got closer, but something about it was captivating. I raised my right hand up to see if it followed, and it did. I kept giving it tests and my reflection continued to pass.

I set down my phone as I continued to walk closer to the mirror, and my reflection continued to mirror me. I started to feel the tension between us and my heartbeat quickened. I heard harsh whispers and voices around me as

269

I stood right before the mirror.

"So this is what you want? What you've been dying for me to find all along?" I asked out loud. I could feel harsh cold radiate off the mirror, like it had just come out of a freezer. But it wasn't the mirror that was cold.

"Come home, Carter," my reflection said, smirking. His bright white eyes hadn't been there before. Black veins started to cover his arms and crawl up his neck. I quickly looked down, but my skin appeared normal. My head started to fill with whispers again, along with voices and words that I didn't recognize.

"Don't be afraid." I looked back up and saw my reflection tilting its head and looking at me. He gave a little laugh and I noticed I was tilting my head with him. I quickly cocked it back up and stared straight back at my reflection as it slowly tilted his head upright to follow.

I slowly started lifting my arm up, feeling a pull to touch the mirror. Seeing my reflection mirror me and go back to normal, I pressed my hand to the mirror and felt sheer cold in that one spot, like someone was doing it on the other side. Something was there, looking at me, waiting for me to touch the mirror. The temperature started to warm up around my hand, but it wasn't from me.

Darkness surrounded me and I was no longer home,

but somewhere behind the mirror. *How do they do this?* This time I wasn't in my old home, but on some road.

Fog covered the road as I started walking down it, not able to see my feet. From a distance I heard a humming noise. I saw my parallel self staring at me from the middle of the road. The moon tried shining through the fog, but only a little light made it through.

From a distance, I saw light coming toward me. When it got closer, I realized it was a truck. The parallel me stepped out of the way as it zoomed past him and headed toward me. I tried getting out of the way, but my foot wouldn't move. It was stuck in what looked like tar on the road.

I grabbed my leg, frantically trying to get my foot out of the tar, but it wasn't budging. I felt the tar cover my toes and it felt like I was stepping on hot gum. The truck came at me as I screamed "Stop!" at the top of my lungs and waved my hands up in the air. As I thought it was going to hit me, it veered to the left, missing me, and continued forward on the road. I turned and watched as it went through a stop sign and hit another car.

I saw a body ejected from the car, which rolled three times before coming to a stop. The truck that almost hit me was smashed up in front, with smoke coming out from underneath the hood. Glass and blood covered the road.

I lifted my foot one more time, broke free and started to run toward the accident scene, feeling my foot stick to the road from the leftover tar. I went over to the truck and the driver was nowhere to be found, and his windshield was completely shattered. Coming around to the front of the truck, I found the driver. His face was beaten in from the glass and blood poured down it, and a bone appeared to be sticking out from his arm. He was motionless. A bottle of beer was shattered all over the pavement nearby. Heat still radiated from the motor, warming my skin.

I quickly ran over to the upside-down car and crouched down to look inside. I put my hand to my mouth as I watched my father cough up blood as he slowly woke from unconsciousness. *Oh no.* I knew how this ended.

My skin crawled and my mind began going to a familiar dark place. I felt eighteen again. All the progress I made with my therapist seemed to disappear. Anxiety was in charge now, but my depressive thoughts wanted to reign. Every wall I built crumbled down and my heart was broken yet again. I felt like I was nothing again. My chest tightened and I couldn't catch my breath.

"Dad . . ." I heard myself say as I started to reach out to him. The smell of his cologne wrapped around me. I was here, at the night of their accident. I felt tears escape. This moment felt real and it made me miss them, miss what I used to have.

He opened his eyes and for a short second they appeared to be normal, but as he hung upside down and looked at me, his eyes started to change to the color of the moon. He undid his seatbelt and dropped to the ceiling of the car, then started to crawl out a shattered window, looking up at me with an evil look.

"I'm bleeding out, Carter, help me." He cackled as he tried to get up, but his leg was broken. "Help me, Carter, help me." He reached his hand out, and then dropped it as he started crawling over the broken glass toward me, with strings of blood dripping out of his nose and mouth. His gray tie was dipped in blood and his powder blue dress shirt looked like a kid painted on it.

I took a few steps back and almost slipped and fell on what appeared to be brain matter. I brought my hand up to my mouth to prevent myself from puking.

"I can't feel anything, Carter." It was my mom's voice. I turned my head and looked into the ditch, where she was lying face down. I was forced to look at her open skull, exposing her brain as gray matter and blood dripped out.

I was horrified. Tears welled up and my eyesight

became opaque. My mind raced a mile a minute as my legs grew weak. My father stopped crawling and lay on the ground lifelessly a few feet before me, a small puddle of blood forming around him. I wanted to wake up, but this wasn't a dream. It was much worse; this was real.

"It only hurt for a little bit, the cops said. Remember?" I turned around and saw my parallel self walking my way. His patronizing tone and look made my blood boil.

"Why did you take me here?" I asked, gritting my teeth in anger and clenching my fists. Everything my parallel self showed me I found abhorrent. I couldn't stand him.

"We're all flawed, Carter. We all make mistakes. I'm showing you demons. But sins aren't mistakes—they're led by choices. Choices we make, like that drunk driver. We're all doomed, because we all sin. God gave us choices, and we never seem to fail with making the wrong one."

"What do you want?"

"Well, that's easy," the parallel me said as he looked down at the ground, then back up at me. "We don't want to *just* become you; we want you to suffer as much as we do here. I just want to know what your insides feel like."

I started taking a few steps back as he walked toward me.

"Come on, Carter, let me out." He ran toward me like a

maniac and I started losing sight of him as the fog got thickened. I turned around and started running away, hearing his heavy footsteps and breathing behind me. This was it. I had to run and get out of here. Fearful thoughts played on in my mind as to what sinister things he would do to me once he caught me. I couldn't let that happen.

"I'm gonna getcha." His voice came from all over in the fog and his cackles filled the air. I continued to run, not knowing where I was headed or how to get out of here. I couldn't help but empathize with Alex, Emily, and Dallas, if this was what they went through on their final days. Guilt and anger washed over me as I turned my hands into balls of fists. They had been all alone, not knowing how to fight this, not knowing where to go. *I'm sorry,* I thought.

After what seemed like miles, I found myself out of breath, wanting to fall over and pass out. I didn't hear the other me anymore, but that didn't make me feel any safer. I stopped to catch my breath for a second and as I did, I started to make out an outline of what looked like a church standing before me.

Without hesitating, I ran inside and felt somewhat safer as darkness and walls surrounded me. Hearing the other me outside, I hid underneath a pew and tried to be as quiet as possible. I heard footsteps enter the church, and there was just enough light from the moon to see his feet and legs through the fog.

I heard his evil laughter fill the church, and his footsteps shook the floor. I covered my mouth as I tried to stay as silent as possible. The footsteps stopped and I heard nothing except my own breathing.

I used my peripheral vision to look left and right, but had no idea where he was. The tension and silence were so raw that the sound of a pin dropping would be heard from anywhere in the church. My heart beat faster than I was breathing as I continued to lie on the cold floor. A bead of sweat ran down my forehead and I held my breath, as if the one drop of sweat could be heard from a mile away.

I slowly turned my head and came face to face with the parallel me. My heart sank and my body froze as I stared right into his bright white eyes.

In a dry, mischievous tone, he said, wearing an unforgiving smile, "Found you." I screamed as I rolled from underneath the pew and started running through the aisles with him following me. I headed back as fast as I could when he grabbed me and put his cold, bony hand over my mouth and his lips to my ear.

"Shhh, church is about to start," he whispered. I tried thrashing my arms and legs to get out of his grip, but it was no use. He had incredible strength that deceived even my looks. He dragged me backward, cackling softly in my ear as he stuck out his tongue and licked the outside of it. I could smell the rotten breath, and the slimy, wet tongue made the hairs on my body stand straight up.

He pulled me to a row and threw me down. I hit the floor and as I slowly got up, I noticed that most of the rows were filled by other people in the parallel universe. Most of them I didn't recognize. Some had faces, and others did not. Some of the guests looked like family and friends, but he moved me away before I could get a better look. They looked too stiff to be real, and eerie, ominous vibes came off of each one, for each was expressionless. The church was completely silent, as none of the people said a single word. They all sat straight up in the pews with their cold, white eyes staring up at the front waiting for the priest to show up.

The parallel me was gone when I looked around, but the church doors closed and I saw no choice but to sit down. The people next to me seemed so lifeless, *inhuman*. They never seemed to blink and gave off no body heat or showed any other sign of being alive. They seemed like dolls, wax figures even, giving off some vibe humans don't possess. Their skin was as pale as snow and they all seemed to hold a dark aura to them.

Organ music caught my attention as I turned to face the front of the room. I saw the priest come out of a side room and step up the lectern. There was applause, but no one moved; instead, it sounded like a recording. This really was a whole other world. My fear and anxiety was through the roof, and had been since I witnessed the car accident. I needed to get out of here and back home.

The organ continued to play as the priest stared out into the congregation, looking from person to person, but not a single one of them took their eyes off the front of the church. *I don't belong here, I don't fit in.* I decided to sit straight up as well and look straight ahead, not moving a single inch.

He continued to look around the whole church, eventually laying his eyes upon me. My heart stopped as he looked right at me for a few moments. I didn't know I was holding my breath until his icy cold stare left mine.

When the organ music stopped and the priest took a few steps forward, I noticed burning candles behind him and scattered around the church. He began to speak, saying, "We all sin. We were born into sin. There's beauty to paying the price for our sins. We have this life to redeem ourselves, to save ourselves. Greater is coming, says the

Lord. We have found a path to not only save ourselves but to live again."

What was he talking about? Everyone looked content to listen to him. He possessed an evil look, and something was awfully familiar about him. But if this was like all the other events, it had to have a purpose.

"'I baptize you with water for repentance, but he who is coming after me is mightier than I, whose sandals I am not worthy to carry. He will baptize you with the Holy Spirit and fire.' Matthew 3:11."

That verse left a chill in the air, and I was confused. There was a reason I was hearing this, but none of the pieces were coming together.

The church doors opened suddenly and my brother walked through and into the church with tears in his eyes. It was the parallel him, but his eyes looked normal. The congregation all turned their heads simultaneously and watched as Alex slowly walked up the aisle toward the priest.

He got down on one knee, and with his eyes closed, he pressed his hands together and said, "Forgive me, Father, for I have sinned."

Chapter 15

Jackson

"Brooke, what is going on?" I asked her, finally cutting through her sobs and pants. I had just gotten out of class, and I hopped in my car and was on my way to Brooke's place.

She finally said, "I just jumped out of my window and landed on the back of a truck. Jade and the parallel me were at my place. Carter won't answer his phone and I think Jade really needs help!"

"Okay, babe, where are you?"

"I'm running down an alley, but I can meet you at the 76 gas station in two minutes."

"Okay, I'll be right there. I love you." We hung up and I stepped on the gas, but I saw Jade walking toward the road. She seemed distraught and it looked like dried blood was matted on her arms. I yelled to her as I rolled down my window, "Jade!"

She wasn't fazed and continued to walk, getting closer to the busy street. I parked my car in a nearby lot, got out, and started running toward her.

"Jade!"

She was almost off the sidewalk when she turned around to face me. "I'm okay, Jackson. I really am. You and Brooke and even Carter have nothing to worry about."

"Jade, look at your arms," I said. "You haven't been yourself; we're all worried about you."

"No one knows what it's like to hide from something from your past," Jade replied. "I don't need to be fixed or saved."

"Dallas lost himself, and I'm not going to lose you, too. This thing becomes you; it feeds off you and gets closer to all of us."

"Even if I did need saving, no one knows how to. This is all way over our heads. My father is going to kill me."

"Jade, your father is dead. Brooke told me when she found that article. I'm sorry for whatever happened to you in the past, but you can't let it affect you. Come with me. I'm going to pick up Brooke and then talk to Carter and we're going to figure this all out."

She shook her head. "No. This isn't some fairytale with a happy ending. If I stay away from mirrors and windows and you guys, it won't hurt me."

"Brooke told me that she just ran away from you, Jade. Where are you coming from?" Her left eye started to fade in color as her right one stayed the same.

"I can't stop seeing them; all of them. This is just the beginning, Jackson, don't you get it? I can't go a second without hearing some unfamiliar voice or feel something underneath my skin." Tears welled up in her right eye and her left one started to change more.

"There's no way out of this. I can't take it anymore. I want my life back!" She cocked her head and moved it from side to side. "It will all catch up to us in the end. No one is safe from it." She let out a deep laugh that didn't sound like her.

"Jade, are you okay?"

She smiled widely at me. "Never better." Her eyes went back to normal, and she no longer seemed confident and carefree, but really concerned and worried.

"Jackson, what is going on?" She put her hands up to her mouth and a few tears slid down her face. "I have no idea what just happened to me." I stepped closer and gave her a big hug.

"Come on, let's go back to my car. We're gonna get Brooke and everything is going to be okay."

Brooke

As I walked down the alley I brushed dirt and dust off me from the back of the truck. My heart was still pounding, and adrenaline raced through my veins. I started walking a little faster, for the gas station was past the alley and down the street.

I had taken a different way than normal because of a fence that ran across two buildings. I changed my route and went through multiple alleys. I was almost out of the last one, when I got a text from Jackson saying he found Jade and they were on their way to the gas station. I put my phone inside my purse and then I heard a noise behind me. I turned around and saw the parallel me coming down the dark, dingy alley. She chuckled deeply.

"Brooke, you think your boyfriend is going to save you?"

"What do you want?" I backed up slowly and threw a few trashcans in between us.

"I just want to tear your body apart—but not how Dallas did to you that night." She laughed maniacally again. "Come on, Brooke, let's have a little fun." I turned around and started to run for it when a pain in my ankle from my jump shot up my leg. I screamed in pain and fell down.

"Aww, Brookey, this is almost too easy, but I guess that kind of describes you." I heard her keep walking toward me as I crawled away from her. My leg burned and

I clenched my jaw in pain.

"This is our world now."

I was almost to the sidewalk when I felt her cold hands grab my legs and pull me backward on the raw cement. I screamed from the pain and fear and felt blood start to seep from my open wounds on my hands and legs. I thrashed about, trying to escape her grip.

"Just accept your demons." I felt her start to lick the blood from the legs and dig her nails deeper into my skin.

I continued to scream and kick, and I finally thrashed enough to get out of her grip, kicking her back and away from me. I cautiously but quickly tried to stand back up and get out of the alley. I got through the pain and heard her continue to come after me, but I made it out and started to limp down the sidewalk. I saw Jackson's car driving down the street and I threw my hands up, waving them back and forth.

My phone started vibrating and I quickly took it out, thinking it was Jackson, when I saw the caller ID read "Dallas." My heart stopped for a second as I stared at it to make sure I was reading it correctly. I pressed "talk."

"Hello?"

"Brooke . . ." Dallas's voice sounded hoarse and weak. "I can't breathe in here. It's so dark. I can feel the maggots eating through the back of my head. They're crawling around my spine. Please come save me. No one else will pick up the phone."

"Brooke! Get in!" I looked over to my left and saw Jackson parked on the side of the road with Jade in the back seat. I quickly hopped in the back and hung up my phone. "Are you okay?" he asked. "What happened?"

"The other me dragged me through the alley. We have to get out of here."

"Oh my God, are you okay?" Jade asked me.

At first I looked at her skeptically, having the evil her in my head from not that long ago.

"Yeah . . . I'm okay."

"I barely got away, too." She leaned in and patted my arm and I involuntarily jerked it away from her icy, unfamiliar touch.

"Can we stop at my place really quick?" Jade asked. "I need to grab a few things." Jackson took her back to her place and she immediately got out of his car.

"Jade, I really think we should come up with you." I said to her out the window.

"I don't think that will be necessary." Her face was expressionless.

"None, of us should be alone right now. Hop in and

we'll all get Carter once I clean up.

Veins in Jade's neck slithered and writhed around until they turned completely black. I didn't want her to be alone but I also didn't want her back in the car anymore.

Jade took a step toward us and bent down to look through the window. "I said that won't be necessary." She gritted her teeth and her voice was deeper. While she looked at me, I saw in her eyes a Jade crying for help and another Jade that was no longer her.

"We'll be back." I told her.

Jackson pulled away from the curb and began driving us back to his place. I looked at Jade through the rearview mirror and saw her standing where we left her; looking at us. I leaned back and rested my eyes until Jackson got us home.

"Brooke, talk to me. Are you hurt? Did anything else happen to you?" Jackson asked me as he grabbed my arms and checked my body for injuries. "We need to get the blood off you. I'll go start the shower."

"No. I mean . . . I'll do it." He let me go as I walked past him and into the bathroom. I turned on the light and went over to the sink. I turned on the water and started to get some of the dried blood off my hands. The cold water stung my raw wounds, and I watched as the dark crimson blood swirled down the sink and let out a few tears. Not just tears of fear, but tears of remorse.

From the corner of my eye, I saw the shower curtain move just a little bit. Looking past the curtain, I saw that the window was closed, and I knew there was no draft in the apartment. My heart began to race as I started to get the vibe that I wasn't alone.

I turned off the light and saw a silhouette behind the curtain. I slowly went up to the shower and got ready to pull back the curtain when my phone went off once again. I looked at the caller ID and saw it was Dallas again. I hit the "ignore" button. A few maggots crawled up the white sides of the bathtub.

"Brooke." Dallas's dry, deep voice filled the silence of the room. "I can't get them off of me; I feel them behind my eyes." I grabbed the curtain and slowly started to pull it to the left until I saw Dallas's naked, bloody body covered with maggots. They were in his eyes and in his head and eating through his body. Pustules covered his skin like chicken pox. The rest of the decaying skin hung off his body like meat falling off a bone. I shrieked, closed the curtain, and bumped right into Jackson, which scared me even more.

"Brooke, what's wrong?" he asked.

I cried into his arms as I told him what I saw. He pushed me behind him as he went up to the shower. He pulled the curtain back and revealed that nobody was behind it.

"I swear! He was there, he called me!" I grabbed my phone and went to my call history, but Dallas's name and number was nowhere to be found. "I swear . . ."

"Babe, it's okay, I believe you. Come on, let's finish getting you cleaned up."

I shook my head. "No, there's something I need to tell you." Tears formed in my eyes again. My throat felt tight, like I didn't chew my food well enough and it struggled to go down.

"What? What's wrong?"

I felt a tear slide down my face and saw it land on the tiles below. "Last summer while you were on vacation, Dallas and I went out to the bars." My hands began to shake.

"Yeah . . . ?"

"Dallas and I fooled around." I put my hand up to my mouth as the truth finally came out.

The look in his eyes told me he was shattered, more hurt than anything else. He took a few steps back from me. Anger and confusion were painted on his face as he tried to keep his mouth from quivering.

"We were both drunk and it happened once. It didn't mean anything!"

"Is that why you haven't told me this whole time? Because it didn't mean anything?" Anger took over his voice. "Is that what you thought about me while you were with him? That I didn't mean anything?"

"No, Jackson, you mean everything to me. We were both hammered and being stupid and I was stressed out about my internship and we were fighting and—"

"And so that gives you the excuse to fuck Dallas? Don't you dare try justifying this! It's been a year and a half Brooke, why are you telling me this now? Is it because he's dead and all the blame and guilt are fully on you?"

"No! It didn't mean anything! We were just going to let it go and never speak of it. We didn't even realize it until we woke up with our clothes on the floor."

"I . . . I can't even believe you."

"Jackson, I'm so so sorry. I wish I could take it back, I love you more than anything."

He looked at me sorrowfully, searching for any sign of a lie in my words. In a monotone voice, he said, "Let's go get Jade."

The whole walk down to his car, not a single word was

spoken. The only noise was Jackson's aggression as he threw his phone down when Carter wasn't answering. Everything was happening so fast. I wished that vertigo was the only thing I was feeling right now, but the pain and guilt hurt so much worse.

Carter

"What have you done, young one?" the priest asked Alex.

"It was an accident," he responded. The air got colder and I could start to see my breath, but no one else's seemed visible.

"God is forgiving. As long as you're honest and open, your sins will be forgiven. But that's what we're all about: sinning. My grandfather used to tell me there is a battle that goes on inside people, a battle between two wolves. One of them is evil; it is anger, envy, jealousy, sorrow, regret, greed, lies, ego, arrogance, and self-pity. The other is good; it is joy, peace, love, hope, serenity, empathy, generosity, truth, compassion, and faith. And I asked him, 'Well, which wolf wins?' And he told me, 'the one that you feed.'"

"I never meant to feed the bad wolf," Alex said. "I didn't mean to hurt anyone. And I can't take it back and I'm really scared."

"What did you do, Alex?"

"I killed someone."

"When was this?"

"Years ago."

"Who?" I said it out loud, and my voice carried through the church. The priest and everyone else turned their heads and looked at me. Their cold, dead stares felt like they pierced right through me. I needed to get out of here. I quickly stood up and started to exit my pew.

"It's awfully rude to leave during church," said the priest. I ignored his comment and started walking down the side aisle, still feeling everyone's eyes on me. "You must pay for your sins."

I walked to the doors, but they were locked and wouldn't budge a single inch. I turned around and saw the priest take a few steps away from the lectern, a long knife in his hand.

"You're in our world now, and this time you won't be getting away." I continued to try to open the doors, but it was no use. I watched as the parallel me took the place of the priest. He let out a dry cackle and started walking down the aisle.

One by one, each candle was blown out, and darkness followed behind him. Everyone else in the church seemed to have disappeared, and it was only him and I left.

"Forgive me, Father, for I have sinned," chanted the other me. I continued to pound and pull on the doors, trying to get them open, as he made his way toward me. I took a few steps back, getting ready to make a run at the doors. I took a deep breath and exhaled as I charged for them, using all my might to break through the wooden barrier. I fell forward until I landed on what seemed to be wet, dewy grass.

I looked in front of me and noticed five gravestones next to each other. I got up and walked over to them. I brushed away dead weeds, and saw the first two were for my mother and father. I went over to the next ones, and saw they were mine and Alex's. Only one more remained. I had almost brushed the weeds off when the parallel me spoke behind me.

"Isn't it sad how we all end up in the ground?"

"Who's the fifth grave?" I asked.

"Why don't you go look for yourself?" I turned back around, crouched down, and was about to remove the weeds when a noise in the distance stopped me. I peeked over the gravestones and saw what appeared to be Jackson and Brooke walking around.

"Carter!" They were calling out for me, but why? I

slowly stood up. They came in and out of view, frantically searching. I began to walk away from the graves and head toward my friends. Their eyes looked normal and they seemed humanlike.

I got closer and closer to them, and then I realized they weren't in Parallel with me but that I was staring at them through a mirror—a mirror in my house. It was the wall mirror that hung down the hall and you could see it from the living room. I was so close to them, but I seemed so far away. They were trying to call my cell phone as they continued to search my place.

I pressed my hands up to the mirror and could feel the cold glass. I began sliding my hands around trying to get them to see me, but it was no use. They couldn't even hear me shouting.

"The only way out is to break it." I turned around and looked at the parallel me, who was smiling satanically. "Let the fun begin."

I turned back to face the mirror, knowing what would happen if I broke this barrier. It was the last thing standing in the way of our world for the parallel me. I started to bang on the mirror. The noise caught Brooke and Jackson's attention and they started to look around for the source. My hands throbbed from the amount of force I had to put onto the thick glass to make a noise. My knuckles began to split open.

"What is that?" Brooke asked. I kept banging on the mirror, feeling it weaken. My friends continued to look around them and then at the mirror as it started to shake.

I noticed Jade wasn't with them, and by the look on Brooke and Jackson's faces, something had happened. Brooke looked like she had been crying and Jackson had never looked so pale.

"I think something is behind the mirror," Jackson responded, getting closer to it. I kept banging on the mirror until the glass started to crack. I brought my arms down one last time, causing the mirror to break, and I fell out of it and onto the floor, glass spilling out behind me.

Jackson and Brooke gasped and rushed to my aid.

"Jesus, Carter, are you okay?" Jackson asked as he helped me up.

"Yeah, I think so," I said as I brushed off glass. I looked behind me but all I saw was the back of the mirror—no parallel world. "Our demons want to be in our world more than we know."

"What did you see?" Brooke asked.

"You're going to have to explain later," Jackson said. "We think Jade is in trouble. We picked her up about a half an hour ago and she was acting crazy, then got back to normal, and then she was crazy again. We dropped her off quick to go back to my place, and now she won't answer her phone or texts. She refused to invite us inside. She threatened us."

"Okay, let's go get her. We can't be alone, any of us." I couldn't help but look back at the mess as we left. If we didn't figure something out quickly, we were all going to die. One by one they we're drawing us in, showing us our past and our secrets, tormenting us with our demons until we became one again, how we were originally created.

We got in the car and I instantly felt the tension between Brooke and Jackson. Something was off, and they hardly even acknowledged one another. Brooke let me sit up in the front, even though Jackson was driving and they always rode side by side. The mood was oppressive. I felt like if I even breathed loudly I would be disturbing something.

"What did you mean by Jade was acting crazy and then she went back to normal?" I asked Jackson.

"She was going to walk into traffic. I found her before she did and she was talking all crazy, telling me how she missed her old life and how her father was still after her. Then her left eye started to fade in color and she started jerking her head left and right, like she was fighting or becoming something else. Her voice even got deeper in the end."

"Like her demon side . . ." I mumbled. Jackson stepped on the gas and raced to Jade's place as dread washed over me.

We pulled up to the apartment and immediately ran inside and up the steps. After what seemed like forever we finally opened the door on her floor, but behind that were more stairs and behind us was the front entrance.

"Did we just go in a circle?" Brooke asked. We all looked around, confused and taken aback.

"This is weird," Jackson added.

"Come on, let's keep going," I started going up the steps once more. The lights began to flicker and we heard a sinister cackle in the stairwell.

"Run, run as fast as you can." We all heard the demonic voice, but no one was to be seen. We got to Jade's floor again and opened the door to her hallway. We quickly found Jade's door and I tried to open it.

"It's locked," I told Brooke and Jackson, turning the knob back and forth.

"Jade, open up!" Jackson called. He switched places with me and tried the knob, but had the same luck as I did.

Jackson angrily kept pushing on the door and twisting the knob.

"Come on in," we heard Jade say, but something was off about her voice. Jackson stepped back as her door creaked open, seemingly on its own, opening into darkness. We all exchanged glances and one by one we made our way into her place. I found a light switch but it wouldn't turn on, so we were left stranded in the dark.

"Jade, where are you?" I asked. Nothing but silence followed. The three of us stuck closely together as we moved around her apartment. I took out my phone and turned on the flashlight feature, shining it all around.

Her kitchen was completely empty and we moved on to her living room, which contained no evidence that she was here. We all carefully started walking down the hallway toward her room. Jackson and Brooke were behind me as I led the way. Something was wrong with this whole situation.

I slowly pushed Jade's bedroom door open, hearing it creak in the silent apartment. My heart beat faster as I slowly made my way in, guided by the little light I had. I looked around her room until something caught my eye. I almost dropped my phone at the sight.

My heart dropped to my feet and my mouth was agape.

Brooke gasped and brought her hands to her mouth as the three of us looked up and saw Jade hanging from her ceiling fan by shoelaces.

She was slowly rotating, with her eyes closed and her lips a dark blue. I looked away at the sight and Jackson pulled me back toward him. We were too late. He hugged me tightly, trying to comfort me. As I tried to hold back the tears, I heard movement within the room. I turned back around and saw Jade's body come to a complete stop as she faced us.

"We need to get her down." Brooke quietly suggested. "She might not be dead."

Jackson quickly left the two of us to go grab a knife to cut the shoe laces.

A smirk developed across her face, though her eyes stayed shut. She laughed and I could hear the bones in her neck crack from the pressure and weight on it.

She abruptly stopped laughing and her smirk disappeared as she opened her mouth to speak. "Our Father, who art in heaven, hallowed by thy name. Thy kingdom come, thy will be done on earth as it is in heaven." She opened her eyes and stared at us. "We're supposed to be delivered from evil, but it looks as if evil found us."

I looked past her and saw her father behind her, smiling at us, not batting a single eye. Jade was no longer alive and no longer herself, and her eyes and her father's shone brighter than the light on my phone.

"I thought you said you weren't going to let anything happen to me?" she asked wickedly.

"Come on, let's go," I said. We walked out of Jade's room, running into Jackson who held the knife with a trembling hand. He looked past us and saw Jade's lifeless body with her demonic father behind her. Jackson quickly closed the door behind us. We ran out of her apartment, down the stairs, and toward our exit. We didn't look back until we made it to Jackson's car.

"Do we call the cops?" Brooke asked.

"I don't know if they'll find the body," I replied. "We need to keep moving." We got in the car and Jackson drove off.

"What do we do?" Jackson asked me. "They're getting us one by one."

"We need to stay together. We'll go back to your place; we'll all stay up and take turns keeping watch until we figure out the best thing to do." We sat in silence until we got back to Jackson's. This had taken over our lives. My girlfriend was dead, nearly everyone I loved was dead, and the ones I kept close kept getting hurt. I couldn't tell if I was desensitized from all the death around me or if Jade's death hadn't hit me yet. I had just met her, but for the time she was alive, she meant everything to me.

I kept my arms close to my body, not wanting to take up much space. If I remained small, everything around me would disappear. My adrenaline fought against my anxious thoughts and only tired out my mind.

The tension in the car further proved the demons were only getting stronger. Like the priest said, the one who lives is the one we feed.

Chapter 16

We got back to my place and I still refused to talk to Brooke, just as Carter refused to talk about Jade. This was real and was becoming a part of all of us. Not all of it made sense yet, and it was hard to believe our closest friends were dying away. I wanted to throw up. I wanted to take pulls from a bottle of whiskey. I wanted nothing more to do with this. I'd forgive Brooke and move on if that meant everything would go back to the way it was. *Grow up, Jackson,* I berated myself. Just for five minutes, all I wanted was to feel five years old again.

Brooke went into the bathroom and Carter sat down by me on the couch. "Jackson, what's wrong with you two?" he asked.

"Brooke cheated on me with Dallas while I was on a family vacation. They were both drunk when it happened," I told him while looking down at the floor. The words stung as they rolled off my tongue. Saying it made it seem more real.

"Jackson, I'm so sorry. What are you guys going to

do?"

"I don't know. I can't be mad at a dead person and I'm in love with Brooke, but it still hurts; it hurts like a bitch. Just when I didn't think things could get worse or hit closer to home, they do."

Brooke came out of the bathroom, and her eyes were puffy and bloodshot. She must had been crying in there. I felt bad for her, but we were all going through the same things and now we were all suffering the consequences. She sat in a chair and silently went through her phone.

"In my Parallel," Carter began, "they took me to where my parents were killed. I saw the drunk driver hit them and their bodies thrown out of the car."

"Carter, I'm really sorry," I told him, feeling my heart tighten.

"It gets worse. The parallel me was talking about how we all sin and make the choices to sin, and then he chased me to this church and made me sit through the service with a bunch of other parallel people. The priest was talking about how there was a way for them to live again and get to us. And we all know that's what they're doing: finding us, bringing us into Parallel and showing us our sins and demons and our past to become us. My brother walked into the church and was talking about how he sinned and that he killed someone."

"Did you find out who it was?" I asked him.

"No, they chased me out of the church, but I ran to a graveyard and I was standing in front of five graves, and four of them belonged to my family, including me."

"But you couldn't see the fifth one?" Brooke added.

Carter shook his head. "And the priest looked so familiar. I stopped going to church years before I graduated high school, but I think it's the same priest who was at my old church before it was abandoned and the church moved."

Brooke made a noise in pain as she grabbed her wrist. I quickly got up and went over to her. I picked up her wrist and saw a cut mark across it.

"When did this happen?" I asked her.

"I got it when I came back from Parallel. It's burning up right now."

"Didn't you say your brother and Emily both had cut marks on their wrists?" I asked Carter.

"Yeah . . . my brother said he did so it would help him not forget who he was. I have them, too, but it was from me going into Parallel a few times. I think it's the demons making their marks on us. I think it's their symbol of getting closer to us."

"Shit, I left my purse in your car; it has a mini first-aid kit," Brooke said.

"Just use the Band-Aids I have in my bathroom," I told her.

"You ran out, remember?" She stood up, but Carter stopped her.

"You're not going alone. I'll go with you. Jackson, you should come with us."

"Let me get my keys. I want to lock up." I said. They opened my apartment door and waited for me in the hall. While they waited I fumbled around the living room for my keys. I couldn't help but start to get paranoid about my mirrors and windows. I didn't want to go into Parallel; there was nothing I needed to see. There was nothing I wanted to see.

"Jackson, hurry up!" Carter yelled from behind the door.

"Coming!"

My head was swimming, my stomach was doing flips and turns, and my temples were throbbing. Everything that had happened made no logical sense. How could there be an evil half of me? How could people get taken to someplace only their worst nightmares could dream of and then fall back here through mirrors? I mean, how much of this world that we lived in did we actually know about?

I didn't want to live every second of my life in fear that my demons wanted to take me back. I just wanted everything to go back to the way it was. But it couldn't, and I had to accept that. I had to accept that my girlfriend cheated on me with my now-dead friend. I couldn't confront him. Hell, it was even hard to confront Brooke. My mind kept telling me that Dallas and I wouldn't have been friends if we never had worked together on a class project. Dallas was never the most popular student in high school. He hit puberty late and he was later known as the butter-faced tenth grader who threw dope parties. His parents were always gone and I felt bad for the kid. He didn't fit in with Carter's or my own social groups. Carter was the one who suggested we hang out with him. Carter also told me Dallas showed early signs of depression junior year and the both of us helped him. But the second time around we couldn't. Instead, we all saw our good friend kill himself.

I swallowed hard and shook my troubling thoughts away as I went to the living room window. From across the street, I saw myself looking out the exact same building and window. He was smiling at me, taunting me. I paced back and forth a few times before I grabbed my baseball bat. Glass flew everywhere as I destroyed all the windows in the apartment and moved on to my bathroom. I dropped the bat on the way and stared into the mirror. I started to hear Brooke and Dallas's laughter and flushed with anger. I scowled, and my hands formed into fists. Dallas was my friend, he was the guy who needed me, the one who would only survive if he was in my social group. The moment he got a full ride to the same college as all of us, I should have known he had his sights set on something else.

"Jackson, what are you doing?" Carter asked horrified. Brooke and him came back into my apartment.

Ignoring them, I clenched my jaw. I didn't remember punching the mirror the first time, but it left blood and shrapnel in my hand. Cracks spider webbed the mirror. I took my other fist and continued to hit the glass, sending shards everywhere. I punched and punched, letting the shards fly and tears of anger flow. I screamed through the external and internal pain of everything I'd gone through.

Carter and Brooke ran into another room to get cleaning supplies and to get out of my way.

Out of breath and with nothing left to punch, I leaned over and let the blood run off my wounded hands and paint the sink red. I looked at the millions of pieces of glass all around the room and realized that was exactly what my heart felt like. There was no turning back and we all had to deal with what we were left with: the good and the bad. They were coming for us, all of us.

I washed off my shaking, bloody hands and grabbed a towel to wrap them in. As I clenched my fists I could feel pieces of glass stuck in my hands, tearing through more skin. I turned off the water and made my way out of the bathroom and into the living room.

I noticed a hanging mirror on the wall that I never had before. It looked brand new. Confused and intrigued, I made my way over to it. Whispers wafted through the air and I felt something evil and sinister around me. I continued to walk to the mirror, getting the feeling something was watching me.

"You guys?" I called out to my friends.

My mind screamed to get away from it, to go get Carter and Brooke, but something about the mirror kept me there. My reflection followed me as I put my hand up to the glass, and for a second I thought I could feel my heartbeat in my fingertips, but it wasn't my own pulse.

I then noticed my reflection was no longer present—all I saw were trees and a gray sky behind me. I quickly turned back around and saw a big body of water behind me. The sun wasn't out, and clouds covered the dark sky. A cool summer breeze drifted from the lake.

I was at RedBone Lake, but I didn't understand why. In the distance I heard laughter coming my way, so I began ran off the sand and into the trees to hide myself. I wanted to be out of there.

I watched as Carter and I came around the corner and started running onto the beach. We looked a few years younger than we were now and wore our baseball uniforms; we must have just gotten done with practice. And I remembered now . . . this was during our junior year. It was a hot summer night after practice and we wanted to cool off in the lake.

We stripped down to our boxers and darted into the water. It was only us there, and our laughter shot into the sky as we swam around and splashed water into each other's faces. I continued to keep low and watch from afar.

I watched as we floated on our backs and talked and whispered; it was kind of hard to hear and I didn't remember what we talked about. We continued to laugh and mess around in the water, and then I started to feel butterflies in my stomach. I saw Carter get closer to me and stand just a few inches away from me. We were both smiling and just looking at each other.

I don't remember any of this. None of this ever

happened, I swear. My heart started to race and the butterflies kept fluttering around inside of me. Without realizing it, I was holding my breath. We were just an inch apart now and everything was silent. Beads of water dripped down our faces and our wet hair lay plastered on our heads.

I shook my head and took a step back, but my foot snapped a twig. The sound interrupted them in the water and they quickly stared off into the timber where I was. I stayed crouched down and started to turn around to go away from the scene when I realized I was now looking through the cracks of a closet door, staring into my bedroom.

I was about to step out of the closet when my parallel self and Carter came bursting into the room, again looking high-school aged. We started taking off our pants to get ready for bed, then lay down and stared up at the ceiling.

"It's about time we made varsity," I spoke.

"I know, I was thinking about quitting if I didn't," Carter replied. "My legs are so sore from practice, though."

"I know. Fucking Coach Kuehl has us running enough killers to pass all the runners on the Olympics. By the way, Anne Marie has been to all of our games so far and I'm pretty sure she wants you."

"Haha, I don't know, dude, I don't think she's really my type."

"You know what my type is? Girls who don't call me back after a one-night stand."

"Jackson, are you ever going to be in a relationship longer than a week?" Carter asked.

"Probably not, but who needs one? I don't need a girl breaking my balls every time I don't text her back right away."

We were quiet for a few minutes before Carter broke the silence. "Thank you, dude, for letting me stay here this week while my parents celebrate their anniversary." My eyes made their way to the air mattress that was on the floor. Secretly, I never wanted him to use it.

"Of course. I get tired of dealing with my siblings and my family shit. But, God, it's so fucking hot." I watched as the parallel me stood up and turned on the fan, then took off his shirt and got back into bed.

My palms started to sweat and the butterflies came back. I remembered this night clearly now. But I continued to watch as I saw myself get closer to Carter.

"What are you doing, Jackson?" Carter asked me.

I started to lean in and Carter didn't stop me as I placed my lips onto his, and before I knew it, we were making out. Beads of sweat formed on my forehead as I watched myself. *I'm not gay!*

I started to get on top of Carter and kept making out with him, feeling our bodies press together. I was ashamed and embarrassed. This was wrong. His lips sparked something inside of me, something I kept buried. My shorts started to get tighter and I wanted more of that which seemed forbidden.

I caught myself holding my breath but I didn't want to release it. This faded memory was about done; I knew what happened next.

"Jackson, stop, I'm not gay," Carter said as he pushed me off him, wiping his mouth with the back of his hand. "What's gotten into you?"

"I know, I'm so sorry, I'm not either. I don't know what I was thinking." But I did remember what it was like. Carter was my first kiss with a boy, and temptation got the best of me that night. The way I felt inside, the way that kiss made me feel was different than how I felt with all the other girls I'd been with.

I looked away for a moment and then back out into my room and the parallel me was gone. I then heard him behind me. "You know you wanted more that night," he said. "Go on, he's right there. Feed your demons."

"NO!" I screamed. I charged out of the closet and ran out of the room, but fell down when a wave of what seemed to be black tendrils envelop me. The current slammed me into the wall across from my open bedroom door, pinning me there while they wrapped around me. The parallel me was on top of Carter in my bed, and we were still making out. *What I secretly wanted to happen,* I realized. I watched as I helped Carter remove his shirt and we rolled around in between the sheets.

"Jackson, I don't know about this," Carter said as he took a moment away from my lips.

"I'm sorry; I just can't keep my hands off of you." I slid them down his toned body and stopped when they reached a hard spot in his boxers.

He moaned softly as I wrapped my hand around it through the fabric. I began kissing his neck while my hands found what they wanted. His boxers started getting wet from the pleasure, but they were stained a deep red. I didn't seem to care. I wanted more, I needed more.

I grabbed onto the sides of his boxers and slid them down his hips. I flung them across the room and went down on him as I began taking off my own pair. *Jackson, what are you doing? This is your best friend. He's not gay and neither are you.* I got my underwear off and as I tossed them off the bed I heard a dark, faint whisper.

"Feed your demons. Give in to what makes you, you."

Experimenting with my best friend gave me feelings of lust and serenity, both of which aren't easily found. Our moans filled my bedroom as we took turns getting on top of each other. I wanted him so badly.

"What are you doing?" Carter asked me.

"What do you mean?"

"You're with Brooke."

"Who's Brooke?"

This was before I even knew her. So why did my parallel self not know anything about her but Carter did? The warm tendrils kept me strapped to the wall while I fought back tears. *I don't want to watch this anymore. This is fucked up. THAT ISN'T ME!*

"Let me go!" I screamed. My voice reverberated off the walls.

"All your friends are dying, Jackson, and you're focused on your sexuality?" Carter asked the parallel me. "You're pathetic. You're just some sad closeted homo who doesn't have any friends because you're a hot-headed meat stick."

"Carter, I don't understand what you're talking about."

"Do you actually think I don't notice you check other

guys out in the locker rooms? That you take extra-long showers just to keep getting a new view? And do you really think that all the girls you've been with actually buy your 'straight' act? I don't know who buys it more, though, you or them. Let me guess. Every day you wake up and tell yourself you're into girls and put on this show so everyone can see. Then you go home and once you're alone you let your thoughts fester. You fear you'll lose your scholarships, your friends that took so long to make because you're not that easy to get along with. You're afraid that your family will disown you and that you'll have nothing left. So, you hide it even more and you tell yourself 'No, not today. It isn't true; I just haven't found the right girl yet.'"

Then, out of nowhere, I watched as blood dripped down from the ceiling and landed right onto my parallel self's body. Blood began to paint our skin as it rained down from the ceiling. Blood droplets started to slide down my sides and legs, falling faster and thicker.

The building wave of blood eventually took the parallel me off of the bed and out of my room. My parallel self looked at me with a smirk as he came rushing toward me. The blood level rose and I tried to catch my breath as my head went under the dark crimson liquid. I was eventually released from the wall, and all I saw was red. The current took me down the hallway and around the corner, and before I knew it I fell through the mirror and back into my apartment. I quickly got back up and looked into the mirror. I saw into my old house again and watched as a wave of blood roared around the corner and down the hall. Before I could react, the blood gushed out of the mirror and into my apartment, beginning to cover the floor.

My parallel self started coming toward the mirror and I watched as the blood stopped flowing as he walked out of the mirror and into my world. I took a step back but I tripped and fell over the baseball bat, landing in a puddle of blood. The mirror behind him started to crack and break as he stepped onto the floor.

He grinned and chuckled as he started to walk toward me. I began to crawl backward. "What's the matter, Jackson, I can't play with you here?" he taunted me. "You didn't want to see your secrets come back to life? Here, let me show you something." He grabbed my legs and pulled me toward him. I screamed and thrashed about, trying to get out of his grasp while digging my fingernails into the hardwood floor.

"Jackson, what are you doing?" Carter yelled at me. I turned and looked at him and Brooke, who had just come back into my apartment with her purse and first-aid kit. I turned back and saw that all the blood was gone, along with my parallel self, but the mirror was still shattered.

"Where did you guys go?" I asked feeling alone and scared.

"We heard you breaking glass so we came back in and saw you going batshit. Brooke rushed to get the first aid kit while I went to find cleaning supplies." Carter explained. "We didn't want to get in your way."

"You didn't see me go into Parallel?" They both shook their heads and walked closer to me.

My hands shook and my heart raced as blood seeped out from underneath my bent fingernails. My chest was tight as I panted, desperately trying to get air back in my lungs. "I didn't want to see anything, I didn't want to be tempted or tormented, so I broke them all, all the windows and the mirrors. But they somehow still got me to go inside. This mirror that I fell out of was new and now it's broken."

"They're going to consume us," Carter said. "We need to stay certain of what is reality and what they want us to see."

Standing up, I said, "Carter, they are reality. This is real."

Diverting my statement, he asked, "It's going to be freezing in here. Should we go to my place or Brooke's?" He looked at the shattered mirror and my bloodied hands with doubt and concern. I was relieved that neither one of them asked what I saw.

"It doesn't matter anymore. Any place is the same. Whether it's at your home or here, they're going to find us. I'm exhausted. I'm going to stay here and if you guys choose to stay we need to have someone keep watch." I walked away and began getting ready for bed.

Carter and Brooke grabbed blankets and pillows once the glass was all picked up. I blew up an air mattress and we all took our spots. Carter took one of the suede couches, Brooke, took the air mattress, and I took the other couch. I turned up the heat and draped blankets as best as I could over the windows.

I started out in the living room with them, keeping watch as they did their best falling asleep. But at some point I subconsciously made it back to my bedroom. I tossed and turned all night, not finding the most comfortable position. I kept thinking about what I saw and what I went back to. I wasn't gay and I never would be. I loved Brooke; well, at least I thought I did. I didn't know who I was anymore.

Pain and heartache ripped through my body again and again, like a bullet to my heart. Thoughts raced through my mind keeping me awake. I was no longer safe and we didn't even know how to stop them. I didn't know if Brooke and I were going to stay together, and life just seemed to be a game of cat-and-mouse.

I used to have a crush on Carter in high school. It was a small one. It didn't last very long but the thought of our kiss always played in the back of my mind. Maybe the reason I slept with girls and struggled settling down with someone was because it wasn't Carter. Not that I wanted to be with Carter, but with someone who made me feel like I could finally be me. Brooke does that but she's not a guy . . .

My underwear grew tight as my thoughts wondered to the scene of Carter and me. What would my parents say if I ever brought home a guy? Not that I ever would. But, if I did . . . would they be happy for me? Would *I* be happy for me?

I readjusted myself not wanting to give into temptation. I turned on my side to get comfy once more and was face to face with my parallel self. He was smiling, staring at me with his white eyes, and he cackled.

"Don't worry, I won't let anything happen to you

while you sleep." I screamed and started to get out of bed, but my legs were tangled in the covers. I thrashed and thrashed until I eventually fell onto the floor. I turned on the lamp and saw that he was no longer on my bed.

My breathing slowed down as I got my legs out of the covers, but as I began to stand up I saw myself sitting in a chair in the corner of the room, just staring at me. The light bulb in the lamp exploded and my room grew dark once more.

A whistling noise filled my room. The tune was similar to a bird's song but it was eerie and ominous, like an early morning fog. I grabbed my covers and jumped back into bed, pulling them over me. I hid underneath them as the whistling stopped, but then I heard my closet door creak open. The hardwood floor creaked as heavy footsteps came closer to my bed. I held my breath. Even though I couldn't see them, I still had hoped they couldn't see me. But I knew better. I knew the fabric of the person I used to be was ripped to shreds. This wasn't God's creation; this was a part of me that I wasn't ready to accept. I didn't know how. This *thing* knew my biggest secret.

I clenched my jaw and prayed to God that this was all a dream. When the creaking of the floor had stopped for a few minutes, I felt someone's breath down my back from within the covers, sending chills down my spine. Something sharp dug into my neck and I was yanked from my bed. I was pulled across the sheets, and then I blacked out.

***

"Jackson, I can't sleep." The sound of Brooke's voice started to wake me up. I slowly opened my eyes and through my blurry vision, I saw her come into my room.

"I know we're not on the best terms and I know that I've hurt you, but I'm scared out of my mind. Carter fell asleep and I didn't feel like keeping watch alone. Can I please sleep with you tonight?"

I blinked a few more times while my head started to throb and spin. I realized I was looking down at Brooke as she was below me, heading toward my bed. I was strapped to the ceiling by barbed wire around my neck, arms, and legs, keeping me in place.

"Of course, babe." It was the sound of my voice, only it didn't come out of my mouth. I looked down at my bed and saw the parallel me covered in blankets facing Brooke. She hopped in bed.

I opened my mouth to say something when I felt barbs run across my face and dig into the sides of my lips. I yelped in pain.

320

"Jackson, what's wrong?" Brooke asked, reaching over to the parallel me.

"Brooke, no!" I yelled. She immediately stopped and looked around for my voice. "I'm up here."

She looked up at the ceiling and immediately got out of bed. "Oh my God, Jackson, how did you get up there?"

"Don't let him down, Brooke. He's the bad one, I spent all night trying to get him up there," said the other me. He pulled the covers off himself and I saw that he looked completely normal.

"Brooke, he's lying!" I called down to her.

The other me looked up at me and then back at her. "I guess you better start running, then." Brooke screamed as she ran out of the bedroom, the parallel me chasing after her.

"Don't fucking touch her!" I yelled.

I started to pull one of my arms through the barbed wire that was wrapped around it, clenching my teeth through the pain as it ripped my skin open. Blood started dripping down my arm and onto the floor below. I began unwrapping the barbed wire from around my mouth, and I moved it up and over my head as best as I could with one free arm. I then worked on getting one of my legs untangled, and as I did, the weight of my body pulled me down and I hung from the ceiling, the coils ripping through my other arm and leg. Grinding my teeth and wincing, I told myself to man up. I quickly ripped my other arm through, and I dangled upside down. I used my upper body strength to pull myself up and wiggle my leg out of the wire, and then I fell to the floor.

Carter came rushing to my aid, helping me into the living room. Brooke was curled up in a chair, practically crying. Carter immediately went through my bathroom and found old rags to give me for my wounds.

"Make it stop, make it stop," she begged.

"Brooke!" I said as I ran up to her, a bloody and bruised mess. "Are you okay? Did he hurt you?" The living room was an icebox. It was brisk and windy from the open windows. I wish I would have never done that. Our breath lingered in the air.

She shook her head no. "He disappeared as soon as Carter woke up. The voices in my head won't stop. And all I hear is constant whistling and screams."

"Jackson, they're not going to stop," Carter said. "The others never got any sleep; they were all trying to run away and hide from themselves. But I think we need to go to the graveyard to see my family. I don't think all of them are there."

Chapter 17

Carter

"What do you mean?" Jackson asked me. Blood slid down his arms and legs like a melting popsicle. I continued to apply the old towels but certain cuts were too deep.

"Remember when I went into Parallel and it took me to the graveyard and there were five graves in front of me?" he nodded. "Well, I think it has to do something with my brother. He did something years ago, something unspeakable."

"You want us to go to a graveyard at night?" Jackson asked me.

"It's better than during the day. This way people won't see us."

"To go look at graves?" Brooke asked.

"No, to go dig them up."

***

After getting Jackson cleaned up and finding a couple shovels, we all hopped in his car and I drove to the cemetery my family was buried in. Something about what I was shown in Parallel was leading me to things that had been buried for too long. Not all the pieces to the puzzle were there, and the closer our demons got to us, the less time we had.

"Did you hear that?" Brooke asked us from the back seat.

"Hear what?" Jackson asked.

"Those voices, what they said," Brooke replied. Tears started to form in her eyes.

"Brooke, we didn't hear anything."

She put her hands up to her ears and said, "Don't let them touch me. They're so close . . ."

"Babe, it's going to be okay."

Jackson and I shared a glance. We didn't need to say it; we both knew what was coming for Brooke. When I looked back at the road, I saw my parallel self a few feet away, standing in the middle of the road and staring at me. I quickly veered over, trying to dodge him. The car went off the road and I slammed on the breaks as the car spun around and almost hit a tree.

"Is everyone all right?" I asked.

"Besides the whiplash and heart attack? I think so," Jackson replied. "You know this is the first time I've let you drive my car. I think you've handled it poorly." From the corner of my eye I thought I saw a figure move through the trees. Not wanting to explore deeper, I pressed on the gas and went back onto the road. I didn't take my eyes off the road until we made it to the cemetery.

We got out and walked toward my parents' graves. The crescent moon didn't give us much light. We brought a few flashlights and would use our phones if needed.

"This place is even creepier at night," Brooke stated. "But nothing like a graveyard to make you feel more alive."

"This is the spot," I said. "Alex is right here, and then my parents, but I think something is buried next to my parents. Did we bring the shovels?"

"They were in the backseat with me," Brooke replied. "I can go back and get them."

"I have to take a piss, so we'll both go back," Jackson said. As they made their way back to his car that was in sight, I looked at the graves. My brother was never crazy. He found Parallel and kept his journal so I could find it and finish what he started.

I missed my whole family. It felt like just yesterday they were still alive and taking care of me and helping me when times got tough. I wished I could crawl into my parents' bed at night and have them comfort me. I felt like a little kid running around in the dark—no direction, completely blind, and with no hand to hold.

If only we could figure all of this out, Dallas and Jade would still be here, and Emily and Alex, and we could have our lives back. We could be planning our trip and just be happy.

Brooke

"Jackson, I don't know what to say about earlier. Seeing you up there and then seeing you in your bed as you . . ."

"It's okay, I would have let you sleep with me. I would have held you all night and I wouldn't have let you go. I cut open my body just to get down to save you," Jackson told me, showing me his bandaged arms and legs. "You're my best friend, Brooke. Carter is my best friend, but when he's not around and even when he is, I turn to you. You've done so much for me."

I shut him up while I gave him a sincere smile and a hug, then he told me he'd be right back as he went over to the trees to go to the bathroom. He held his flashlight in his armpit while undoing his pants. I grabbed the two shovels from the car and slammed the door. He was still going as I walked around the car.

"Hey, Brooke, come here quick, come check this out," he called.

"Babe, we really shouldn't leave Carter by himself," I yelled back to him.

"I want to show you this!" He zipped up his pants and started walking into the woods. I looked over at Carter, who was kneeling by his parent's graves. Biting my lip in hesitation, I rested the shovels on the car and quickly jogged over to Jackson.

"Jackson, it's really dark and creepy here," I said as he led me into the woods. "Where are you taking me?" All I heard were my heavy footsteps and twigs and leaves crunching.

"We're almost there, babe," he said, still about twenty feet ahead of me. Fog rolled in as the night began to grow colder.

"Jackson, I don't want to be in here anymore, not after what's been going on."

The fog wasn't anything to mess with. It was as thick as clouds, and before I knew it, he was gone in the white smoke and I was lost and left alone right in the middle of it. Everywhere I turned looked the same. I began to hear digging noises from afar, and they seemed to get more and more aggressive.

"I don't see you." I felt eyes on me, and the agony of it all drew beads of sweat to my forehead. I felt six years old again and scared of the dark. My flashlight did nothing, for the fog swallowed up all the light.

"Come on, Brooke, you don't trust me? That's not fair. Look what you did to me." The fog cleared a little bit and I saw him with his back toward me about ten feet away, just standing there.

Then all of a sudden, my phone rang. I pulled it out and saw that it was Jackson calling me. My heart stopped. *Not this again.*

"Babe, why are you calling me?"

"Don't pick up, it's not me. Now, come on, I have to show you something." I ignored the call and continued to follow him, but my phone kept going off. *What are you doing, Brooke?*

"What do you have to show me? Jackson, we can't leave Carter alone."

A long moment of silence followed my question as I tried to keep up with him. Why would he tell me not to pick up? Jackson would never leave Carter like this.

"I have to show you where they put the body."

"What body?"

The phone rang again and I quickly answered.

"Brooke, where are you?" Jackson asked.

"I'm right behind you. I followed you into the woods; you had to show me something."

"Brooke, I'm with Carter. That's not me. Get out of the woods!" I froze in my tracks, like I was turned to stone. I hung up, then turned around and started to run when I ran into the parallel Jackson. We were eye to eye and his cold, white eyes stared right through to the marrow.

"Yours," he finally answered. He pushed me down and I fell into an open grave

I looked up and saw my parallel self next to Jackson, both looking down at me and smiling. "You wanna have some make-up sex, Brooke?" Jackson chuckled to himself. "Nothing like a graveyard to make you feel alive. I thought you were a lot smarter than this, Brooke. It was almost too easy to lure you into the woods like that. You're easy, right, Brooke? But of course, you're so vulnerable I can smell the desperation on your breath as you hope for my forgiveness." I watched as the parallel me cackled and jumped down into the grave with me. "No one's gonna hear you scream."

Carter

"She's in the woods?" I asked.

"Yeah, I have to go get her," Jackson said.

"Jackson, wait, they're playing games with us. They're using us against each other. You don't know what you're going to see in there."

"I can't just let her die, Carter! I could never live with myself!" "When I went to the bathroom my parallel self must have appeared from behind a tree and caught Brooke's attention.

"Carter, they're getting stronger . . ." Jackson put his hands up to his mouth. I heard a twig snap from a distance behind me and I turned around and saw my parallel self emerge from the woods. "Why are we here?" he asked.

"I need to see who the fifth grave belonged to."

"Carter, I don't see a fifth grave."

We both watched as Brooke and the parallel Jackson came out of the woods a few yards from the car. She was screaming and covered in dirt while she looked around for us. Jackson and I appeared to be hidden behind a divide that was conjured up by the parallel Brooke and Jackson. We could see her but she couldn't see us. We were free to move around as we pleased but we would never meet her face to face. It was like a two-way mirror.

"Brooke!" Jackson yelled but his voice went right past her. He began running her direction while I was close behind.

We watched as the parallel Jackson's eyes changed and went to his real, normal ones; that was something we never knew the demons could do. He said something to her and caught her attention. She turned around and looked at him. Confused, she stopped running and stood still.

"Brooke, are you okay? He said. "Did you see where he went off to?"

She remained quiet, traumatized even. He took another step closer.

Before Jackson and I got too close to the divide, I told him to stop running.

"Why?" said Jackson, out of breath.

"What if this is a trap? What if they've set this entire thing up and they're trying to get us closer to them. What if that's not Brooke?"

He opened his mouth to counter but closed it and said nothing. He held his clenched fists at his side. The both of us stood a good twenty yards away.

The parallel Jackson continued, "Brooke, I know you must be freaking out, but this, this is really me." Tears formed in his eyes. "I still love you and want to be with you. You're my best friend. Don't you think that we can get passed what happened?" He held out his arms welcoming her for a hug.

"Brooke, don't!" The real Jackson screamed.

"I'm tired of this. I'm so scared." She began crying as she walked up to Jackson and met him for the embrace. He hugged her tight while his eyes reverted back to white circles. The parallel Brooke came out of nowhere and drug a knife straight through Brooke's back. The parallel Jackson then pushed her deeper into the knife. She let out a scream as she fell from the other Jackson's embrace. She landed on her back and looked up at the two of them while blood ran down the sides of her mouth. Seconds went by as Brooke quickly bled to death.

"Oh my God. Brooke . . ." Jackson whispered. Brooke was now one with parallel Brooke as she stood up and wiped the blood off her mouth. Her eyes were instantly white and we watched as she and Jackson charged at us.

"Come on, let's go to the car!" I yelled as we both started running to Jackson's vehicle. We accidently dropped our flashlights but didn't care. We hopped in and started the car, making our way out of the cemetery. I turned down the gravel road and stepped on the gas.

"Where are we going?" Jackson asked, trying to keep his composure.

"In my Parallel, they took me to a church. I'm pretty

sure it was my old church that my family and I went to. I think we can find answers there. I can find out what my brother did."

"Carter, that church has been abandoned for over ten years; no one is going to be there."

I ignored his comment and continued to drive, cautiously looking behind me and in the rearview mirror. "Jackson, what did you see earlier tonight?" The car was silent and he looked out the window.

"Just something we promised to never talk about," he mumbled.

"Dude, you can be honest with me. I just want to know what you went through. I'm here for you, Jackson. Always."

He started to get antsy and looked uncomfortable. I tried to think about what we promised to never talk about. As I ran through our past, I remembered what it was.

"Jackson—"

"I'm not gay. Can we drop this?" he harshly asked.

"I don't think that, I never have. I just want to know what they showed you."

"It doesn't matter."

"It does matter, Jackson. Our friends are dead because of what that stupid place showed them. They're showing us our past and all the trials that have been hard for us. Whatever internal demons you're fighting, you don't have to fight alone."

"Carter, I don't know the life I'll have if I leave the old Jackson behind."

"Being gay is not a sin and it is certainly not a demon. You battling with your thoughts about your sexual orientation, that is the demon. They are using that against you because it makes you weak. You haven't come to terms with what your parallel self already knows or doesn't know."

He bit his lip as his mouth trembled. "I'm not . . . I can't be gay. I don't know how to live my life in that way. What would my parents think? What would—"

"Jackson, I'm your best friend, always have been. No matter who you decide to bring home and date has nothing to do with our friendship. I want you to be the happiest guy alive and if another guy does that for you, then so be it. You don't have to admit or accept anything now or even tomorrow. Just know that I'll always be here for you and that a sexual orientation doesn't define you. And it certainly isn't a sin."

He remained silent and looked pained. I looked ahead as the old church came into view. Shards from broken windows caught the headlights, and I saw decaying bricks, glass, and shingles scattered around it. Loose shingles hung off the eaves, and parts of the roof had caved in. The 1930s-era white siding had lost its glow. I pulled into the gravel driveway, and the old oak trees cast shadows along the ground and the side of the church. It was exactly how I pictured it and how the town left it.

"I can't keep doing this, Carter," Jackson said.

"Can't keep doing what?"

"I can't keep seeing dead bodies." Tears began to form in his eyes. "I'm not like you. I just watched my girlfriend take a knife to the back and watched her bleed out. I can't just put it behind me. I need time. I need closure. I don't want to go into that church and watch my best friend lose his mind and his life. *I* don't want to go in there and lose my mind and my life."

His words hung in the air. The moonlight shined down on half of his face, and I could see his hands were trembling and he was breathing heavily. Jackson looked exhausted.

"Jackson, this isn't easy for me either. I don't know what I'm doing, but I do know that our time is running out. So, the only thing for me—we—to do is to keep moving forward. I don't have much of a plan, but all I need is a little faith that I'm hoping we can find inside that church."

"You're not going to die in there," Jackson promised me.

"Neither are you."

I parked the car but left it running so it could shed light into the church. We both stepped out and made our way to the front doors, walking up the crumbling cement steps. We pushed open the doors, and the aroma of must and mildew filled the air. Rotten wood was all that remained of the broken rafters and pews. Cobwebs hung from the ceiling and covered the pews so thickly it looked like the first snowfall of the year.

The headlights shone through an unbroken stained glass window, casting a rainbow of vibrant colors across the church. We slowly started to walk forward, hearing the weak wooden floor moan beneath us. The church was exactly the same one in my parallel universe. The confession box was worn down, and the pews looked like they were about to collapse at any second. Animal feces were scattered all over the floor. An eerie feel that we weren't alone hung in the air.

"Hello?" I called out. The only thing that answered back was silence.

"Carter, they're going to find us," Jackson said.

Shadows seemed to move from the other side of the stained-glass windows, but it was too difficult to make out what it was.

"We just need to look around for a little bit." I continued to walk forward. "If these really are demons, maybe we can get a priest's blessing. We need anything we can get."

"So you chose to go to an abandoned church for that?" Jackson acted insulted.

"This place was in my parallel and I had a hunch we wouldn't be the only ones in here. I don't know. I felt like the other me wanted me to come here."

"Must be a pretty strong hunch." Jackson grumbled.

We made our way farther into the church, but there was no sign of anyone being up here. We went up onto the altar and I walked into the sacristy behind it.

Old, half-burnt candles were stuck on the tables like gum. Old newspaper articles littered a table, and bible verses were engraved into the wood. But I saw no sign of recent activity.

"Hey, there's a staircase to the basement right here," Jackson called. I walked out of the room and saw Jackson staring down the stairs in the corner of the church. I made my way over to him and peered down them with him. For a split second, it looked like my old priest was at the bottom of the stairs, looking at us from around the corner. I blinked and he was gone. The sense of foreboding and negative energy within the church told me to get the hell out of there, but I had to be valiant.

"Carter, we are not going down there," Jackson told me.

The headlights on the car went out and we were left in the dark, eerie church.

"We don't have a choice." I carefully found my way back to the sacristy and grabbed a candle, lit it, and rejoined Jackson.

"Where's your phone?" Jackson asked me while taking out his and turning on the flashlight feature.

I felt around my pockets but it wasn't in any of them. "I left mine in the car, I think. I took a step down the stairs, but Jackson grabbed my arm to stop me. "We have to be brave," I said.

Hesitant, Jackson joined me on the step and we began going down the rest of the cement stairs. When we got to the bottom and turned the corner, we encountered a wooden table in an open, dingy room. If I remembered right, this used to be the room for kids' Sunday school.

What looked like the priest was sitting down at the

table with his back toward us, murmuring about something. He wore a black gown, and his thinned-out brown hair seemed home to a few gray ones as well. The candlelight danced on the walls, showing us other doorways and decayed debris covering the floor. The smell of the basement was not only of mold and mildew, but of death.

Jackson shook his head in fear. "Carter, we are not going to talk to him," he whispered harshly. "We are going to leave." Jackson's voice trembled with every word.

Ignoring him, I walked to the front of the table to look straight at the priest. Jackson eventually made his way over to me. The priest was looking down at the table, still mumbling nonsense, and I noticed a small puddle of blood form by his hands. It looked like blood was dripping from his nose.

"Father David?" I called out.

He immediately stopped whispering and he tilted his head up and looked up at us. His eyes seemed bloodshot, and his irises looked faded. Deep wrinkles covered his face, and sorrow as dark as the blue in his eyes masked the rest of his look.

He slowly stood up from his chair, and my heart almost flew out of my chest. I hardly recognized him as the priest. He looked more sinister now than he did in my

Parallel.

"We need your help," I continued. "Demons have been coming after us and our friends, and now they're dead, and we don't think they're going to stop until they become us."

"You shouldn't be here," Father David said in a deep, raspy voice.

"We have nowhere to go; we don't know what to do!" Jackson fumed, clearly impatient with the priest.

"They're going to wear you down, one by one, until you can't fight them anymore."

"Father, my brother left this journal telling us what he discovered and what happened to him," I said, "but it doesn't tell us how to stop them or where they came from."

He took the candle from the table and started walking away from us. For a split second I saw my and Jackson's parallel selves on the steps, but in an instant they were gone. Dread washed over me, and the feeling of us being safe was gone.

"I can't help you," he added. Jackson and I slowly walked around the table and carefully followed him into the other room. We watched as wax dripped off the candle and onto Father David's hand, singeing his flesh. His neck twitched from side to side and then stopped.

"Why can't you help us?" I asked.

"I'm not an exorcist," he spat.

"We're not asking for one. All we're asking for is some help or answers that can help us stop this," Jackson lashed out.

"You can't."

"What do you mean we can't?" I asked.

A swift breeze came rushing down into the basement, making the flame on the candle dance. Goosebumps covered my skin and my hair fell back on my forehead. Jackson and I exchanged worried looks as the air dropped in temperature. Father David turned back around and faced us, the light from the candle casting shadows on his half-lit face and on the walls.

He turned and looked behind him at an old, rustic-looking mirror pushed up against the wall. Cobwebs and dust covered parts of the glass, as the mirror looked as old as he did.

"For years I would come down here and pray, right in front of this mirror. I would pray to keep my soul, pray for forgiveness, pray to see the sun rise again, but what I got was worse. You can't just expect the past to go away like a faded memory. The past is permanent and it will follow you. For years I tried hiding my past, hiding what would keep me up at night, hiding every trace of the mistakes I committed. Until one day I saw myself in the mirror, but the reflection was not mine. That mirror is a gateway to my hell. Everything that makes me human was reflected back at me. And so I go there, I go to where my worst fears and sins are held. I go back and back and feed off what they give me so they can feed off me in return. Truth is, I don't know why I'm still fighting. I can feel them under my skin like it's burning my insides, but my body is cold to the touch. I'm forgetting who I am and what I look like. I sit in the dark hoping that they won't see me, and as exhausted as I am, I keep fighting, but the closer they get the weaker I become." He sighed. "What's the point? I'm old enough to be dead."

"Where did these demonic entities come from?" I asked him.

"According to legend, it goes way back to when the first sin was committed, which caused the universe to split in two: our world and theirs. We were born with four arms and four legs, but due to the splitting of the worlds we were split, as well, to be rid of sins and demons, forced to find our other half. So for centuries, our demon selves have been searching for us, to become us. They stay dormant until we err and hide the things that we can't get over; actions that cause us the most pain and strife, actions that destroy the most vulnerable lines that run through us. Parallel is their sanctum, their home, but it's also home to our demons and sins, the ones that we feed. Parallel doesn't lie. But be careful, for it is our minds that make up the rest."

"Wait, but if they're just entities and if they need a body to inhabit, what if there's no body to possess? Where would they go?" I asked.

"I would assume they would be obliterated. These battles that we're facing, they have nothing to do with God."

"Isn't there a way we can refuse to give up our body to them?" Jackson asked.

"Even if Parallel is destroyed, they already have their marks on you. You can't be unseen, and they're not going to stop until they become whole with you again."

"So just like that, there's no way to save ourselves?" I asked.

"We're all sinners; we're all going to sin, that's inevitable. To be saved, you can be baptized in fire and the holy spirit."

"So, if you burn the bodies, the demons have nowhere else to go," I mumbled.

Jackson and I watched as what appeared to look like

black tendrils crawl up the priest's skin. It looked like his veins were alive and moved around underneath his skin. Behind us, the old mirror began to crack and fall apart. Father David's eyes were even more discolored whiter than before.

"You need to go," he told us.

"Wait!" I said, while Jackson pulled my arm to get away from the priest. "My older brother, Alex, he came and saw you. I saw him in my Parallel; he was talking to you about the sin he committed."

"I remember."

"What did he do?"

"He accidently caused someone's death."

"Who?"

"Years ago, he killed Spencer."

"Who's Spencer?"

He began twitching involuntarily, switching back and forth from his human self to who he was becoming. With pursed lips, he scoffed and answered, "His younger brother."

Chapter 18

"What did you say?" My stomach churned and my head spun as I tried to make sense of what he just said. *His younger brother? That would make him my older brother, as well.* I never knew I had another older brother. My mouth grew dry and his bitter words hung in the air.

He cackled sadistically and threw his head back, causing bones to break in his neck. "Spencer died before you were born."

"Carter, let's get out of here." Jackson tugged on my arm and we walked out of the back room and headed toward the stairs. As we ran up the stairs, I looked back and saw myself sitting at the table, watching us. He was getting closer to me.

Reaching the top, I jumped off the priest altar and began running down the aisle, Jackson right behind me. All of a sudden the floor started to break beneath us. The snapped wood tripped me and sent me tumbling forward into a pew, and Jackson broke through.

"Help!" Jackson cried out as he tried frantically to grab hold of the floor. Only his chest, arms, and head remained above the wood.

Pain shot up my arm, which had landed on the edge of the pew, as I quickly got up and ran to aid my best friend. I grabbed his arms, but that made the floor crack and break even more from the added weight. I heard a sinister laugh and looked up to see my parallel self come up around the corner from the stairs.

"Come on, get me up!" Jackson pleaded.

"I'm trying, but you're slipping," I said as I gritted my teeth and continued to tug.

Jackson let out a blood-curdling scream as he was pulled downward. I jolted forward from the force of the pull and tried my best to keep both of us above the floor.

"Carter, they're grabbing me!"

"I'm not letting you go!" I heard the parallel me grow closer, laughing as he watched us struggle. I grunted from exertion as I tried to get Jackson out of the hole, but the strain of his weight began to exhaust me. I pulled and pulled, but all of a sudden a voice stopped me.

"You didn't really love me, Jackson." I turned my head and saw Brooke coming down the aisle. Blood dripped down her mouth and the back of her legs. Her chest had been oozing out blood from where the knife went through. Her bright white eyes pierced into us.

Seeing her so close to me made me jump, and Jackson

dropped a few inches farther into the hole.

"You're right." It was Jackson's voice, only it didn't come from him. The parallel Jackson was right behind me now, pulling one of my arms off and away from Jackson, leaving me to hold onto him with only one arm. Brooke had repositioned herself and tried helping the parallel Jackson. She started pulling the same arm as he was. I let out a cry as pain shot up my arm, burning my muscles and tendons. The other Jackson tried to pull me away as Father David continued to pull Jackson down from below.

"Carter!" Jackson called out. I kicked parallel Jackson away, and he stumbled backward. He released my arm as he fell to the floor, breaking it beneath him and sending him and Brooke tumbling to the basement below.

With both my arms and all my might, I steadily and carefully pulled Jackson out of the hole until he got one of his knees free. He then used that knee to push up and get his other leg free. I helped him stand up but the force made him fall into me, but I caught him and held him up. I gave him a big hug and we carefully made our way out of the church and back to the car.

"Carter, where are we supposed to go?" Jackson asked, trying to catch his breath. I pulled out of the driveway, sped off, and got back onto the main road.

"I have to find where they buried Spencer. I mean, I can't believe my ears." My hands trembled as I tried to keep my composure behind the wheel.

"You're really going to believe that old, senile priest?"

"Jackson, I don't know what else my brother would have talked about with him, let alone why my Parallel would show me five graves. This is all fucked up, but it could be accurate."

"Yeah, but why would your Parallel show you what Alex did?"

"To tell me that he killed our other brother!"

"It's just strange to me that you've gone all your life not knowing you had an older brother." Jackson bit his lip. "We need to find out how to stop them, Carter. We're going to die like this. And if the priest can't save us and if he said this fight isn't with God, then I don't know what else to do."

Jackson's comment got me thinking. I collected my thoughts and went through my own personal timeline. My memory flashed to when they took me to Parallel. My mother was bloody from the waist down; as if she had a miscarriage . . .

"My mother had a miscarriage before I was born." I said.

"And after Alex was born?"

I nodded. "My parents brought it up once to me years ago. And for some reason I was told to not talk about it to Alex."

"Why would that be?"

"It traumatized him. He was only a few years old at the time. I think Alex believed he killed his younger brother."

"How?"

"I don't know. But I have an idea of how to end this. Jackson . . . I know what we have to do," I realized.

"What?"

"He said 'I will baptize you in fire.' So I think, Jackson . . . we need to burn our friends."

"Carter, what are you talking about?"

The cold truth made me sound heartless. "Jackson, think about it. Our friends are just going to keep coming after us. That's not them—they're not living, and their demons are just going to stay in their bodies because they need them as a host. They can't survive without a body. We can set them free."

The car grew silent, and for a split second I actually thought I was going crazy. But I did think that was best for all of us; for them. To set them free. And I didn't know what else to do. We're running out of time.

"Carter . . . I just don't know about that. That seems so fucked up. No matter what happens in the end, you know nothing is ever going to be the same again."

I started to realize the drive was taking longer than I expected. We were still on a gravel road in the middle of nowhere. I wasn't sure if our conversation distracted me, but this all seemed unrecognizable. Getting antsy, I began digging around my pocket for my phone to use its GPS.

"Do you see that?" Jackson asked. His tone was flat from fear. I took my hand from my pocket and directed my eyes back to the road.

"See what?"

Jackson pointed. "There, on the side of the road." His eyes never moved, which made me not want to look. I swallowed hard and moved my eyes in the direction of his finger.

On the side of the road was a dark figure dressed in an all black, hooded robe and walking away from us. It was the coldest night of the year so far, and that was definitely not enough to keep warm. The movements were stiff, and the person walked with purpose but no direction. There weren't any houses for miles and it was almost one in the morning. Why were they out here?

"Should I pull over and ask if they need help?"

Jackson looked at me like I was crazy. "Fuck no. And even if tonight didn't happen, I would still say fuck no. No one should be out here by themselves this late, and especially not dressed like that."

I didn't respond and kept driving, leaving the mysterious dark figure in my rearview mirror. Jackson and I both tried to get a good look at their face, but it was too dark to see anything. My heartbeat slowly lowered the farther away we got. My grip on the steering wheel was so tight I could see the whites in my knuckles. I just wanted to be home. After a few left turns, I saw what looked like a highway in the far distance. *Thank God.*

"No fucking way . . ." Jackson sat straight up in his seat as we both saw the hooded figure again. "Carter, you need to drive."

"Did we just go in a circle?"

"Carter, please get us out of here." I pushed the pedal down farther but was careful not to speed too much, as the gravel was loose. I made a few more turns and started to feel better the farther from the figure we got. Our surroundings looked familiar, but I wasn't sure if I really knew where we were. Five minutes went by and the gravel roads continued. They never ran this long. Something wasn't right.

Chills ran up my spine and took the breath right out of my mouth as I brought the car to a screeching halt. The hooded figure was back, but walking our way this time. When the car stopped, so did they. I drowned out Jackson's horrified, demanding questions as I crept slowly toward the figure. There was no way any of this was possible. I had to see who it was. My foot hovered over the gas pedal, prepared to fly out of here, and I made sure the doors were locked. I rolled down Jackson's window, for the person was on his side of the road.

"Carter, what the fuck are you doing? Roll up my window!" Jackson leaned toward the middle of the car, scooting as far away as possible from the rolled-down window. The figure was now by the right-side headlight. All I needed was to drive one more foot. "Carter, please stop, I don't want to know who it is!" I drowned out his cries and my quickened heartbeat and drove until the figure was right next to Jackson's window. They were too tall to be human and their head went above the car. The scene was unnerving, and my instincts told me something was off with everything from the road to this figure. "Carter!" Jackson tried rolling up his window, but I had locked it. I leaned down, trying to get a good angle to look at the face, when Jackson stopped me.

"Carter, look . . ."

I looked out the windshield and saw something that made my stomach do flips and my blood run cold. I had made a horrible mistake stopping here. In the near distance stood the church. It was like we drove in circles just to come back here. But I knew it wasn't me who took us back here. The figure by the window was gone when I looked again, but we weren't alone. Shadowy figures moved around throughout the trees, and humanoid creatures circled the church. A loud humming noise reverberated through the air like a choir. They were all humming to a dark, deep tune. Everything seemed backward. It looked like we had driven into a parallel universe, or that our two worlds were merging. I couldn't tell if this was real of if they were playing with our minds. The church was on the wrong side of the road, and even though it was the middle of the night, it looked a lot darker.

Suddenly the four car doors flung open and the windows in the back shattered in a loud crescendo. Glass and our screams flew through the air. "Carter, get us out of here!" Jackson yelled at the top of his lungs, and in two seconds I turned us around and drove the opposite way.

It took us five minutes to get back to the main highway, the time it should have taken us originally. I didn't know what we saw or where we were, but it seemed like we crossed the line between our world and theirs. We drove to my house in silence, our hearts in our mouths.

"I'm just so upset." Jackson pouted as he folded his arms. "I now have so many windows to replace and this wouldn't have happened if I would have driven! Seriously, Carter, you're never driving my car again."

Arriving at my house, we ran inside, and I went to my room where I kept Alex's belongings and started going through them again.

"What are you doing?"

"I'm trying to see if there are any clues about Spencer and if there are any records on him. Could you hand me my laptop quick?" I asked, pointing to it and continuing to skim through Alex's journal and the box he left for me.

Jackson handed me my laptop and I quickly logged on and went to the obituaries to search for Spencer. I asked Jackson if he could read through my brother's journal again to try to find any hidden messages or clues. He shook his head, gave me his unnecessary cocky grin, and read through it.

"Carter, I don't think your mother's miscarriage would be in the obituaries.

"You never know."I continued to search. Before I

came across anything I needed, a familiar cackle went through the air. I stood up and looked around the living room until I saw my parallel self down the hallway. He was next to the mirror I shattered. Jackson and I quickly looked around to make sure no other parallel demons were around.

"Let me show you what your brother did." He smirked as he put the pieces of the mirror back together. All he did was look at it and it was magically back intact.

I walked closer to the mirror while Jackson tried grabbing my arm. I shook his hand off of me until I was content with where I stood. The parallel me didn't leave the side of the mirror as I watched a few feet away.

The glass lit up like a TV and it began showing us an unfamiliar scene. My mother fell asleep on the couch while reading a book titled, *Becoming a Mother of Two*. The sound of a commercial was in the background. Her hair was long and curly; a style I never saw her wear. She was wearing the same exact white dress she was in my parallel. What appeared to be Alex as a three-year old came running into the living room holding a toy car in his grubby, left hand. He was trying to get her attention as Dad seemed to be in another room. Dropping his toy, Alex climbed on the couch and jumped on her, right over her stomach. She instantly woke up and groaned in pain while grabbing Alex and setting him on the floor in a quick motion. Alex lost his balance and knocked over a burning candle that was on the coffee table.

She winced in the pain as she held her arms close to her belly. She called out to Dad not noticing the candle until a small flame caught on the white linen cover. Alex stood there crying not knowing what was going on. Dad came into the room and put out the small flames right away then comforted Mom.

The scene then took us to a hospital later that day and showed us Mom and Dad crying from the doctor's news, she must have been pregnant. My heart hurt for them. It hurt for all of them. They never told me the story, only the part where she had a miscarriage. The vision in the mirror ended and when I looked over the parallel me was gone. The glass in the mirror shattered once again and fell on the floor.

"It was all an accident . . ." I murmured.

"How would your brother remember that at his age?" Jackson asked.

"It was a traumatic moment in his life; in my parent's lives. I'm sure it was brought up between the three of them while he was growing up. That's not something you just sweep under a rug." I turned around and walked back into the living room.

"I guess I'm still confused on how an accident like that led to your brother's death."

"I have no idea, Jackson." I raised my voice.

"I know, Carter. There is so much to take in and it's hard to believe, but I'm here for you. I know there's not really any closure, and it's not like there's an easy way to go about what happened to him. But it makes sense why you didn't find a fifth grave, but were still showed one." Jackson sat next to me and put his hand on my shoulder.

"I know, but there has to be something more like you said. I am not understanding this—" I cut myself off, glancing at the picture of my brother and I that I found. And then it all hit me. I picked up the picture and looked at the back of it, rereading what my brother had written on it. *"Keep the ones you love hidden."*

"I know what we have to do next."

"You do? What?"

"What happened to my brother is still hidden; literally and metaphorically. I think something else is underneath his floorboards."

Jackson looked at the picture I was holding and made the connection as well. I knew what we had to do.

"Why do you think that?" he asked.

I shook my head and bit my lip. "I have no idea what but I know that something isn't finished. We have to finish what my brother started. I can only imagine what Alex went through, all the guilt, and his parallel self showing him time after time what he did. But something tells me that what the parallel me showed us was not the same story Alex believed. We're going back to Alex's apartment."

Jackson stood up and paced the floor while he talked. "Carter, this is hard, dealing with all of this. What have we gotten ourselves into, and what we will be getting ourselves into? I never would have thought it would be going down like this."

I walked up to Jackson and looked him in the eye. "Don't you give up on me, Jackson, not yet. We're going to make everything okay, okay? We're going to finish this and stop them. Do not let them win."

He nodded and reassured me that he wouldn't give up. I grabbed my car keys, getting ready to leave, when I noticed Jackson was still standing where I left him, staring down the hall. I followed his eyes and saw his parallel self staring back at us, giving us a wicked smirk.

"Come on, Jackson." I grabbed his arm.

"I thought your mirror broke?" He froze where he stood.

I pulled him away. "Don't look at it." I opened the door and we left my house, and headed toward Alex's old apartment.

***

"What if nothing is there?" Jackson asked me.

"Then we take this show somewhere else."

"Hey, forget something?" he asked, giving me his stupid old grin and holding glass bottles. He carefully placed them in a backpack.

"No, that's why you're carrying it." I shot him a grin back and walked to the fire escape ladder. Jackson threw the backpack over his arms and got ready. I began climbing up it first, and then stopped to look down at Jackson. "You don't have to do this."

"I want to. Besides, we're both already too far in to go back now." And with that being said, he followed me up the ladder. We made our way to the broken window and carefully climbed inside. "So, where is that floorboard?"

"In his room, right under where his bed used to be." I started to make my way over to the bedroom when I noticed a trail of white rose petals that led to a mirror in the living room that never used to be there. Looking back I remembered I had left a white rose at Alex's grave awhile ago. Was he doing this on purpose?

"Can I ask you something?" Jackson spoke.

"Of course," I said, turning my attention back toward him.

"How are you so strong? Like, all the time. You don't cry, you don't talk about how you feel about the past, you just keep moving forward. How do you do it?"

"I've learned to accept what is and not what it could have been. I'm okay with what has happened, even if it does hurt. And I've learned you have to not look behind you but at what lies ahead of you, even if you can't see it."

"Do you ever regret anything?"

"No. I try not to live life that way. Regretting things is wasted energy. You have to learn what means the most to you in life and what you can live without."

"Brooke was my everything and now she's gone, and our friends—" his voice cracked. "It's hard to believe and it's hard to cope with. They're not something I can live without. I'm not like you, and I'm sorry."

"I'm not saying I can live without those people. It was more a generalized statement. And I understand, but it's all going to—" A harsh knock at the front door interrupted us, making us jump back. We started making our way to the door when Jackson stopped me.

"Wait, don't open it!" The knock came again, only this

time it was more urgent and louder. I was almost to the door when Emily came out of nowhere from behind me and opened it. She stepped to the side and got out of the way. I took a step back as Alex ran in with what looked like someone's charred, smoking body. We watched as he ran into his bedroom and closed the door. Getting ready, Jackson took his backpack off and set it on the floor.

"What just happened?" Jackson asked, standing near the mirror. Before I could respond, arms came out of the mirror and started pulling him into the glass. "Carter, help!" he cried.

I quickly ran over to him and grabbed hold of his arms, but the force was too strong and I was starting to lose him. I looked behind him and saw an evil, sinister Jackson grabbing onto him, eagerly pulling him through. His dark, gruesome arms and hands wrapped around Jackson and I watched as his bony fingers dug into his neck and chest, latching on tightly. Jackson let out a painful cry and gripped onto me even tighter.

I lost my grip on Jackson and flew backward crashing into the floor. "Hold on a little longer, Jackson!" Adrenaline moving through my veins I stood up and went toward the backpack. I reached my hand in and pulled out a bottle. I turned around igniting the cloth and sent the

Molotov cocktail flying into the air. It smashed onto the floor, sending a wave of flames across the room and toward the front door as the other Jackson pulled him through the mirror.

"Noooo!" I cried. I ran to the mirror and pounded on the cruel glass, hoping I could make them come back. I heard Emily's screams as the flames engulfed her body. I turned and watched as she slowly fell to her knees before hitting the ground.

I ran toward my brother's room, dodging the flames. I opened the door and knelt by the floorboards where I earlier found the photos. I picked up the floorboards and set them aside and began digging through the crawlspace, taking more boards off and making the hole even bigger. I pulled out my cellphone and used its flashlight feature to shine down there, looking for anything, but it all seemed so bare.

As I kept looking under the floorboards, I heard the door shut behind me. I quickly turned around as Alex came up to me and pushed me into the hole. I fell down father than I thought I should be able to, hitting cold, hard cement at the bottom. I looked up and saw I fell about a good ten feet. I forgot fifth floor had higher ceilings, and more space, in between the sixth level.

I rolled over and groaned as I tried to get my breath back; the wind had been knocked out of me. I looked for my phone, and while I did, I started to hear this deep, eerie humming noise a few feet away from me. I heard bones cracking and feared I had found what I was looking for.

I found my phone and shined the light in the direction of the noise. I found the charred body, still smoking, and watched him slowly get up. I smelled burnt, rotting flesh, and saw his skin was starting to fall off his body. One of his eyes was completely burned away, and his other one had dark yellow pus in it with just a few dark veins going through it. His teeth were a dark wooden brown, and only a few hairs remained on his head.

"Who are you?" I asked petrified.

He let out a deep cackle and started to stand up. "I know what you're thinking, and you're right: underneath the floor, no one can hear you scream."

Chapter 19

I started backing away, looking for a way out of this hole. I tried jumping up and down, reaching for anything to grab onto. His laughter taunted me as he watched me struggle to get out.

"I'm Spencer."

"How can that be? You were never born."

"No, but it was Alex who created me." He belted out laughter.

"What do you mean?" My back was now pressed up against the wall.

"Alex was traumatized by what he did when he was younger so his mind made up a different way to help cope with his stress. At that age he had no idea what a miscarriage was." Spencer said. "He had flashbacks to our mother's pain and saw the fire he started on the coffee table. So what did kid Alex do? He created this fictional story of me burning to death. He got it in his head that a small fire was what killed me. He pictured me like this." Spencer flew his hands up and watched me take everything in. "He buried his little secret not only in the back of his mind but underneath these floorboards."

"You're not real. This isn't possible."

"It's ironic. Your brother killed me, but it was I who killed him on the inside. He grew up with all this guilt and dread and believed a story that never happened. But I am real. I am your brother's demon. I am your brother's sin."

"You don't have another half so there's no way you can be here."

"Our brother believed in his story so much that his parallel self conjured up me as well; making me come to life in the parallel world. I became a part of your brother." He tilted his head and stared at me.

"How did you get down here?" I asked.

"Once Alex broke the barrier between the worlds, his parallel self brought me through, and came here to hide me underneath these floors. I waited until the time was right for you to find out the truth about me. All those times you smelled me but had no idea what and where it was coming from. And now you know how strong Parallel really is."

He started to walk closer to me, looking more and more satanic. His eyes started to change, and anger grew across his face. More of his skin started to slowly fall off his body. His bones showed through the rotten flesh in his arms and legs, and even his jawbone became more visible.

"Now come give your older brother a hug." He opened

his arms and moved in closer. I quickly jumped up and grabbed a hold of a two-by-four and started hoisting myself up. Spencer grabbed my leg, but I kicked him away and climbed on top of the plank. I reached up and grabbed the sturdier floorboards around me, using my upper-body strength to hoist myself up and out of the floor.

I got half of my body out when Spencer latched onto my legs and began pulling himself up. I could feel his flaky, dry skin brush against my legs as he gripped tighter onto me. I started dragging myself across the floor, slowly inching my way out of the hole, with Spencer still on my legs. Spencer was only about four feet tall but had more strength than anyone could guess. He could move faster and grip tighter than anyone I know.

I turned to look over my shoulder and started kicking him, trying to get him off me. I kicked him in the shoulder and watched as the force sent him back down the hole. I quickly finished dragging myself out and onto the solid floor, when all of a sudden Spencer popped up out of the hole and pulled himself up as well.

I ran to the door and opened it but before I could get out, I felt him latch onto my arm, dragging me back toward him.

He pulled me down closer to his mouth and breathed

into my ear, and I could feel his warm, humid breath on my neck as he said, "Add one more demon to your list."

The flames had made their way into the room. I reached for something to get him off of me. My eyes darted to a burning plank dangling the ceiling, and I wrenched it free, bringing it over my head and onto Spencer's, causing him to fall off my back.

He grunted as he hit the floor, but I didn't stop there. I walked over to him and shoved the burning plank into his abdomen. He screeched in pain as fire crawled across his body. I went back over to the door as I heard him stand up and begin running toward me. I ran out of the room first, slamming the door behind me. He screamed as he tried to bash the door open, but the sounds died thirty seconds later as I heard his body hit the floor. I took a short moment to catch my breath, though it was difficult with all the black smoke in the air. I noticed more breathing and whispering behind me. I slowly turned around and saw the fire engulfed most of the room, and flames danced up the walls.

The blaring sounds of smoke detectors on the floor and in this unit flooded the air. The noise of fire trucks could be heard in the distance. Noises of residents' screams and panic rang through the whole building as they tried to run to safety. I had put everyone's lives in danger but I didn't care. I had to finish this. I had to save the souls of my friends and family.

A few feet away from me I saw my parents and Alex staring at me. It looked like they were standing in the flames themselves. They wore their evil smirks. In the background I heard the familiar humming noise begin. I couldn't tell if they were doing it or if I was.

"Welcome home," my brother said.

"Bring Jackson back," I demanded.

They all cackled and tilted their heads, as if in confusion.

"Bring him back!" I yelled.

"What's wrong? Because if he dies, then you're really all alone?" my mother asked.

I looked around and saw Brooke sitting in the corner, on fire, just watching me. Jade was hanging from the ceiling fan, with flames going up her body. Dallas was lying on the kitchen floor surrounded by flames and a puddle of blood from his neck.

"You can't get rid of us," Alex said. "We're your demons now." His eyes burned with hatred and a snarl spread across his face.

Pieces of the floor started to crumble beneath us and bits of the ceiling crashed to the floor. I had to get out of here or I was going to die with them.

All at once they began to chant, "Thy kingdom come, thy will be done on earth as it is in heaven."

"Let him go!" I yelled. The mirror shattered and Jackson was hurled out onto the floor. The humming immediately stopped, and the sound of the crackling fire took over. Jackson coughed up a little blood, and his arms and face were scratched up. I ran over to him and helped him up.

"Look around you," Alex hissed. "You really think this will ever end? Your sins and demons will always find you. They will always catch up with you. It's because we're human. Well, we were."

Jackson and I stumbled toward the window, trying to dodge the flames that engulfed the apartment. I was coughing so much that my chest and throat started to ache. My lungs had a hard time taking in air. Jackson and I tried to see our way out through the smoke and haze.

All of our friends' bodies were burning. It was a painful sight to see, even though they were already dead. We came here to find the rest of the truth but unfortunately, it hadn't gone so peacefully.

I looked back at my family. My parents' bodies were all beaten up, like they were the night of their accident.

Blood and pus oozed out of my mother's cracked-open skull, and my father's forehead was cut open and his nose bled.

"This isn't real . . ." I mumbled.

"Carter, it's always been real." I turned around and saw my parallel self grab Jackson, throwing him out of the window and to the hard ground below.

"Noooo!" I yelled. My parallel self grabbed me next, bringing my arms around to my back as I clenched my teeth in pain.

"It only hurts for a little bit," Alex taunted.

I felt my parallel's cold, rotten breath brush up against my ear as he said, "Come on, Carter, let me in." His slimy tongue ran across my neck and up to my ear. He let out a sinister cackle.

"We can all be together soon," my father said. "Just feed your demons."

In the deepest tone of voice I ever heard from myself, the other me yelled, "GIVE ME YOUR SOUL!"

The floor continued to burn around us, and I could no longer breathe. I began coughing, and my eyes burned from the dryness and the heat.

"It's going to be okay, Carter. Haven't you ever played with yourself before?" Alex chuckled. The other me started pulling me across the room, away from the window and toward me family.

"You're getting weaker," the parallel me taunted.

Bits of the ceiling continued to fall around us, and I heard sirens in the near distance. My body was starting to burn, but I wasn't sure if it was from the fire or from the other me trying to get inside. I watched as the flames started to envelop my family, their flesh starting to melt off. They all looked at me and smiled. Beads of sweat started to drip down my forehead, and I grew exhausted. I couldn't tell if I was passing out or dying. I used the rest of my strength to push myself away and took a few steps back. I almost lost my balance as the floor continued to break beneath my feet.

I got ready as the parallel me started to come my way and I threw my fist at him, hitting him across his face and sending him back and onto the floor. A smirk formed as he looked up and an evil glare filled his eyes as he quickly stood and charged right at me.

We both hit the ground and rolled a few times, each of us trying to stay on top. He ended up on me and started to wrap his bony fingers and hands around my throat, closing off my air. I was legitimately scared to look at myself and see such an evil, crazy face. I never knew I could look like

371

that.

"No more running. No more hiding behind that mirror of yours. I have finally found you," the other me spat. I could feel myself grow weaker as my vision deteriorated and I became light headed. He got right down in my face and stared at me with his moon-colored eyes, smirking.

I brought my hands up and pierced my thumbs through his eyes, giving me enough time and energy to push him up and off me. I got up but before I ran too far, he grabbed my leg and dragged me back down, crawling on top of me and pushing me into the ground. The scorching hot floor began burning my face. I clenched my jaw as I let out a painful grunt. The floor creaked and cracked below us. My stomach was in knots and my heartbeat quickened.

I saw feet to the side of me and heard a heavy object bash into the parallel me's head. He went flying off me, and I rolled over and saw that Jackson had come back for me. I reached out for his hand and grabbed onto it as he helped me up. We made it back over to the window, and I looked over once more at my family. They were burning, but they never took their evil, soulless eyes off me.

The two of us climbed down the ladder and landed on the safe, hard ground below, taking deep breaths of fresh air. Fire trucks were already parked with water spraying away. Screams and sobs filled the parking lot as policemen began taking names. Jackson and I exchanged glances and started walking back to my car.

"I thought you were dead so many times," I admitted.

"I thought I was, too." He let out a little chuckle in relief.

"Thank you for coming back for me."

"You know how many times you did that for me?" He gave me a grin. "I just figured you'd be pissed if I didn't so . . ."

Despite all we'd just gone through, I couldn't have been happier. My family and friends were at peace. I didn't really know what was next or what any of this meant, but I had a good feeling we had gotten rid of their demons and put them to rest.

***

I lay down in my bed and groaned as I saw the sun would be coming up rather soon. The noise of the shower running helped soothe me and almost put me to sleep. For some reason, it made me feel safe.

I called out to Jackson, "Hey, if you don't mind me asking, what did you see when you went back into Parallel?"

He didn't answer me, but I thought maybe the running

water was too loud. I let the question go until I started to hear mumbling come from the bathroom. I got up and made my way over to the bathroom door, laying my ear on it and trying to listen as best as I could.

"It's a lie. I love Brooke. No one else. It was one kiss and it didn't mean anything," Jackson said. Who was he talking to? I tried to see if I could hear anything else come from the bathroom, but it only seemed to be his voice. "Dead, dead, dead. Get out, get out." The humming tune came back, only this time it was from Jackson.

I had taken a step back from the door when it opened. Jackson stood in the doorway smiling at me, only in his underwear. He stepped out of the bathroom and into the hallway with me. I turned to go back to my room and noticed myself in the mirror down the hall. The mirror was put back together once more but that's not what got me. My heart dropped as I realized I was the only one reflected in the mirror. I turned back and looked at Jackson, who was still smiling at me.

"You okay?" he asked me. Water dripped down his body and onto the hardwood floor.

"Yeah, I just need to go to the bathroom," I lied.

"It's all yours." He stepped out of the way so I could go in. I did my thing and took a quick breath and walked back out. I found Jackson rummaging through my fridge, looking for something to eat.

"Oh, hey, dude, I'm sorry but I haven't gone grocery shopping in a few weeks. I don't think anything is good in there," I said. "If you want, we can head somewhere to get breakfast."

"No, it's all good," he said, taking out a gallon of expired milk. As he set it on the counter and unscrewed the top, I saw chunks move around in it. "I just wanted something to drink."

"Jackson, that milk is expired," I said. He nonetheless brought the gallon of milk up to his mouth and started gulping it down. He set the jug back down and wiped his face off with the back of his hand, removing the curdled milk there.

"It tasted fine to me." He then went and sat down on a chair in the living room, and started looking from side to side and then up at the ceiling. "Man, I can hear them move around. Doesn't it ever get annoying living with those noises?"

"What noises?"

"Nevermind. I didn't know you had a record player," Jackson said, humming to a nonexistent tune.

"I don't." Goosebumps started to crawl across my

arms. I watched as Jackson shivered multiple times.

"I shiver every time they touch me." His voice seemed a little deeper now.

"Jackson, are you okay?"

"I'm fine, Carter," he said firmly. "We had a crazy night. I'm exhausted. We should go to bed."

I watched him get up and head toward my room, but before he went down the hallway, he stopped for a few moments, staring at the corner of the living room. He finally went into my room, and I heard him get situated under the covers.

I made my way down the hall cautiously and walked into my bedroom. I noticed the curtains covered the windows now and the room was dark except for a little bit of light from my alarm clock.

"Did you close the curtains?" I asked him, wondering if I did it earlier without realizing.

"Yeah, I didn't want to be woken up by anything, ya know? Having windows is like having a gateway into our life. But you would already know that." He gave me a familiar, subtle grin.

I ignored his comment and got into bed with him, but stayed as far away from him as possible. I kept one of my legs out from underneath the covers in case I needed to get out and sleep elsewhere. Normally the sheets were cool to the touch, but when I touched them it was as if I placed my body onto ice. Immediately my skin grew numb and my body trembled.

I kept waking up to the feeling that he was watching me sleep, whether I was rolled over facing the opposite direction or on my back. Sometimes I caught him shiver in his sleep, and a few times he mumbled about how he had no place to go. I was almost asleep again when I heard him roll around and sit up on the edge of the bed.

"I'm so cold . . ." he whispered. He started rubbing his skin and rolling his neck around. I listened as he got up and began walking around my room.

I carefully turned my head so I could get a good look at what he was doing. He went over to a picture I had of the two of us on my dresser, and he picked it up and started laughing at it.

"You know, it's funny to think that when you look at something it makes you think of something else. I hardly remember who the person is in this picture. What I *do* remember is one time when I was little I got sick. I coughed so much I broke three ribs, and they never seemed to heal properly."

I watched as he looked down at his abdomen and

started feeling the bones, which were sticking out farther than usual. He pushed his palms down on his ribs and tried forcing them to go back to how they should be, and I heard snapping and crunching noises. The sounds made me wince, but Jackson's face didn't move a muscle.

"I was sick enough that my mom took me to the ER. I was cold, always cold. I remember fading in and out of consciousness and when I blacked out I was greeted by something; a man, perhaps, maybe more than just one, but maybe something else. He told me I had to leave, that I wasn't allowed to be there and that something went wrong. I was sad. I didn't want to leave, so I asked them if I could come back. They told me when I was ready. Then I started feeling warm again. And just like that, I woke up to what I thought was my mom and she saw what she thought was her son. And here I am."

He shot me a cynical look through the dark, and I felt an instant rush of chills through my body. He set the picture down and stomped out of my room. I was going to just lie in bed and let Jackson do whatever he wanted, but then I started to hear him rummage through cupboards and closets. It sounded like he was beginning to make a mess.

"Where is it?" he murmured. "To warm the soul." I got myself out of bed and found him in the kitchen, rummaging through the cupboards. I looked down at the floor and saw that pieces of Jackson's hair seemed to be falling out. As I got closer to him, a few lights in the house seemed to flicker. Something was off in the air and paranoia seeped in.

"Jackson, what are you looking for?" I asked him.

"I know you have it," he replied.

I looked over my shoulder at a mirror and saw that Jackson still wasn't showing up in it. I turned back around and noticed he was gone. None of this was adding up. What did Jackson see in his Parallel?

"It'll become you." I turned back around and saw my reflection talking to me. "We'll become one again."

I quickly left the view of the mirror and started looking around for Jackson, frantically going from room to room checking everywhere possible, but he was nowhere to be found. I went back to my room and sat down on my bed and took a deep breath. I was exhausted. I forgot what it was like to sleep. Just for a minute; one minute was all I wanted, to rest my head down and forget about what life had become and what it was going to be. I didn't care anymore. I wanted to help Jackson, but this was way over my head. My dark thoughts made me feel helpless, telling me not to help Jackson. My mind told me to go to bed and to wait till later. The sanity that was left told me that would be too late.

I spaced off, looking at the ground, when all of a sudden a burned hand came out from underneath the bed. I quickly stood up and moved away as I watched the hand slide back under. I slowly made my way back over to the bed and kneeled down. I found myself holding my breath as I started to grab the sheet to lift it up. I almost had the sheet lifted when I heard a loud crash come from the garage. I dropped the fabric and ran toward the noise.

I went into the garage and saw cans and boxes knocked over, my things spilled all over the floor. The garage door was open and Jackson was standing out in the driveway. I carefully made my way over to him, confused.

"Jackson, what are you doing out here? Let's go back inside." As I got closer, I saw that he was dripping wet from head to toe. He was standing in a puddle, and my mouth dropped open as I noticed an empty can of gasoline right next to him on the ground.

"I told you, I'm cold," Jackson said in a dry voice. I noticed that one of his eyes had faded in color. I brought my hand up to my mouth as I saw him holding a box of matches from my cupboards.

"Jackson, put down the matches. Let's get you cleaned

up. I can get you some blankets." I started walking closer to him.

"DON'T COME ANY CLOSER!" he warned. His voice kept changing from his normal one to a darker, more sinister one.

"Let me help you."

He shook his head and I started to see tears form in his eyes. "No, Carter, you can't help me. I am who I am."

"What do you mean by that?"

"I can't un-see what I saw. I don't want the life that it showed me. I'm not like that." His voice started to crack as a tear slid down his face. "I can't accept it. Not yet."

"It doesn't have to be like this! Jackson, fight it!"

"Our friends are all dead. They're all ashes now."

"Jackson, you're my best friend and I am not going to let you suffer like everyone else did. Jackson, don't leave me . . . I have no one else."

As he cried, he started to laugh manically, changing from his normal self to his demon side, then back and forth.

"I didn't want this," he cried. "Any of this. You're my best friend, Carter, but I can't accept my demons. I can't live like this. To live in fear, regret, pain, and everything else that kills you. Father David even said this isn't a battle with God. Carter, you're going to be just fine. You always have been." He sniffled as snot and tears ran off his face. He swallowed hard and gritted his teeth as he spoke once more. "The moment you let it in without actually accepting it is the moment you are no longer yourself."

"Fight your demons, Jackson," I pleaded. His hands shook as he held a match and the box. "Jackson, don't do this."

"It hurts. It hurts like hell. I feel like I'm being ripped apart as *he's* trying to claw his way out of me. It burns and all I hear are voices in my head and this tune that I can't stop humming." His eyes started to lose more color and I saw a little more of his hair fall out as he shivered a couple of times. "They're saying 'do it.'" He started shaking his head, sending droplets of gasoline everywhere. He then stopped and tilted his head, looking at me at an angle. He threw the box of matches at me and they landed on the cement.

"Set me free, Carter," he said sorrowfully, yet with his old effusive charm.

"Wh-What?" I stammered.

"Come on, do it. I know you can."

"Jackson, I'm not setting you on fire. Things are going to get—"

"NO! They're not going to get better, don't you

understand? Did things get better for you when your family died and you were left alone?" His words felt like knives.

"They didn't right away, but I know they will—"

"Face it, Carter, you never needed any of us. You had your therapist, and that was all she wrote. You've always been strong. I don't want to look in the mirror at myself and take a field trip back to memory lane where I used to have friends and a girlfriend but now I'm scared to death to see the demon in the mirror, and the demon that is me. So do it. Set me free."

"Jackson, I can't."

Jackson cried and clenched his teeth. It looked like he was fighting something. He shouted out in pain and the noise filled the sky. His cry for help rang like bells as he continued to twitch and shiver.

"Please, Carter," Jackson's voice seemed to go back to normal. "I can't live like this. Save my soul . . . please. I don't want to come back. Don't let them take my body. Do this for me." His cold, teal eyes fell on me. His sobs filled the air, and tears welled up in my eyes as I stared down at the box of matches and went to pick them up. I slipped the carton out and grabbed a match, watching as a tear fell out of my eye and onto the cold pavement below. Jackson looked sad and in pain and he needed me to put him out of his misery, to baptize him in fire. I swiped the match across the side of the box with a shaky hand and felt the warmth radiate off the flame onto my face. I looked at the flame and then back up at Jackson. We both had tears in our eyes, but his eyes slowly went all white.

"What are you waiting for?" he yelled in the last bit of his human voice that he had left. "DO IT!"

I couldn't stop the tears from flooding my face. I looked back down at the lit match, and I took a moment and a deep breath before I threw it at Jackson. "I'm sorry," I mumbled. I watched it soar through the air and hit Jackson's chest. In a blink of an eye I watched as flames engulfed his body, like he was a human torch. His screams filled the morning sky as he ran around my driveway screaming in pain but laughing satanically.

His normal voice came back only to say, "Thank you," those were the last words I ever heard him spoke.

I turned around, stopping myself from watching, and headed back inside, sobbing. Everything finally hit me, and I was still trying to take in what just happened. My heart was crushed and I was breathless, devastated, destroyed.

I was all alone. My family, my friends: all gone. If there was any way I could get them back, I would. I didn't know how I was going to cope with this, let alone move on.

All their screams running around in my head, their memories burning in the back of my brain. I set fire to my best friend. But I told myself it was okay because I saved him. He wanted to be saved, and I had to do what I had to do.

I missed my friends and family like crazy, but I was okay with being broken. I was okay with being alone. Sometimes you have to break to really know what makes you whole. Although, I could feel my broken heart it should be hurting but it ain't yet.

I turned on the shower and hopped in, letting the almost-scalding water pour down my body. I was exhausted, but I was afraid to go to sleep and see something that wouldn't be there when I awoke. I scrubbed my body multiple times to wash away how I really felt. Steam filled the room, and I felt hidden. I felt safe, cloaked almost, and for those very short moments I found myself taking a breath.

I got it now. I understood everything. And that was exactly why I was still here. We all were going to mess up, but we were the ones who decided at the end of the day if we liked who we saw back in the mirror, and if we could live with and move on from the choices we made.

No matter what we did or where we were, the past

would always find a way to catch up with us. Just because we could no longer see it didn't mean it wasn't there. Parallel was a dark place and maybe, just maybe somewhere in there I could find a place that shed light. Parallel was nothing more than a place that reflected back onto humanity. But who was I kidding; didn't we all like to feed our demons sometimes? We gave power to the things that had power over us. And if we didn't get over it and move on, it would consume us and we would become one again.

I turned off the water and grabbed a towel to dry off. I put my clothes on and went over to my mirror, which looked normal, and wiped off the condensation. I waited for something unordinary to happen, but it was just me looking back.

I walked out of the bathroom and into the kitchen to look for something decent to eat. The sun shone through the windows, lighting up my house. I saw the picture of my brother and I and smiled as I picked it up. I took it over to one of the end tables and laid it next to a picture of Jackson and me. At least I'd have these relics of my friends. Even if my memory faded, I knew I could count on what was real.

I eventually found some coffee, and as it was brewing I walked over to the hall closet and pulled down a box. I was preparing to place my brother's journal and a few other items into it. I closed the door and stopped halfway down the hallway, for a swift breeze came along and brushed up against my face. My heart fluttered a little; I didn't know how I would feel a breeze when there were no windows in the hall. I laughed at myself. *What I knew was no longer what I know.* I thought I had a grasp on everything that was thrown at me, but our world wasn't as rigid as I once thought it was. I knew now that we were never alone, and the things we buried didn't always stay there.

I brought the box over to the coffee table and noticed a sketch I had started a while ago. I sat down on the couch and picked up my pencil. I wanted to finish what I started. I stuck my tongue out as I concentrated on the outlines, my vivid thoughts running through my mind like a wildfire. *It's almost done.*

I smiled at my work. I set the pencil down and felt clean. I traced the finished piece, as if touching it allowed me to accept what I knew. I closed the gray book and placed into the box, then stood up and put everything back in the closet.

After shutting the closet door, I looked at myself in the mirror but was interrupted by a knock at the door. I held my breath and started to make my way toward it. For a moment, I was no longer scared of what was behind that door, or what lurked under my bed or in the corner of my house.

Sometimes we lose our humanity, and it's those who fight who can get it back. Our past tends to hold us down by chains we don't have keys to, and all our scars and all our demons make us who we are. We all have our days where we feel like others are dragging us down, but we look behind and see that the one holding the chains is ourselves. But to those who do lose their humanity, I wonder where it goes. I wonder where the warmth of life fades to. Where does the soul go if our body remains? I won't have the answer to the age-old question of what happens to us when we die. That energy doesn't just go away. Maybe my friends went to their own parallel universes, only this time where they were actually happy. I will always hold onto the humanity I have left, but I'll also sometimes wonder when I'm feeling cold where the other part of me went.

I knew I was going to be okay and I wished my friends were still around, because I would tell them that one day you will make peace with your demons, and all the fears and pain in your heart will cease. I would want them to take every step with strength, and maybe for the first time in their lives they could open the door to themselves and see them smiling right back, welcoming you home.

I took a big deep breath and opened the door.

Acknowledgements

In order to adequately acknowledge the individuals that helped *Parallel* become what it is today, I am compelled to provide you with some background insight in my start to writing novels. When I was younger, I would handwrite novels on pieces of scratch paper that I would beg my mother to bring home from work. I am unable to tell you how many paper books there are; several boxes at least, each one hand stapled, by me, to creatively make a binding. The books were so long, I had to get creative stapling the pages because staples can only hold so much paper. That being said, no matter how terrible the idea was, I would write… and write…. and write… until I felt I was able to pour everything into that story. Whiteout was my best friend, to say the least.

Fast-forward and now I have completed a novel, not with pen and paper, but with hours and hours of typing, reviewing, and editing. I replaced whiteout with the, ever so frequently used *delete key*, and a professional editing company. To say I am so proud of myself for this accomplishment is an understatement; it feels incredible to share *Parallel* with you. The anticipation of releasing this has been KILLING me as I have waited to share this idea for years. I am humbled, honored, and blessed to finally be able to share my first novel with you.

There are so many people to acknowledge for their assistance helping me create *Parallel*, it is daunting. I will start by giving a very personal thank you to my close friends, Andrew and Nadia, for always listening to me (yes, I know I can talk), letting me bounce ideas off you, and seek constant reassurance that my ideas are sound. I need to thank my grandmother, Diane, for taking each hand-written paper book and personally reading them during my younger years. That simple task motivated me to continue this passion. I need to give an obvious thank you to my mother, Shelley, for being a constant beacon of positivity, support, and remaining my biggest fan. A major thanks to Anne, at Inkstand Editorial, for turning my jumbled thoughts, run-on sentences, and several misspellings into something understandable. You have done incredible work to this novel, and I could not be any happier.

Lastly, I want to thank a special someone who helped guide me in getting this crazy idea off my computer and into the reader's hands. Tyler, I want to thank you for being that voice of reason, providing me love and support, and encouraging me to keep making dreams become a reality.

To say the least, this novel is the first step in accomplishing my dreams. Parallel is living proof that if you work hard enough, and really want something, *you,* the reader, have all the power to make it happen. This is something that isn't taught, but learned. Just know, that whoever and wherever you are, anything can happen as long as you don't give up.

Made in the USA
Las Vegas, NV
10 August 2021